# TRANSFORMATION

Benjamin Samuel Brasford

INTELLIGENT PUBLISHING

Columbia, MD
https://intelpub.com

## THE WORK SERIES

Portions of this book are works of nonfiction. Certain names and identifying characteristics have been changed.

Book Design by Intelligent Publishing
Editors: Jude A. Daya, William Bernhardt

Publisher's Cataloging-In-Publication Data
(Prepared by The Donohue Group, Inc.)

Names: Brasford, Benjamin Samuel, author.
Title: Transformation / Benjamin Samuel Brasford.
Description: Columbia, MD : Intelligent Publishing, [2019] | Series: The work ; volume 2 | Includes bibliographical references.
Identifiers: ISBN 9781732942523 (paperback) | ISBN 9781732942530 (ebook)
Subjects: LCSH: Brasford, Benjamin Samuel--Religion. | Spirituality. | Self-realization. | Christianity. | Metaphysics.
Classification: LCC BL624 .B73 2019 (print) | LCC BL624 (ebook) | DDC 204/.4--dc23

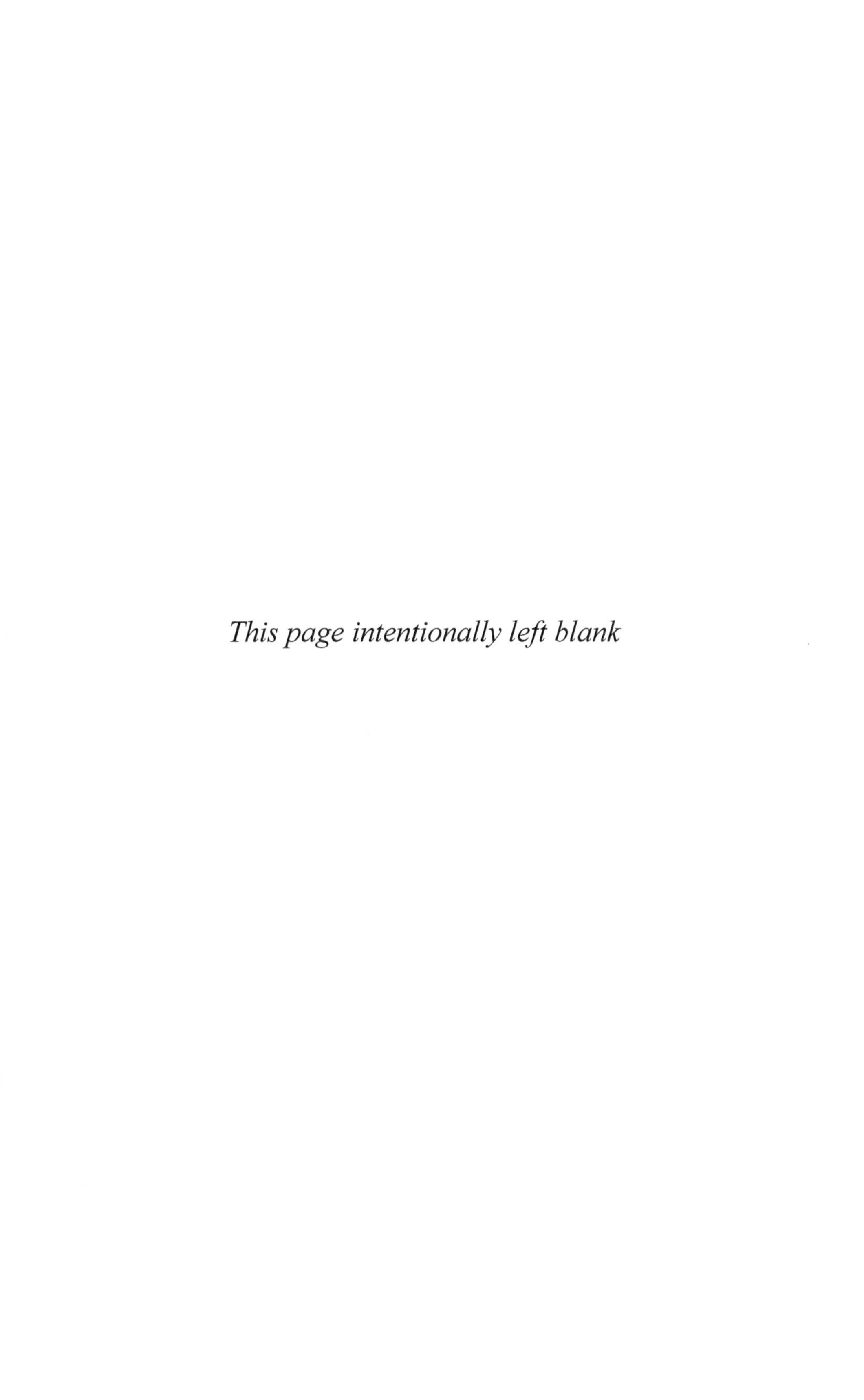

*This page intentionally left blank*

# DEDICATION

This book is dedicated to those who did the right things, listened to those, for the most part, that reared them directly and indirectly, yet still somehow went through abnormal things at a time when they just didn't quite know where they did or would fit in this world.

Table of Contents

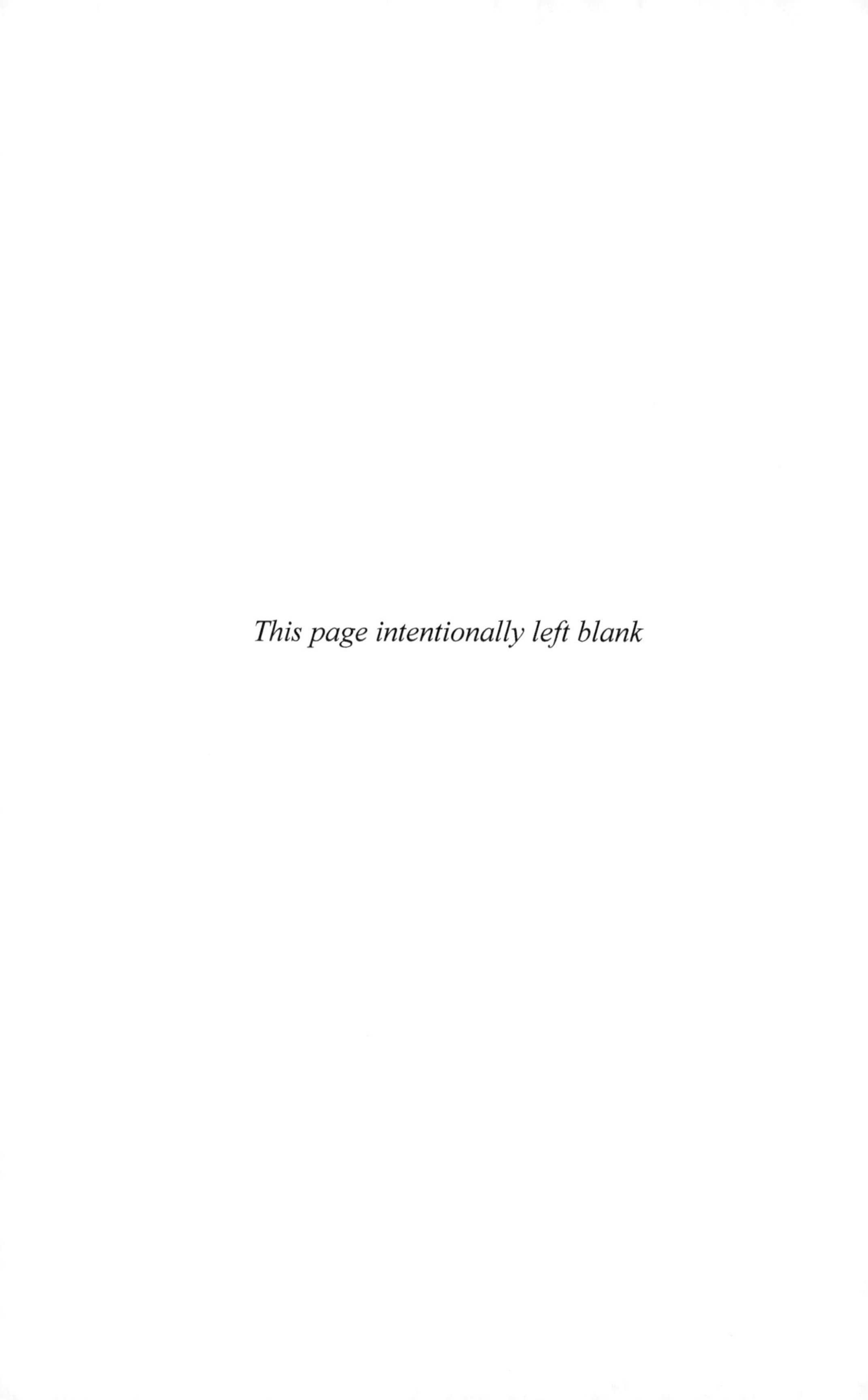

*This page intentionally left blank*

# ACKNOWLEDGMENTS

Thanks to all that were involved in this project, specifically Volume II of The Work.

Thanks to Horace Butler for his sage advice in providing some pointers and touch up.

Thanks to Will Barksdale for his assistance during the research process and his friendship.

Thanks to Gabriel Lightner who is the best friend and brother that I have ever had who has been an inspiration to me in more than words can express.

Thanks to Mary Hoekstra in her wonderful editing assistance and our enjoyable intellectual conversations.

Thanks to Ahmad Jason Deus (A. J. Deus), who when I came across his work which has been helpful over the years, has been an inspiration into intellectual matters like no one else.

# PERMISSION ACKNOWLEDGEMENTS

Special acknowledgement is made for permission to reprint the following copyrighted material. The Works of Philo by C. D. Yonge, copyright 1993 by Hendrickson Publishers, Peabody, Massachusetts. Used by permission. All rights reserved. A Serious Look at New Age Spirituality Used with permission of The Chronicle of Higher Education Copyright© 2018. All rights reserved. The Mosaic of Christian Belief : Twenty Centuries of Unity & Diversity by Olson, Roger E. Reproduced with permission of IVP Academic in the format Republish in a book via Copyright Clearance Center. Revelation Four Views, Revised & Updated Taken from Revelation Four Views, Revised & Updated by Steve Gregg Copyright © 1997, 2013 by Steve Gregg. Used by permission of Thomas Nelson. www.thomasnelson.com. Delbert Burkett, An Introduction to the New Testament and the Origins of Christianity © Delbert Burkett 2002, published by Cambridge University Press, "Reproduced with permission of the Licensor through PLSclear." Brian P. Copenhaver (Ed.), Hermetica, The Greek Corpus Hermeticum and the Latin Asclepius in a New English Translation, with Notes and Introduction © Cambridge University Press 1992 "Reproduced with permission of the Licensor through PLSclear." The Essenes, Qumran, and The Dead Sea Scrolls." The Rosicrucian Digest No. 2 (2007), Copyright (c) 2018 by the Supreme Grand Lodge of AMORC, Inc. All Rights Reserved. Used with Permission. Excerpt(s) from THEY CAME BEFORE COLUMBUS BY Ivan Van Sertima, copyright © 1976 by Ivan Van Sertima. Used by permission of Random House, an imprint of Penguin Random House LLC. All rights reserved. The Hebrew Bible Today: An Introduction to Critical; Book Author: Graham, Steven L. McKenzie and M. Patrick Page Numbers/Description: pages 193-194; Used with permission by Westminster John Knox Press. Total Word Count: 453, The Old Testament between Theology and History; Book Author: Neils Peter Lemche; Page Numbers/Description: xvii; Total Word Count: 78, Used with permission by Westminster John Knox Press. From: Against the Spiritual Turn: Marxism, realism and critical theory, Sean Creaven, Copyright (© 2010) and Routledge, an imprint of Taylor & Francis, reproduced by permission of Taylor & Francis Books UK. © Geza Vermes, 1998, The Complete Dead Sea Scrolls in English Revised Edition, Sheffield Academic Press, an imprint of Bloomsbury Publishing Plc. FORGED by BART D. EHRMAN. Copyright (c) 2011 by Bart D. Ehrman. Courtesy of HarperCollins Publishers. The Evolution of Civilizations : An Introduction to Historical Analysis. New York: Macmillan Company, 1961, "With permission." Ehrman, Bart D. "Chapter 1 The Text of Scripture in an Age of Dissent: Early Christian Struggles for Orthodoxy." Ehrman, Bart D. The Orthodox Corruption of Scripture. New York: Oxford University Press, 1993. 3-46. Book "Reproduced with permission of the Licensor through PLSclear." "I HAVE ALWAYS LOVED THE HOLY TONGUE": ISAAC CASAUBON, THE JEWS, AND A FORGOTTEN CHAPTER IN RENAISSANCE SCHOLARSHIP by Anthony Grafton and Joanna Weinberg, with Alastair Hamilton, Cambridge, Mass.: The Belknap Press of Harvard University Press, Copyright © 2011 by the President

*This page intentionally left blank*

## PREFACE

An ordinary boy, who grew up partly within a big city and partly within a town of slightly less than 3,000 people, I was raised traditionally Christian, under the old-school Pentecostal Holiness brand of Christianity. Women had the greatest of restrictions under this brand, not being allowed to wear earrings, make-up, nor pants and shorts. After some time, my mother would entertain other brands of Christianity, having an epiphany of her own involving what we thought with God revealing to her that he loved all people and not just who were considered holiness followers. This was another transition for me in realizing that the world is bigger than what I had come to understand.

As I grew up within the rural town and atmosphere of Woods, Atlantis, I began to realize that my options were limited and that a change of scenery was needed. My only way out that I could see at the time was to join the Army. So, I did join the Army which placed me within an entirely different environment. Through this environment an opportunity provided me an avenue to become an adult, one which my parents alone could not provide me with. It afforded me with life skills and avenues for travel and experience that I could have never been exposed to had I stayed within my home environment. I learned that different opportunities bring new challenges as well.

How I came to my belief system through upbringing and what I accepted and did not, brought opportunities as well. One such opportunity was to join a church that appeared to me through my Army job at the time, which was in Communications. This opportunity seemed innocent on the surface but over time proved altogether something different. With this opportunity to join this church named Soul's Last Stop came also an opportunity to marry someone that I did not know. The church leadership headed by a man named Dying and his wife Death, presented to me promises that would provide long lasting benefits. Promises were made to my soon to be wife, Conflict who had a son from a previous marriage, at the time that seemed plausible to her as well. I took it to mean, whether implied by the leadership or something that I contrived on my own, that God wanted not only for this church to be a significant part of my spiritual development, but to also be accompanied by a marriage union and family formation that he personally ordained. I would find out years later that how ever I came to this position, it did not afford me with the benefits that I was promised nor believed to be something that would fulfill the long held emotional holes that I did not realize that I had that stemmed from my childhood rearing.

After strange dealings with the leadership of Soul's Last Stop, Conflict and I realized that this church was not what Dying and Death had made it out to be.  It took a few years for us to piece together enough details to decide to leave this establishment and try to stay together on our own terms.  We also decided to not only remain Christians but to also continue to pursue God and church.  I would find that some of the later churches had similarities to Soul's Last Stop in key areas.  I would also realize that Conflict used her own tactics in dealing with me that were in no way to my own personal benefit.  Like the churches who utilized tactics for trapping me through utilizing my unrealistic beliefs, Conflict too decided to utilize my unrealistic beliefs against me for her own personal gain.

After recognizable patterns through church, niceness on the surface, manipulation and control, and working to utilize the beliefs that I had in order to keep me locked within the marriage to Conflict, I had come to realize that the time had come for me to deal with my beliefs.  I had to ask myself was it God that led me to the understanding or was it something or someone else.  The only logical conclusion at the time was to deal with Christianity itself by finding out what it meant historically and fundamentally.  Opportunities presented themselves for me to do so.  I began initially with reading the Bible for myself until I went to specific authors that had written on the subject of Christianity from different viewpoints, some were Christian themselves and others were not.  I had no idea that my studies would lead me down a rabbit hole that would take me on a course of going far deeper than I had originally intended to go.  I later dealt with other related and unrelated subjects that lead me to different understandings of life in general.

My purpose for writing this particular work is to demonstrate my journey through beliefs, opportunities that came as a result for dealing with my beliefs, recognizing life patterns, and coming to altogether different conclusions that I had never intended to come to.  This work is to serve as an expansion of Volume I of the Work Series "The Life of Benjamin Samuel Brasford," as well as a continuation.  It will expand upon parts of my story that are not within Volume I of the Work Series, as well as present Volume I from a different perspective.  That perspective will go into detail that largely focuses upon the last five years of my marriage with Conflict which leads to the ending of not only our marriage union, but also my parting ways with Christianity and church whether temporarily or permanently.  I have gone through great lengths and detail for selected subject matter in an effort to demonstrate what specifically led me to come away from my long held Christian beliefs that I had obtained through childhood rearing and adulthood.  I thought that this was necessary because making such major decisions would definitely need some explanation.  Whether my conclusions are right nor not, this work serves to show how I have arrived to where I am.

*This page intentionally left blank*

# INTRODUCTION

From as early as I could remember, I believed that by becoming a Christian, all of my problems would be taken care of. I believed that all of my problems and issues whether psychological, emotional and even the physical ones, would be fixed. All that I had to do was to get saved and God would do the rest. Whether it was directly or indirectly, this understanding entered into my conscious or subconscious at a very early age. In time, I found out that I was not in fact mistaken enough.

After I got saved, I believed that everyone who was saved were good to go. I believed that I could trust them with my secrets, even my life. I did not vet anyone who was Christian. I believed that I had arrived at the greatest accomplishment of life. I could finally lay down my head and that the life of ease and service to God would carry me from them on. When I look back, I realize just how much of a fool I was.

By the time that Death and Dying approached me with the promises that they made to me about marrying Conflict, I was already had. I had already enslaved myself within a mindset of complete naivety, laziness, and delusion. If they were in fact predators, then I was easy prey. I was like a gazelle that did not even bother to run from the lion. They did not even have to lay a trap for me for I had willingly walked right into it. I made it so easy for them that they could have told me anything and I would have believed them. Such a sad state of affairs. I did not then understand the term "Burden of Performance," that I would find out about many years later. The term that I would never be able to get away from. If I wanted respect in this life, then I would have to earn it. I would have to earn trust, love, and reliance. I would have to demonstrate character, behavior, and actions that would be indicative of others seeing me in a light to yield to me, willingly, their friendship, loyalty, and love.

I began to realize over time that most, if not all, issues spring from a childhood event. Perhaps a set of occurrences over a process of time took place during childhood that led me into this ridiculous line of thinking. I would later find out that childhood rearing was paramount to the success or failure of an individual. It is up to that individual to at some point realize their error and decide to, if they are able, do something about it. So, I decided to do something about it.

After years of marriage and experiencing similar negative patterns, I had had enough. With this new mindset, an opportunity came for me to become aware of an entirely different world. This would not come easy for I had to do much work to face my pathologies and to decide to overcome them. This work took place in a sequence that led me to a far greater understanding of life, for which I am now a perpetual student of.

Volume I of the Work Series is an introduction to the author, Benjamin Samuel Brasford, my life and character to my early adulthood. The previous Volume depicted the struggles that Benjamin went through and eventually overcame from a broad perspective. This volume will serve as an expansion and continuation of Volume I to include the actual discovery that I went through that led to my transformation. Chapters 1, 2, and 7 of the current Volume foreshadow different parts of my story prior to discovery; while Chapters 2 and 7, also report how I navigated that discovery. The remaining chapters reveal what I learned during my discovery period.

The context for this work is in the style of a classroom. It is an intellectual journey and is not to be taken as fact or truth. Rather, the journey's purpose is to show the process of my learning. This book can be read as one unit, or it can be approached from the individual subject matter material, depending upon the reader's subject knowledge. The subject matter that is directly related to Christianity and Biblical Archaeology is included within chapters 3 through 6. The subject matter within Chapter 8 is directly related to metaphysics and atheism. The subject matter within Chapter 9 is directly related to genetics, anthropology, ancient history, and general truth-seeking. A series of later works

# INTRODUCTION

will provide further ideas from the various subjects presented here.

Instead of providing a glossary, the definitions to certain terms are provided within the footnotes.  Key information about individuals' themselves and their work(s) are also provided within the footnotes.  An endnotes section is provided with references to ancient works, whether they are from the B.C. or A.D. period, to include their actual quotes at times.  Other selected modern individuals' works are included within the endnotes section as well.  A detailed bibliography is provided at the end of the work.

Every effort has been made to properly accredit all sources of the material within this work and provide as detailed and accurate a bibliography as possible.  We hope that you are enriched by this story continuation and find the information presented useful and enlightening.  Without further delay, let us discover.

# TRANSFORMATION

# 1 NIGHTMARES

Soul's Last Stop in Losem, NW was the church where leaders Death and Dying had arranged my marriage with Conflict. During my tenure there as a member, I encountered weird happenings. I found myself at times simply sitting, minding my own business, when my mind went places over which I had no control. I beheld weird visions of lust that caused me to desire every woman I laid my eyes on, to include those women I was fighting to not see. I experienced uncontrollable laughter that came out of nowhere, then ended abruptly. At other times and in an effort to isolate myself, I laid down very early at night to sleep. I recognized my need for isolation but was unaware of why the need existed. I felt as if some outside force was guiding me, and frequently felt that something or someone else controlled my mind and thoughts. The force was comparable in weight and gravitas to a heavy presence that moved me.

# NIGHTMARES

All I could do was yield to the heaviness and control. Despite having no idea what it was, I chose not to fight it. This phenomenon occurred here and there over time; eventually it would cease with my having no recollection of it. It was at bedtime when I witnessed the strangest things.

After a year into my church membership, the church leaders left their home to me and Conflict, while the remainder of the congregation moved to Ocean, Flat to establish themselves there. Conflict and I were both in the Army at the time, so we had to remain where we were until our next assignments.

One night while asleep, an unseen presence awoke me and restrained me to the bed: I could not move a muscle. I tried to yell Conflict's name, but was unable to move my lips. Strangely, I could hear myself in my own mind. After this event subsided, I called Dying, the male church leader, to explain the event.

Dying told me, "You should have pleaded the Blood of Jesus three times instead of calling your wife's name. Next time that happens, never call your wife's name again." After this phone call, I felt that I was armed with adequate knowledge in case this event took place again.

Sometime later on another night, while Conflict and I slept, I awoke to very loud footsteps. I was again restrained by a presence similar to the one before. This time my eyes were open while I listened to the footsteps of this presence but I was unable to move my head or any part of my body. I listened in silent immobility as the sounds of the invisible footsteps arrived at my side of the bed, then the presence leapt upon me, restraining me further. This time I remembered what Dying had advised and recited over and over, "The Blood of Jesus! The Blood of Jesus!" After the fourth repetition, the presence immediately finished. I sat upon the bed, awed by what had taken place.

There was another night, a while after Conflict and I were asleep, when I dreamt that me and a man whose face I could not see were walking and talking during what appeared to be nighttime. We walked through an alley in a neighborhood that had no residents. There was no activity and it was dark and cold. The man and I were having a conversation, yet I was unable to recollect it later when I recounted my dream to others. After walking and talking for a while, the man made a statement I apparently found offensive. I looked at the man's unseen face and exclaimed loudly, "The Blood of Jesus!" The man, though obscured, looked me in his eyes and replied, "What is that going to do?" Then an unseen presence leapt upon me, waking me out of my dream and prompting me to recite loudly, "The Blood of Jesus! The Blood of Jesus! The Blood of Jesus!" The presence immediately left me.

After Conflict and I received our military orders to move to Fairway, Flat which was about an hour and a half from Ocean, Flat where the church had moved, I did not experience these things again. The funny thing was - the very bedroom in the church leaders' house, where Conflict and I slept, was the same bedroom where the church leaders had slept.

# 1 NIGHTMARES

It became apparent to me, having had watched many a horror movie growing up, that the specter of haunted houses was probably more than just a concept.

## 2 SOUL SEARCHING

After arriving in Fairway, Flat it appeared a new job and what looked like a new start in life might present themselves. Dying had coerced me into getting out of the army. I had no plan to do so though, and Conflict and I had two children to support. Times became rocky financially and I had it rough finding employment. I learned the hard way that when your relationship is already bad, lacking stable income does not aid the situation. Conflict and I still attended the church services on the weekends in Orange, Flat, rejoining the remainder of the church members. It was in Orange, Flat, that the church eventually dissolved altogether.

After quite some time, I landed an industrial job at a lumber mill. The job was tough at first, what with my being new to the lumber industry.

Months passed and I not only got the hang of the work, but also realized that this was something that I wanted to consider doing long term. I stuck with the lumber industry and made contacts with other companies. I moved from job to job a few times, seeking my way to move up to the management side.

While on the job one day, I met a preacher who was going through a rough time. He told me that his brother had set him up on the job and that his brother was a pastor of a different church where he himself attended and pastored. Some time passed and I was invited to his church. Conflict and I began attending regularly. It only took a matter of a few months for me and Conflict to realize that this preacher was very much similar to Death and Dying. This preacher's name was apropos: Abracadabra. A motto me and Conflict gave him was, "Now you see it, now you don't," for this preacher had a great many magic tricks in his top hat and up his sleeves!

One of Conflict's past coworkers, Passive Aggressive, reconnected with her after a while. Passive Aggressive was a preacher in another church in another city called Mobtown, Manor, which was several states away.

Abracadabra possessed an ability, or so it seemed, to foretell future events. He even seemed to be able to explain past and present events as well. He knew things that Conflict and I had not told him. Conflict and I found Abracadabra's gift so exciting that after Passive Aggressive and Conflict talked for a few weeks, and I got acquainted with Passive Aggressive, we introduced Passive Aggressive and

# TRANSFORMATION

Abracadabra via the telephone. After their discussion, even Passive Aggressive was convinced that Abracadabra was a true man of God.

It did not take long after that telephone conversation and affirmation for the veil to be lifted and the truth to be revealed about Abracadabra's intentions. At that time, I was unfortunately unaware that familiarity breeds contempt. I did not grasp that people got quite comfortable after a while and that was when their true colors shone through like the risen sun!

Abracadabra apparently had a thing for Conflict and even made passes at her. She hid this from me until it culminated in Abracadabra's divulging to me that it was Conflict, and not he, making the passes. Conflict and I were still unaware of who we were individually and jointly, nor did we know our capabilities. I, being vulnerable and naïve, trusted Abracadabra the preacher. This led to immediate problems within my marriage. On her part, Conflict confided in Passive Aggressive, while I confided to Abracadabra. It took some time for Conflict to divulge her side of the story to me and I was not at all happy that she had hidden this entire ordeal from me. After a heated discussion, I left our home for a time but eventually we reconnected. All of that took place before both Conflict and I fully realized we had been had yet again by church leaders. As a consequence, I learned a hard lesson about spiritual things and people. That lesson was that relying on the gifts of other people can and had proved disastrous. Things had gotten better between me and Conflict. We had parted ways with Abracadabra but remained in contact from time to time with Passive Aggressive.

Not long after parting ways with Abracadabra, I had inadvertently learned of another church from a coworker, Wesley, who attended it. I attended a few times and later invited Conflict. The name of this church was Solace and things were different this time. Solace was quite unlike the first two churches in which we had been entangled. At Solace, for the first time in our congregation-starved lives there was relief. There was no funny business at this place. It was a time of recovery. Conflict and I never got close enough to get to know the leadership of Solace.

Unfortunately, Conflict and I had not attended Solace very long before she received military orders to move to Cedrick, Manor, which was about two hours from Passive Aggressive's church in Mobtown. As we had done before while living in Fairway and driving the distance to Ocean, we drove on the weekends to Mobtown to attend Obscure Delivery, the church Passive Aggressive pastored. We remained at this church for quite some time. I began working full-time for  the federal government as an administrative assistant, while attending night classes working towards an associate's degree in business. During our tenure at Obscure Delivery, we recognized that it was a controlling, superficial environment. One thing Passive Aggressive knew how to do was put on a good show. Her heart seemed like it was in the right place. The problem was her insatiable need to be right and the excessive dominance she displayed.

After three years, Conflict received military orders for reassignment to Green Pastures, Southland. Passive Aggressive was not happy about this news; so galled was she that she suggested that Conflict trust God and separate from the army. Conflict and I knew that was not an option but the turn of events was a strong wake-up for both of us. We decided to part ways with Passive Aggressive and the Mobtown church. Passive Aggressive did genuinely love us, as we did her, but no matter how much you may love someone, your best interests for them are not the same as their own. There was just no way that Conflict could get out of her assignment: she even tried, to no avail.

I had begun my studies in Christianity after this third negative church experience, ending with Obscure Delivery. I knew nothing else but the Bible. So I started there. I was able to obtain my AA prior to leaving Cedrick, Manor and moving to Green Pastures.

After relocating to Green Pastures, I began attending classes towards obtaining a bachelor's degree in business. Conflict and I had our third child, our third boy. I did not work during the day, having taken on a full daytime courseload at Green Pastures University. So I shouldered the homemaker role, attended classes, and continued my personal studies which, at times, kept me up until 2 or 3 am. I became consumed by my studies. When I could not read, I downloaded podcasts to replay throughout the day. When I could, I would watch YouTube videos. After a while I began contacting the authors of the books directly, whether via e-mail or Facebook Messenger. There was not a soul I contacted who did not get back to me at least a few times. I was so consumed by learning that I often neglected my homemaker duties. My learning took on a faster pace, and though I did not understand why, I refused to do anything to shut off that faucet. My ardor began causing problems between Conflict and I. Because the two older boys were old enough to help out with their younger brother, I would often have them assist me.

I found another church that was very close to where we all lived in Green Pastures. The church was called Globalism. It was the largest church Conflict and I had ever attended. As at Solace, Conflict and I never got close to the leadership of Globalism. I was slipping away from church attendance as I progressed in my personal studies. I managed to pass my college classes. After a while, I stopped attending church and eventually even Conflict stopped attending.

I came to a realization after studying Christianity that prompted me to look back at my congregational choices. I began to reflect on my three negative church experiences. I saw that there were similarities between all three places: Soul's Last Stop; Abracadabra's church; and Passive Aggressive's church, Obscure Delivery. They all had patterns that began with enticing through niceness, causing individuals to enjoy the show, then to interference with personal lives, and then the familiarity would set in. In each church, the issues were lessened each time from the first to the third. I saw myself running from one church to another, never sitting down to consider that maybe the problem wasn't the churches or anyone or anything else; I considered that maybe I had had a problem all along.

While the churches interfered with Conflict and my lives, we had to realize at the end of the day that each of them was still responsible for our own decisions. Others are only able to do what you allow them to do. We saw how the three negative churches' atmospheres were oftentimes breeding grounds for control and manipulation. We realized that some people should not be in positions of power. The goal for many, while they may have been and may be followers at this time, should be to eventually become leaders, even if they decide to only lead themselves and no one else.

At Green Pastures, Southland is where I met my crossroads: a decision that would not come easy, but one that I could no longer delay. One that would cause me to face whether or not God was worth holding onto any more - or at least as I had come to understand it at that time. After having gone through many years of negative church experiences, the time had come to do some searching. I realized that the problem could not be with the churches and the people that I encountered alone. I had to consider that I, too, had a problem. It was a few more years that passed before I would come across a quote,

*"That we do not become," he answered, "haters of reasoning as some become haters of men; for no greater evil can happen to any one than to hate reasoning. 88. But hatred of reasoning and hatred of mankind both spring from the same source. For hatred of mankind is produced in us from having placed too great reliance on some one without sufficient knowledge of him, and from having considered him to be a man altogether true, sincere, and faithful, and then after a little while finding him depraved and unfaithful, and after him another. And when a man has often experienced this, and especially from those whom he considered his most intimate and best friends, at length, having frequently stumbled, he hates all men, and thinks that there is no soundness*

*at all in any of them. Have you not perceived that this happens so?"*

*"Certainly," I replied.*

*"Is it not a shame?" he said, "and is it not evident that such a one attempts to deal with men, without sufficient knowledge of human affairs? For if he had dealt with them with competent knowledge, as the case really is, so he would have considered that the good and the bad are each very few in number, and that those between both are most numerous." [1]*

This was one of the "aha moments" for me in my spiritual and intellectual development. Moments of clarity are golden: the clear golden moments for me required courage and curiosity to embark upon a journey with an enticing, unknown destination of my own choosing.

---

1        (Plato, Phaedo Section 88.)

# 3 UNEXPECTED ESCHATOLOGY

One afternoon in Mobtown, I was downtown, in the basement of a library attending a seminar for affordable housing. As I was leaving the basement of the library, something led me to a section where I noticed a book entitled, *The Rapture Exposed: The Message of Hope in the Book of Revelation* by Barbara R. Rossing. Having grown up having learning about the Rapture, I never knew that people wrote books about the subject, or that they wrote books to dispute what I understood to be the Rapture.

So I picked up the book and began scanning through it. To my surprise, I came across a word the author said was from Christian studies: "Eschatology."[2]   The only thing I

---

2     Eschatology - The part of theology concerned with death, judgement, and the final destiny of the soul and of humankind. (Press, Eschatology, n.1)

learned growing up was that we must be saved so that the wrath to come, which was the judgment of God through Jesus Christ would destroy and place within hell all those who chose not to come to the salvation of Jesus Christ. The common scriptural passages that I heard resoundingly were,

*[16] For God so loved the world, that he gave his only begotten Son, that whosoever believeth in him should not perish, but have everlasting life.*

*[17] For God sent not his Son into the world to condemn the world; but that the world through him might be saved.*

*[18] He that believeth on him is not condemned: but he that believeth not is condemned already, because he hath not believed in the name of the only begotten Son of God.*

*John 3:16-18 KJV*

Holding the book in my hand, I hearkened back to my childhood. I remembered I was taught that the end of time was near, that the world would be destroyed and all the saved would go to heaven and worship God all day.

I left the library and later made a note to buy a copy of the book for myself. I had gone through the last bad church experience that I could endure. By this time, I had decided to begin doing my own investigation instead of continuing to trust others with my spiritual development.

# TRANSFORMATION

Once I purchased a copy of Barbara R. Rossing's book, I learned that the predominant view of eschatology in the United States existed around 1859 to 1877. During that timeframe a man by the name of John Nelson Darby, an English clergyman, developed this view from the vision experienced by a 15-year-old girl in 1830, during a healing service at the Port Glasgow Scotland church. From this young lady's vision, Darby began teaching a two-part return of Jesus Christ. The first return would be in secret to take many Christians off the planet, which is an explanation of the Rapture. The second return would be the final return, to be viewed publicly throughout the world. At the end of a seven-year period of global tribulation, during which the rule of the Antichrist would occur contemporaneous with that seven years, Jesus would conquer said Antichrist,[3] and then establish a physical kingdom that would last 1,000 years.[4] This latter view is entitled, "Dispensationalism".

I learned that, of the several views of eschatology, there are four main ones. In general, all the others branch from them.[5] Dispensationalism became so ingrained in people's minds that they refuse to even have an honest discussion about it, and are often emotional about it, to the point some may be willing to harm others, or wish harm. This hearkens to the concept of ego investments.[6] My understanding of this concept is when someone believes something very strongly, they embrace that idea to the point it becomes a part of their

---

3 Antichrist - 1(in some Christian teachings) a personal opponent of Christ expected to appear before the end of the world. (Press, Antichrist, n.1)

4 (Rossing, 2: The Invention of the Rapture 22-23)

5 (Gregg)

6 (Tomassi, The Rational Male 4)

identity.  Within this line of reasoning, if someone disagrees with an ideology, and they counter it in any way, it's as if the person with the ideology is under attack, because the idea has been so internalized and engrained on the individualist level of their psyche.

The views of the clergyman Darby were also popularized by Cyrus Ingersoll Scofield, via a reference Bible published in 1909, *"The Scofield Reference Bible"*, which was a version of the King James Bible that included headings and notes from the dispensational system of eschatology.

## Four Views of the Book of Revelation

Eschatology is significant to the understanding of Christianity.  In fact, without eschatology, there really is no Christianity.  Christianity is very much concerned with the belief in the return of Jesus Christ from heaven to gather those who have accepted His salvation and punish all those who have not.  The end of the world, the last days, and various demonstrations of imminent language, pervades the writings of the New Testament.  The four main views of eschatology are Historicism, Preterism, Futurism, and Idealism.  Utilizing *Revelation: Four Views, A Parallel Commentary* by Steve Gregg and other sources I will lay out the four main views of eschatology that all other views spring from in one form or another.

## Historicism

The Historicist approach to the Book of Revelation is a Reformed view.  This approach, according the Historicist

Research Foundation[7], *"... was the standard interpretation from Wycliffe to Spurgeon (500 years) and is known as the Protestant interpretation in distinct contrast to Preterism and Futurism, which were Jesuit interpretations contrived during the counterreformation.  The Reformation confessions have adopted the Historicist interpretation, including the Irish Articles (1615), the original Westminster Confession of Faith (1646), the Savoy Declaration (1658), and the London Baptist Confession (1688)."*[8]

By and large, it is not as popular as it was during the days of the Reformation Era.  The Reformation Era was *"the religious revolution that took place in the Western church in the 16th century. Its greatest leaders undoubtedly were Martin Luther and John Calvin. Having far-reaching political, economic, and social effects, the Reformation became the basis for the founding of Protestantism, one of the three major branches of Christianity."*[9]   The three major branches of Christianity are *"... the Roman Catholic Church, the Eastern Orthodox churches, and the Protestant churches; in addition to these churches there are several independent churches of Eastern Christianity as well as numerous sects throughout the world."*[10]

Those that teach the Historicist view believe that God revealed, in advance, events spanning the entire church age;

7      The Historicist Research Foundation has a mission to promote scholarship and foster understanding about the Historicist interpretation of Biblical prophecy, internationally and is a service of the Puritan's Network.
8      (McCarter)
9      (T. E. Britannica, Reformation)
10     (Matt Stefon)

the disclosing of events was through symbolic visions of the Apocalypse, another name for the Book of Revelation.[11]   A line of interpretation utilized by the Historicists system of eschatology involves the "year-for-a-day principle," which denotes time periods that are to be taken literal and exact, though are cast in a symbolism that represents a year as a day.  This brings to mind the scripture in II Peter Chapter 3 verse 8, which says,

*"But, beloved, be not ignorant of this one thing,
that one day is with the Lord as a thousand years,
and a thousand years as one day;"*

from the King James Version, which appears to echo Psalm Chapter 90 verse 4, which says,

*"For a thousand years in thy sight are but as yes-
terday when it is past, and as a watch in the night."*[12]

Historicists take these two verses literally.  As Gregg [13]states, they appeal to Ezekiel Chapter 4 verses 4 to 6, which shows that the prophet was required to lie on his left side for 390 days and upon his right side for 40 days, which represented the same number of years of judgment that God decreed upon Israel and Judah respectively.  This is used to extrapolate something referred to as "prophetic time" in regard to the book of Daniel and the book of Revelation.

------

11      (Gregg)

12      All biblical references from this point forward are from the King James Version, unless otherwise noted.

13      (1997, 2003)

# TRANSFORMATION

One of the most common names and interesting subjects concerning the "end times" is the concept of the "Antichrist", which by name itself, is never once mentioned within the book of Revelation. The term is found in First John chapter 2 verses 18 and 22, chapter 4 verse 3, and Second John chapter 1 verse 7. This concept of the Antichrist is applied differently and taken for meaning from certain verses, such as Second Thessalonians chapter 2 verses 1 to 4 which shows,

*[1] Now we beseech you, brethren, by the coming of our Lord Jesus Christ, and by our gathering together unto him,*

*[2] That ye be not soon shaken in mind, or be troubled, neither by spirit, nor by word, nor by letter as from us, as that the day of Christ is at hand.*

*[3] Let no man deceive you by any means: for that day shall not come, except there come a falling away first, and that man of sin be revealed, the son of perdition;*

*[4] Who opposeth and exalteth himself above all that is called God, or that is worshipped; so that he as God sitteth in the temple of God, shewing himself that he is God.*

This man of sin, or as understood by some as the Antichrist of the New Testament, is a topic hot enough to have been included in in *"Left Behind"* the book and movie series by Tim LaHaye and Jerry B. Jenkins.

According to a website that puts it succinctly, *"In Christianity, the Antichrist or False Messiah is generally regarded as a figure of evil that will claim to be the Christ (Messiah)."* [14]The site continues, *"... Jesus, whom Christians believe to be the Jewish Messiah (the Christ), will appear in his Second Coming to Earth to face the Antichrist, who will be regarded as the greatest false messiah in Christianity. Just as Christ is the savior and the ideal model for humanity, his opponent will be a single figure of concentrated evil."*

## Preterism

Preterism, is a view of eschatology stating that the events described by Jesus in Matthew 24-25, Mark 13, Luke 21, and parts of the book of Revelation were all either partially or completely fulfilled in the past. The books with those chapters mentioned,  excluding, according to some, the book of Revelation, are referred to as the "Olivet Discourse."[15]  Those who see it partially fulfilled in the past, are generally called partial preterists. Those who see it all fulfilled in the past are called full preterists. Preterism *"... is attributed to being formulated by Luis del Alcázar (Ludovicus ab Alcasar, Louis of Alcazar) (1554–1613), a Spanish Jesuit theologian, in his work entitled, "Vestigatio arcani sensus in Apocalypsi" (1614) published after his death. Alcázar's method was for the Book of Revelation, and was shortly taken up by Hugo Grotius. John Donne cites him in a sermon. Henry Hammond was an exception, among English Protestants, in following Alcázar's interpretation."*[16]

---

14    (_Star_ The Star of Jews, who is the Antichrist?)
15    (Russell 49)
16    (Wikipedia, Luis del Alcázar)

Some hold that Alcazar[17] formulated this view as a counter to the Historicist view of eschatology.[18]  Preterism, along with Futurism, which we will discuss later, are both counter views to the Reformer's views of eschatology, viz., Historicism.  There were those, though, who held preterist leanings earlier than Alcazar.  The church historian, Eusebius of Caesarea who lived during the time of Emperor Constantine within the 4th A.D. or C.E,  wrote the first "official" church history; Andreas of Cappadocia, who also lived within that century and others.[19]  Moving forward, C.E. will be used.

## The Dating of the Book of Revelation

The dating of the Book of Revelation becomes paramount in regards to eschatology whether it was partially or completely fulfilled in the past or will be partially or completely fulfilled in the future.  For the discussion of dating the Book of Revelation, we will be referring primarily to the work of the late John A. T. Robinson, *"Redating the New Testament"* (1976).[20]

---

17    Alcasar broke with earlier Jesuits in stressing a preterite and historical reading that held that everything in the Apocalypse, with the exception of the last three chapters, had been fulfilled in the early centuries of the Church. (Amanat)

18    (Gregg, Revelation Four Views 62)

19    (Gregg, Introduction to the Book of Revelation 62-63)

20    John A. T. Robinson - an English New Testament scholar, author and the Anglican Bishop of Woolwich.  He was a lecturer at Trinity College, Cambridge, and later Dean of Trinity College until his death in 1983 from cancer. Robinson was considered a major force in shaping liberal Christian theology. Along with Harvard theologian Harvey Cox, he spearheaded the field of secular theology and, like William Barclay, he was a believer in universal salvation. (Wikipedia, John Robinson (bishop of Woolwich))

# 3 UNEXPECTED ESCHATOLOGY

One of the most profound statements in Robinson's book, is, *"One of the oddest facts about the New Testament is that what on any showing would appear to be the single most datable and climactic event of the period - the fall of Jerusalem in AD 70, and with it the collapse of institutional Judaism based on the temple is never once mentioned as a past fact."*[21]

So, the dating of the book is very important regarding preterism. The historical and climactic event Robinson spoke of was the Jewish war between the citizens of Judaea and Rome. It began in 66 CE under the reign of Emperor Nero and ended with the destruction of Jerusalem in 70 CE, under the reign of Emperor Vespasian; his son Titus was the army general who led the destruction. Many Jews were killed, and others were taken captive into slavery. Flavius Josephus was born Joseph ben Mattathias circa 37 CE in Jerusalem of a priestly and royal family.[22] He wrote about this war in his histories, *"The Jewish Wars"* or *"Wars of the Jews."* He excelled in his studies of Jewish law and studied with the Sadducees, Pharisees, and the Essenes, eventually aligning himself with the Pharisees. In 62 CE he went to Rome to free some imprisoned priests. After accomplishing this mission through the intercession of Nero's wife, Poppaea, he returned to Jerusalem in 65 CE to find the country in revolt against Rome. Hare states, *"... Josephus was an*

---

21    (J. A. Robinson 19)

22    Flavius Josephus, original name Joseph Ben Matthias, (born AD 37/38, Jerusalem—died AD 100, Rome), Jewish priest, scholar, and historian who wrote valuable works on the Jewish revolt of 66–70 and on earlier Jewish history. His major books are History of the Jewish War (75–79), The Antiquities of the Jews (93), and Against Apion. (Poole)

*eyewitness to history, and his writings are considered authoritative. These texts are key to understanding a pivotal point in world history, which has tragic repercussions even to this day."*[23]

The pivotal point in world history spoken of by Hare is the same datable and climactic event that Robinson spoke of in "*Redating the New Testament.*" Following the destruction of Jerusalem, Josephus returned to Rome with Titus and began his literary endeavors. He completed "*The Jewish Wars*" or "*Wars of the Jews*" among other works. Since 70 CE is the date of the destruction of Jerusalem, the Book of Revelation is either dated prior to the destruction of Jerusalem during the reigns of Nero and ending with Vespasian, or dated afterwards during the reign of Domitian around 95 or 96 CE. Some say that the Book of Revelation was written after the destruction of Jerusalem, by relying on the works of St. Irenaeus,[24] who is estimated to have lived from 120/140 CE to 200/203 CE.[25] Those called "classic preterists" date

---

23      (Hare)

24      Saint Irenaeus, (born c. 120, /140, Asia Minor—died c. 200, /203, probably Lyon; Western feast day June 28; Eastern feast day August 23), bishop of Lugdunum(Lyon) and leading Christian theologian of the 2nd century. His work Adversus haereses (Against Heresies), written in about 180, was a refutation of Gnosticism. In the course of his writings Irenaeus advanced the development of an authoritative canon of Scriptures, the creed, and the authority of the episcopal office. (Wingren)

25      We will not, however, incur the risk of pronouncing positively as to the name of Antichrist; for if it were necessary that his name should be distinctly revealed in this present time, it would have been announced by him who beheld the apocalyptic vision. For that was seen no very long time since, but almost in our day, towards the end of Domitian's reign. (Irenaeus). Also see, "Before Jerusalem Fell" and

the book of Revelation prior to 70 C.E.  Details within Revelation are used to demonstrate how certain events took place prior to 70 CE, while later details are viewed as the prediction of the fall of Rome and beyond to the Second Coming of Christ.  Some preterists see Revelation as having taken place prior to and ending within the destruction of Jerusalem.

There are what are referred to as the "101-time statements" throughout the New Testament.[26]  I will concentrate on the main Bible verses that lead to the understanding, as many have demonstrated, of Jerusalem's fall in the war with Rome; it culminated in 70 CE and has been the focal point of the preterist view.  The Olivet Discourse that is recorded within the synoptic gospels, viz., Matthew, Mark, and Luke, is in chapters 24 to 26 in Matthew, chapter 13 in Mark, and chapter 21 in Luke. Below is a side-by-side comparison of some of the verses from the aforementioned books of the New Testament.

---

"The Beast of Revelation" by Kenneth L. Gentry
26      (Green)

| Matthew 24 | Mark 13 | Luke 13 |
|---|---|---|
| 1 And Jesus went out, and departed from the temple: and his disciples came to him for to shew him the buildings of the temple.<br><br>2 And Jesus said unto them, See ye not all these things? verily I say unto you, There shall not be left here one stone upon another, that shall not be thrown down.<br><br>3 And as he sat upon the mount of Olives, the disciples came unto him privately, saying, Tell us, when shall these things be? and what shall be the sign of thy coming, and of the end of the world? | 1 And as he went out of the temple, one of his disciples saith unto him, Master, see what manner of stones and what buildings are here!<br><br>2 And Jesus answering said unto him, Seest thou these great buildings? there shall not be left one stone upon another, that shall not be thrown down.<br><br>3 And as he sat upon the mount of Olives over against the temple, Peter and James and John and Andrew asked him privately,<br><br>4 Tell us, when shall these things be? and what shall be the sign when all these things shall be fulfilled? | 5 And as some spake of the temple, how it was adorned with goodly stones and gifts, he said,<br><br>6 As for these things which ye behold, the days will come, in the which there shall not be left one stone upon another, that shall not be thrown down.<br><br>7 And they asked him, saying, Master, but when shall these things be? and what sign will there be when these things shall come to pass? |

Different parts of Revelation are said by some authors to coincide with the verses within Matthew, Mark, and Luke that discuss the *Olivet Discourse*. The "101-time statements" issue relates to the obviously expected nearness of the events to take place within the lives of those who lived either during or near the time of Jerusalem's destruction. Some scholars explain that the Olivet Discourse was a prophecy about the end of all things and the days of vengeance that were to fulfill all things written throughout the Old Testament concerning God's promises to Israel. This view seemed the closest to taking what the writers said in general to explain what they meant by what they wrote. Preterists, in general, let the Bible speak for itself, if such a thing is even possible. They generally don't add to or take away from the text, except when it seems that there is no other way.

## Dispensationalism

We visit again, *"The Rapture Exposed: The Message of Hope in the Book of Revelation"* (2004) by Barbara R. Rossing. By the time I had stumbled upon this book, and after many failed or at least negative church experiences, I became open to the possibility that perhaps it wasn't the churches that had the problem. I considered that I had the problem. Rossing discussed the four main views of Revelation, just as Gregg did in his book. I had spent the greater part of my life in church and had never heard of differing "views" on the book of Revelation. I always thought that we were living the end times and that I would be raptured if I did not die and go to heaven. I became devastated at the things that I saw in Rossing's book.

At one time, dispensationalism was the dominant view on the book of Revelation in the United States, the Western world in general, and perhaps throughout the world. It has dominated the Christian media and the world to the point that many Christians and non-Christians alike are unaware of the existence of other approaches, as I was unaware. [27]Dispensational teachers such as John Nelson Darby, Cyrus Ingersoll Scofield, Clarence Larkin, Charles Ryrie, John Walvoord, Hal Lindsey, Jack Van Impe, J. Vernon McGee, Chuck Swindoll, David Jeremiah, most of the main Christian denominations such as the Baptists, Pentecostals, Calvary Chapel Movement, Plymouth Brethren, Evangelical Free Churches, and most non-denominational, evangelical churches, all teach this view.

The placement of the Rapture is the major difference between dispensationalism and other views within Futurism. [28]Dispensationalism uses Revelation 4:1 for the placement of the Rapture, while other futurist views utilize other passages of scripture to explain the Rapture.

*"After this I looked, and, behold, a door was opened in heaven: and the first voice which I heard was as it were of a trumpet talking with me; which said, Come up hither, and I will shew thee things which must be hereafter."*

*Revelation 4:1*

The majority of Revelation is seen as future to us within futurist views, especially dispensationalism. Most of Revelation appears to be continuous, though it is not a chronological work which at times tells a similar story in different parts. The futurists generally take a literal approach to the

---

27      (Gregg, The Futurist Approach: Everything after Chapter 3 Awaits Fulfillment in the Future 64-68)
28      Futurism will be discussed below.

visions within scripture, while others with differing views take a somewhat allegorical or spiritual approach. One of the main things that I discuss below in the pre-millennial, a-millennial, and post-millennial views is the "tribulation," which is generally understood from chapters 6 to 19 in Revelation. The futurists also take into account the book of Daniel chapter 9 verses 24 to 27.

*24 Seventy weeks are determined upon thy people and upon thy holy city, to finish the transgression, and to make an end of sins, and to make reconciliation for iniquity, and to bring in everlasting righteousness, and to seal up the vision and prophecy, and to anoint the most Holy.*

*25 Know therefore and understand, that from the going forth of the commandment to restore and to build Jerusalem unto the Messiah the Prince shall be seven weeks, and threescore and two weeks: the street shall be built again, and the wall, even in troublous times.*

*26 And after threescore and two weeks shall Messiah be cut off, but not for himself: and the people of the prince that shall come shall destroy the city and the sanctuary; and the end thereof shall be with a flood, and unto the end of the war desolations are determined.*

*27 And he shall confirm the covenant with many for one week: and in the midst of the week he shall cause the sacrifice and the oblation to cease, and for the overspreading of abominations he shall make it desolate, even until the consummation, and that determined shall be poured upon the desolate.*

*Daniel 9:24-27 KJV*

This tribulation is a seven-year period, after which there will be a thousand-year physical reign of Christ when He returns on earth; this seems to be discussed in chapters 19 and 20 of Revelation. There follows a renewal of all things discussed in chapters 21 and 22.[29] This rather complicated system has different explanations, depending upon the particular dispensationalist. Dr. David R. Reagan[30] does a good job of explaining it on the Lamb & Lion Ministries website. We will go into detail from Rossing's point of view below.

Futurism[31] is said to have originated from Francisco Ribera in 1585 as a refutation to the Historicist view as spoken

---

29    (Reagan, Daniel's 70 Weeks of Years : When did it start? Has it ended, or is there a gap in it?)

30    Dr. David R. Reagan serves as the Founder and Director for Lamb & Lion Ministries. He is a native Texan who resides in a suburb of Dallas. "…Dr. Reagan is a Phi Beta Kappa graduate of the University of Texas in Austin. His graduate degrees were earned in the field of International Relations from the Fletcher School of Law & Diplomacy of Tufts and Harvard Universities. Dave — as he prefers to be called — was the founder of Lamb & Lion Ministries in 1980." (Reagan, Dr. David R. Reagan)

31    The 16th-century movement called Futurism, expounded by the Jesuit Francisco Ribera, stressed the future fulfillment of the prophecy of the End as mentioned in scripture with both the rise of the Antichrist and the return of Christ. (Stefon)

of above.[32]  Ribera apparently taught that the Antichrist had no yet come and that he would arrive within the last days which were understood by him to be in the future.  This view did not gain prominence until it was introduced in Protestant circles by Samuel Maitland in 1827, and then popularized by John Nelson Darby, a British evangelical preacher and founder of the Plymouth Brethren in 1830.

This "rapture" doctrine had its origins possibly from the vision of a young girl, Margaret MacDonald in Port Glasgow, Scotland.[33]  To reiterate, Rossing reported that John Nelson Darby used this vision in his system to explain that Christ would return twice.  Christ would return and rapture his "church" to heaven which is supposedly stated in Revelation chapter 4, the tribulation of seven years would begin, end, and then Christ would return as supposedly stated in Revelation chapters 19 and 20.

Darby's eschatological dispensationalism pieces together various parts and passages of scripture, since not one single verse within the Old or New Testaments ever men-

---

32     Francisco Ribera (1537–1591) was a Spanish Jesuit theologian, identified with the Futurist Christian eschatological view.  He was born at Villacastín.[1] He joined the Society of Jesus in 1570, and taught at the University of Salamanca. He acted as confessor to Teresa of Avila. He died in 1591 at the age of fifty-four, one year after the publication of his work In Sacrum Beati Ioannis Apostoli, & Evangelistiae Apocalypsin Commentarij.[2]  (Wikipedia, Francisco Ribera)

The 16th-century movement called Futurism, expounded by the Jesuit Francisco Ribera, stressed the future fulfillment of the prophecy of the End as mentioned in scripture with both the rise of the Antichrist and the return of Christ. (Encyclopedia Britannica)

33     (Rossing, 2: The Invention of the Rapture 22)

tions the word rapture.  He explains that the word "rapture" comes from the Latin, *raptio*, a translation of Greek for the word "caught up," which is used in I Thessalonians 4 by the Apostle Paul.

Apparently between 1859 and 1877, Darby made a number of mission trips to the United States to push forth his rapture ideas and he gained many followers.  The dispensations that Darby came up with consisted of seven different periods, or dispensations, of history, during which God dealt with the people of different times; some preachers have utilized Revelation to discuss the churches of Ephesus, Smyrna, Pergamos, Thyatira, Sardis, Philadelphia, and the church of the Laodiceans.[34]  These seven churches represent the seven different ages, or dispensations.  Sometime later, Cyrus Ingersoll Scofield was instrumental in producing an annotated Bible with the headings and notes based on Darby's system.  Scofield had achieved notoriety for nefarious deeds, including embezzlement of money and forgery, for which he served six months in jail.  He reportedly abandoned his wife and children, but became a Christian.  This Bible became the Bible, selling in the millions, with many people reading the headings and notes along with scripture as though they were of the same "authority."  Over time, this system of dispensationalism, became the main eschatological view.

With the earlier reference to Daniel 9:24-27, the dispensationalists use it to describe God's "stopwatch" for fulfilling Israel's promises.  We are apparently living within a parenthesis or gap in time due to the 70th week of Daniel 9, stopping beforehand at the 69th week.  Apparently, this

---

34     (Bible Study Tools)

parenthesis or gap was created by God or as a response from God for the Jews having Christ killed on the cross under Pontus Pilate, the Roman procurator or the Roman prefect. [35]So Christ's crucifixion, in the dispensationalist system, supposedly stopped God's prophetic "clock" for Israel as supposedly described by Daniel 9:24-27 wherein this discusses the 70 weeks.

The dispensationalist view has more lately received impetus by Tim LaHaye and Jerry B. Jenkins in their book series and movie series *"Left Behind,"* (2008) and within the book *"The Late Great Planet Earth"* (1970) by Hal Lindsey.

## Idealism

According to Steve Gregg in his *Revelation Four Views* (1997, 2013), the idealist view is one that does not seek an individual or specific fulfillment of the prophecies of Revelation in the historical or futuristic sense. Instead, idealists take the approach that the prophecies within the Bible are to be seen as spiritual lessons and principles that could continue throughout the course of history. Additionally, the Bible contains spiritual lessons depicted in the visions.[36]  This view does indeed take into account the highly symbolic and so called apocalyptic language throughout the Old and New Testaments.

---

35    Pontius Pilate's title was traditionally thought to have been procurator, since Tacitus speaks of him as such. However, the inscription on the so-called Pilate Stone refers to Pilate as "Prefect of Judaea". The title used by the governors of the region varied over the period of the New Testament.  (Hanson)

36    (Gregg, Introduction to the Book of Revelation - The Idealist Approach)

Idealism does not force one to try to and make consistent or harmonize specific passages of scripture with specific fulfillments.  It does however, make every passage relevant to every Christian for any time.  The problem comes in when or if the specific passages were meant to be fulfilled specifically, perhaps as understood by those who originally wrote those passages.

There are times when those who hold the other three views mix their views with the idealist approach when systematizing or harmonizing is not or does not seem plausible.  Preterists, whether classic or full, at times mix their views with some degree of idealism.  The idealist view is held by Barbara R. Rossing herself.

## The Millennial Views on Revelation Chapter 20

In our approach to the different millennial views, some postulate four, while there are only three main views that are described by Steve Gregg and others.  These views of the millennial period as mentioned above are pre-millennial, a-millennial, and post-millennial.  A fourth millennial view described by others is historic pre-millennial.  For our purposes, we will stick to the three main millennial views discussed by Steve Gregg and others.

Before we describe the views themselves, let us take a look at this supposed millennial period as approached within Revelation.

[1] And I saw an angel come down from heaven, having the key of the bottomless pit and a great

chain in his hand.

² And he laid hold on the dragon, that old serpent, which is the Devil, and Satan, and bound him a thousand years,

³ And cast him into the bottomless pit, and shut him up, and set a seal upon him, that he should deceive the nations no more, till the thousand years should be fulfilled: and after that he must be loosed a little season.

⁴ And I saw thrones, and they sat upon them, and judgment was given unto them: and I saw the souls of them that were beheaded for the witness of Jesus, and for the word of God, and which had not worshipped the beast, neither his image, neither had received his mark upon their foreheads, or in their hands; and they lived and reigned with Christ a thousand years.

*⁵ But the rest of the dead lived not again until the thousand years were finished. This is the first resurrection.*

*⁶ Blessed and holy is he that hath part in the first resurrection: on such the second death hath no power, but they shall be priests of God and of Christ and shall reign with him a thousand years.*
*⁷ And when the thousand years are expired, Satan shall be loosed out of his prison,*

*⁸ And shall go out to deceive the nations which*

*are in the four quarters of the earth, Gog, and Ma-gog, to gather them together to battle: the number of whom is as the sand of the sea.*

*⁹ And they went up on the breadth of the earth, and compassed the camp of the saints about, and the beloved city: and fire came down from God out of heaven, and devoured them.*

*¹⁰ And the devil that deceived them was cast into the lake of fire and brimstone, where the beast and the false prophet are, and shall be tormented day and night for ever and ever.*

*¹¹ And I saw a great white throne, and him that sat on it, from whose face the earth and the heaven fled away; and there was found no place for them.*

*¹² And I saw the dead, small and great, stand before God; and the books were opened: and anoth-er book was opened, which is the book of life: and the dead were judged out of those things which were written in the books, according to their works.*

*¹³ And the sea gave up the dead which were in it; and death and hell delivered up the dead which were in them: and they were judged every man according to their works.*

*¹⁴ And death and hell were cast into the lake of fire. This is the second death.*

# 3 UNEXPECTED ESCHATOLOGY

*<sup>15</sup> And whosoever was not found written in the book of life was cast into the lake of fire.*

*Revelation 20:1-15 KJV*

What is this millennial period? *"Some see this as a future earthly theocracy by which Christ will rule over the nations for a thousand years.  Others see it as a time during which Christ will rule earth from heaven through the life-changing power of the Gospel.  Still others look at it in another way.  And the multitude of others holds a multitude of other interpretations.*

*One's final interpretation of the thousand years from Revelation 20 depends more upon certain factors related to a Christian's hermeneutic than the strict text of the ten much debated verses.  There are several ways in which orthodox Christians choose to come to Scripture and depending on which of these methods is used, ones' understanding of eschatological issues – and a host of others as well – will experience changes both significant and trivial.  And since one interprets Scripture primarily through the filter of his understand of other passages in the Word, one's millennial view does have an effect (whether small or great) on the way in which he lives his life. "*[37]

There are reasons why the aforementioned four views of Revelation, in general, cannot be applied, or are not applied, to Chapter 20 of Revelation.  The final chapters of Revelation, chapters 20 to 22, are approached differently in regard to interpretation.  *"... the interpretation of these final chap-*

---

37      (Blue Letter Bible)

"

*ters comprises what is arguably the controversy in eschatological studies, if not all evangelical theology.*"[38]

While each of the three views that will be discussed can be presented with impressive exegetical arguments in their defense and have enjoyed their own period of prominence within the thinking of the Western Church, every view has had its embarrassing supporters who claim to act from their beliefs but represent something altogether outside of Christianity.

## Premillennialists Approach

Premillennialists understand the 1,000 years to follow the return of Christ, just after a time of great apostasy and tribulation. The dispensationalists and the premillennialists hold this view but no longer side with one another where the modern nation of Israel comes into play. The British Government supported the establishment of Israel as a nation state in Palestine in the year 1917.[39] On May 14, 1948, Israel was declared a nation state in Palestine.[40] The dispensationalists hold that modern-day Israel holds a significant role in the redemptive work of God for the end times, where a third temple in Jerusalem is to be completed to include the reestablishment of the Levitical priesthood, the same priesthood that is discussed in the Old Testament. The premillennialists see the church as opposed to the "ethnic" Israelites as a major focus for the millennial period. This method is considered grammitico-historical, with the church being the

---

38    (Gregg, The Millennium Chapter 20 516)

39    (T. E. Britannica, Balfour Declaration)

40    (Office of the Historian)

fulfillment of Israel and the kingdom of God being present from the day of Pentecost[41] to be experienced during the millennium after Christ's return; the rapture takes place prior to the millennium, and Christ will reign literally on earth for 1,000 years.

## Post-Millennialists Approach

The post-millennialists see Revelation 20 as a consummation of history in the 1,000-year reign of the saints, though Christ will accomplish this through the church fulfilling its gospel mission,[42] just before Christ's return. They generally do not hold this as a literal 1,000 years, but see this timeframe as representative of an era, age, or indefinite period of time. After the gradual Christianization through the fulfilling of the gospel mission, Christ will then return and immediately usher the church into its eternal state after judging the wicked. So, in the post-millennial view, Christ returns after the millennium.

This method is considered covenant-historical.[43] The church is seen as the fulfillment of Israel, the kingdom of God is a spiritual entity through the mission of spreading the gospel message, and the millennium being a golden age previous to Christ's return with the vast majority of people becoming Christian. Due to the fact that there are higher degrees of interpreting the first century CE events in light of prophecy, preterism is often a good view that goes alongside

---

41      Acts Chapter 2.

42      For the gospel mission, some hearken to Matthew 28:19-20, and other passages within the New Testament.

43      (Bible)

post-millennialism. There is even a view of governments becoming Christianized as a theocracy having Christian rulers, better known as the reconstructionist view, which is said to now be gaining the most popularity in the world today.[44]

## A-Millennialist Approach

The a-millennialists approach takes the position that there is no millennium specifically. There is no golden age period before the 1,000 years or after in the a-millennialists view. Chapter 20 of Revelation is taken spiritually, or symbolically, as if the reign of the saints depicts either the vindicated martyrs reigning from heaven in the present age, or earthly believers achieving spiritual victory over personal sin during the same period.[45] The timeframe is the whole time between Christ's first and second advents, where the binding of Satan at the beginning of the millennium is associated with the first coming of Christ. The "fire from heaven" at the end of the millennium is associated with His second coming. This method is redemptive-historical, with the church being the eschatological fulfillment of Israel, the kingdom of God being a spiritual reality in which all Christians partake. This is seen presently by faith, but will be grasped by sight at the consummation, and the rapture (the saints, living and dead, shall meet the Lord in the clouds and immediately proceed to judge the nations with Christ and then follow Him into their eternal state).[46] The idealist view of the book of Revelation goes well with the a-millennial view due to the fact of

---

44    (B. Robinson, Christian Reconstructionism etc. Beliefs and practices)
45    (Gregg, The Millennium Chapter 20)
46    (Bible)

the spiritual or symbolical approach to prophecy fulfillment.

## An Unexpected Conclusion Reached on Eschatology

Reading Barbara R. Rossing's book, "*The Rapture Exposed*," opened up an entirely new world. Something intrigued me about the understanding that some things may have already happened. By that time, I was already transitioning out of attending church services regularly. At work, I would listen to three men who went by the title of apostle. They all had decent-sized platforms within Christian circles. They all had series everyone was able to watch on YouTube and other websites at their leisure. One of them in particular, was discussing preterism, which he called fulfilled eschatology. What captured me was his method of delivery. He never elucidated his views entirely in the particular series I viewed several times. I remember him mentioning a book written by the late David Chilton,[47] "*The Days of Vengeance*".[48] He also had other series which went into more detail about his views, still without stating which of the four main views he held. I then put the other two apostles in the backseat, so to speak, and only listened to him. All three apostles were quite distantly located geographically. Later I learned about the Preterist Archive, a site maintained mainly by Todd Dennis.[49] I would subsequently learn about

47    He was a self-taught economist of the highest order. He was a self-taught theologian of the highest order. He was the most gifted author I ever worked with. His books required no editing. They could be typeset and sent to the printer. (North)

48    (Chilton) (2006)

49    DEVELOPER AND CURATOR of PreteristArchive.com (Est. 1996)

various other sites on preterism. I became aware of people like Philip Mauro,[50] Henry Grotius,[51] and others to include Sir Isaac Newton.[52] After months of study, I had partially accepted the understanding of preterism, but I did not discontinue or limit my learning by settling there. I continued to pay attention to the works by people such as Kenneth L.

---

50      Mauro was born in St. Louis, Missouri.[3] He was a lawyer who practiced before the Supreme Court, patent lawyer and also a Christian writer. He prepared briefs for the Scopes Trial. His works include God's Pilgrims, Life in the Word, The Church, The Churches and the Kingdom, The Hope of Israel, Ruth, The Satisfied Stranger, The Wonders of Bible Chronology, The World and its God, The Last Call to the Godly Remnant, More Than a Prophet, Dispensationalism Justifies the Crucifixion, Evolution at the Bar and Things Which Soon Must Come to Pass. (Wikipedia, Philip Mauro)

51      Hugo Grotius, Dutch Huigh de Groot, (born April 10, 1583, Delft, Netherlands—died August 28, 1645, Rostock, Mecklenburg-Schwerin), Dutch jurist and scholar whose masterpiece De Jure Belli ac Pacis (1625; On the Law of War and Peace) is considered one of the greatest contributions to the development of international law. Also a statesman and diplomat, Grotius has been called the "father of international law." (Onuma)

52      Sir Isaac Newton, (born December 25, 1642 [January 4, 1643, New Style], Woolsthorpe, Lincolnshire, England—died March 20 [March 31], 1727, London), English physicist and mathematician, who was the culminating figure of the scientific revolution of the 17th century. In optics, his discovery of the composition of white light integrated the phenomena of colours into the science of light and laid the foundation for modern physical optics. In mechanics, his three laws of motion, the basic principles of modern physics, resulted in the formulation of the law of universal gravitation. (Westfall)

Gentry,[53]  R. C. Sproul, [54] and others.  I would then come across Charles Coty's website,[55]  where he had a wealth of information about preterism, more from the fulfilled perspective.[56]  I also found a video entitled, "Are You Kidding Me?"[57]

In a short time, after having learned of Samuel G. Dawson,[58] Don K. Preston,[59] William Bell,[60] Sam Frost (who at

---

53     Kenneth L. Gentry, Jr., Th.D., is a conservative, evangelical, and Reformed lecturer and writer. He is committed to the Reformed faith as set forth in the Westminster Confession and Faith and Catechisms. Though retired from pastoral ministry, he holds his ordination in the Reformed Presbyterian Church General Assembly, a conservative and Reformed denomination.

54     Robert Charles Sproul (/sprool/ SPROHL; February 13, 1939 – December 14, 2017) was an American theologian, author, and ordained pastor in the Presbyterian Church in America. He was the founder and chairman of Ligonier Ministries (named for the Ligonier Valley just outside Pittsburgh, where the ministry started as a study center for college and seminary students) and could be heard daily on the Renewing Your Mind radio broadcast in the United States and internationally.  (Wikipedia, R. C. Sproul)

55     (Coty)

56     Another way of saying full preterism.

57     Over eighteen months in production, we are excited to provide this tool for introducing Preterism to others. You've Gotta Be Kidding . . . Right? chronicles Brian L. Martin's (General editor of Fulfilled! Magazine) journey to Preterism. Join him as he encounters scriptural principles like audience relevance, apocalyptic language, cloud-comings, and more.  (Martin)

58     Samuel G. Dawson has several books available via Amazon at: https://www.amazon.com/Samuel-G.-Dawson/e/B001KCIAA4

59     (Preston)

60     (Tree of Life Ministries)

the time held the full preterist view),[61] Kelly Birks,[62] and others, I could no longer hold preterism in a partial form and maintain a consistent hermeneutic.[63] Proper exegesis [64]as taught by many a preterist and those that held one of the other three views on eschatology, would not allow a partial position. Based upon the "101 timing-statements" within the New Testament and the apparent expectancy of the coming of Christ within that first century generation, full preterism was the only view that I could maintain. I accepted full preterism (which is called by various other names, including covenant eschatology, and fulfilled eschatology) because it answered many questions, while obviously opening the door for the mind to replace the answered questions with unanswered questions.

An entire new world of thought had opened up once I started looking. I had conversations via social media with the one apostle who was directly, yet indirectly, discussing this view of eschatology. I thanked him for what he did. It's amazing how people with several states in between them, having indirect contact, can still learn from one another. I subsequently learned that there was a growing interest for the differing positions within preterism, even full preterism. Eschatology was one of those subjects that was all inclusive. It causes you to study the entire Bible and take more seriously what you once may have, or may not have, ever known. I had gained an entirely new perspective and re-

---

61      (Dennis)

62      (Birks)

63      Hermeneutic - Concerning interpretation, especially of the Bible or literary texts. (Oxford Dictionary Online)

64      Exegesis - Critical explanation or interpretation of a text, especially of scripture. (Oxford Dictionary Online)

spect for the Bible in general, but as often happens when questions are answered, the door opened for new questions. After a while, full preterism wasn't enough for me anymore. I figured that if all things are fulfilled, then why should I not only no longer continue attending church, but why remain a Christian?  Still, I could not negate the spiritual experiences that I had.  Now I would visit book stores to see what was on the shelves in regard to Christianity from different perspectives in general.  I grew up worshiping within the Pentecostal brand of Christianity.  The gifts of the spirit were still apparently operative and operating I thought, though I could not deny the clear language within the texts of scripture.  So, I kept searching.

# 4 IN COMES TEXTUAL CRITICISM

Some months down the road after having accepted full preterism, I found myself in a Barnes and Noble looking through books in the Religion section. I came across a book by Bart D. Ehrman,[65] a PhD professor who taught at the University of North Carolina Chapel Hill, entitled, *"Forged: Writing in the name of God-Why the Bible's Authors Are Not Who We Think They Are."* I grabbed it and read, *"... the dead in Christ will rise first; then we who are alive, who remain, will be caught up together to meet the Lord in the air." Read the verse carefully: Paul expects to be one of the ones who will still be alive when it happens."*[66]

---

65     See https://www.bartdehrman.com/barts-biography/ for Professor Bart Ehrman's biography.

66     (Ehrman, Chapter 3: Forgeries in the Name of Paul 106)

It then became apparent that not only preterists and others who held the differing views of eschatology were aware of the nearness of expectancy within the New Testament. Professor Ehrman specialized within a field called Textual Criticism.[67]  I would subsequently learn from professor Ehrman that there are no originals to any New Testament letters but only copies, much of which were written in the Greek language.  As professor Ehrman states on page 57 of *Misquoting Jesus: The Story Behind Who Changed the Bible and Why,"… once a scribe changes a text-whether accidentally or intentionally-then those changes are permanent in his manuscript (unless, of course, another scribe comes*

---

67     The process of attempting to ascertain the original wording of a text. The New Oxford American Dictionary.  Textual criticism, properly speaking, is an ancillary academic discipline designed to lay the foundations for the so-called higher criticism, which deals with questions of authenticity and attribution, of interpretation, and of literary and historical evaluation.  This distinction between the lower and the higher branches of criticism was first made explicitly by the German biblical scholar J. G. Eichhorn; the use of the term "textual criticism" in English dates from the middle of the 19th Century. (Kenney)

"One of the leading questions that textual critics must deal with is how to get back to the original text-the text as the author first wrote it-given the circumstance that our manuscripts are so full of mistakes.  The problem is exacerbated by the fact that once a mistake was made, it could become firmly embedded in the textual tradition, more firmly embedded, in fact, than the original." (Ehrman, Chapter 2: The Copyists of Early Christian Writings 57)

Biblical criticism, discipline that studies textual, compositional, and historical questions surrounding the Old and New Testaments. Biblical criticism lays the groundwork for meaningful interpretation of the Bible.  (T. E. Britannica, Biblical criticism)

*along to correct the mistake)."*[68]

So, the understanding is, that scribes would get their hands on the documents, place comments within the margins or near the text, and later scribes would incorporate those comments within their scriptural translations of the text; from that point on, you have a new reading. The original writing was mixed with the commentary of scribes who would copy from the original or earlier copies.

The discipline of textual criticism fascinated yet perplexed me at the same time. P46, the forty-sixth catalogued papyrus and first reasonably complete copy from the book of Galatians, the New Testament letter, is dated circa 200 CE. Professor Ehrman, *"... states that the reconstruction of the copy from which P46 came from, cannot be made."* [69]

To be fair, modern scholars or writers have not been the only ones to figure out issues with the texts of the New Testament. Even Origen[70] found mistakes in his day, as he notes, *"The differences among the manuscripts have become great, either through the negligence of some copyists or through the perverse audacity of others; they either neglect to check over what they have transcribed, or, in the process of check-*

---

68    (Ehrman, Chapter 2: The Copyists of Early Christian Writings 57)

69    (Ehrman, Chapter 2: The Copyists of the Early Christian Writings 60)

70    Origen, Latin in full Oregenes Adamantius (born c. 185, probably Alexandria, Egypt—died c. 254, Tyre, Phoenicia [now Sūr, Lebanon]), the most important theologian and biblical scholar of the early Greek church. His greatest work is the Hexapla, which is a synopsis of six versions of the Old Testament. (Chadwick, "Origen")

*ing, they make additions or deletions as they please."[71]*

The final major New Testament example that I witnessed by an early writer was, again from Origen and from someone named Celsus who opposed the Christian faith at that time. Celsus is reported to have said, *"The Christian believers, like persons who in a fit of drunkenness lay violent hands upon themselves, have corrupted the Gospel from its original integrity, to a threefold, and fourfold, and many-fold degree, and have remodeled it, so that they might be able to answer objections."[i]*

The textual critic essentially detects and, to the extent possible, removes the effects of discrepancies within an ancient work. A text is said by some scholars in the field to be an abstract idea or concept rather than a concrete artifact. The textual critic attempts to reduce the discrepancies and, to the best of their ability, restore the document to its first or original state. This is of course based upon the text and how it was transmitted.

Textual criticism is not concerned with theology in any way. Its focus is document restoration by way of removing variants within the texts by comparing the remaining available extant texts.

---

71      Commentary on Matthew 15.14, as quoted in Bruce M. Metzger, "Explicit References in the Works of Origen to Variant Readings in New Testament Manuscripts," in Biblical and Patristic Studies in Memory of Robert Pierce Casey, ed. J. Neville Birdsall and Robert W. Thomson (Freiburg: Herder, 1968), 78-79. (Ehrman, Notes: Chapter 2: Note 9 221)

I eventually saw that even the Old Testament had no originals but was from copies as well. So, an entire field of textual criticism was devoted to the Old and New Testaments. This is something that after several years attending church, I had never heard of. I actually felt cheated that I was now learning more outside of church than I was in church. I'm sure that this was/is not everyone's experience. I found that church in general, or at least in my experience, was largely focused on devotion and not knowledge. Schodde states that, *"...the actual state of the text furnishes its own evidence that corruptions have found their way into the text."*[72]

Textual emendations were seen to have been made when careful study by the student of textual criticism was applied. This helped me realize that the "doctrine" of Biblical Inerrancy and infallibility had to be revisited if any amount of genuineness would be considered in approaching the study of the Old and New Testaments.

A formal statement called the Chicago Statement on Biblical Inerrancy was formulated by the International Council on Biblical Inerrancy by more than 200 evangelical leaders at a conference held in Chicago in 1978.[73] It seemed that Article X of the above referenced document, which is found within the Journal of the Evangelical Theological Society, is what the doctrine of inerrancy and infallibility is based upon largely if not entirely.

This states that the extent of the Word of God based on available copies and translations faithfully represent the

---

72      (Schodde 45)
73      (Chicago Statement on Biblical Inerrancy)

original, though we do not have any of the originals to the Old and New Testament texts. This is apparently why they had to make this statement in Article X, though the average Christian is unaware of what doctrine of Biblical Inerrancy this is based upon. The essential elements of the Christian faith being affected by the knowledge that its texts are not in fact original is a tell-tale sign that this statement is an obvious mechanism devised to ease the minds of those who are unaware of the science of textual criticism. There would be no need for science to represent the original documents of the Old and New Testaments if the original intent or reading and understanding of said documents were apparent and demonstrably possible. The Protestant tradition of Biblical scholars relied heavily on the notion of sola scriptura, a concept introduced by Martin Luther,[74] an Augustine monk who studied for many years and was then appointed Professor of the Holy Scriptures at Wittenberg University.[75]

"Luther discovered texts which formed the basis of the Reformation principle "sola gratia" (by grace alone), while studying and making notes on Paul's epistles : man's salvation comes by God's grace alone and does not in any way depend on his works (which was not the teaching of

74    Martin Luther, (born November 10, 1483, Eisleben, Saxony [Germany]—died February 18, 1546, Eisleben), German theologian and religious reformer who was the catalyst of the 16th-century Protestant Reformation. Through his words and actions, Luther precipitated a movement that reformulated certain basic tenets of Christian belief and resulted in the division of Western Christendom between Roman Catholicism and the new Protestant traditions, mainly Lutheranism, Calvinism, the Anglican Communion, the Anabaptists, and the Antitrinitarians. He is one of the most influential figures in the history of Christianity.  (Hillerbrand)

75    (Virtual Museum of Protestantism)

the Roman Catholic Church). This was the basis of Luther's disagreement with traditional doctrine, and it was taken up by all the other Reformers. According to Luther, Scripture could only be read in the light of 'sola gratia' which opened the reader's mind and led to 'sola scriptura.'"[76]

Others clarify the concept of sola scriptura this way, *"The Reformation principle of sola Scriptura has to do with the sufficiency of Scripture as our supreme authority in all spiritual matters. Sola Scriptura simply means that all truth necessary for our salvation and spiritual life is taught either explicitly or implicitly in Scripture. It is not a claim that all truth of every kind is found in Scripture."*[77]

Faith had to be maintained, so authorities crafted statements that would gloss over the eyes and ease the minds of others who were unaware of this, because the reconstructions through textual criticism of the remaining copies could not prove the inerrancy doctrine.[78]

## Old Testament Textual Criticism

When I dove into the Old Testament and the scholarship on it, mistakes were found in many places.[79] With no originals to these documents, and only surviving copies by scribes with variations, the idea of faith began to wane. The New Testament is said by some to have as many as 3,000 surviving Greek manuscripts, many versions translated into

---

76    (Virtual Museum of Protestantism)
77    (MacArthur)
78    (Ehrman, Chapter 4: The Quest for Origins 105)
79    (Schodde)

various different languages, and quotations found in the patristic writings, which are writings written by the early church fathers of the Ante Nicene period.[80]

The idea of variations in the copies of the texts was evident and no one could argue it away.[81] The Protestants still relied upon faith, regardless of the copyists errors, which removes the reliance of that faith without caution.[82] If the original words of scripture have not been preserved, how could we rely on the texts as they have come down to us? So, what had to happen was a guiding interpretative principle, or better yet, a philosophy that had to be created and implemented to guide how people "see" these scriptures. On one hand, it is innocent, or could appear that way. On the other hand, it could be seen as a cover up to hide the mistakes and perhaps deliberate lies of those that preceded us.

Concerning the Old Testament, Shodde stated, *"The state of affairs of the Old Testament is rather peculiar, quite different indeed from the New Testament or other literary remains of antiquity the restoration of whose original form is attempted. ...Our oldest Hebrew MSS. date from the ninth or tenth Christian centuries, and are thus thirteen and more hundred years removed from the autograph copies of the writers. .... Notably is this the case of the Septuagint, which stands in matter of time at least as near and even nearer to the original writings than do the oldest and the best of New Testament manuscripts to the of the apostles."[83]

---

80    (The Center for Hellenic Studies)
81    (Simon 105)
82    (Kummel 104)
83    (Schodde)

# TRANSFORMATION

From studying this discipline, I learned about the Masoretic[84] and the Septuagint[85] texts of the Old Testament. "The name Septuagint (from the Latin septuaginta, "70") was derived later from the legend that there were 72 translators, 6 from each of the 12 tribes of Israel, who worked independently to translate the whole and ultimately produced identical versions. *"... The best known of these are the Codex Vaticanus (B) and the Codex Sinaiticus (S), both dating from the 4th century ce, and the Codex Alexandrinus (A) from the 5th century. There are also numerous earlier papyrus fragments and many later manuscripts. The first printed copy of the Septuagint was in the Complutensian Polyglot (1514–22)."*[86]

As far as the Masoretic text, *"This monumental work was begun around the 6th century ad and completed in the 10th by scholars at Talmudic academies in Babylonia and Palestine, in an effort to reproduce, as far as possible, the original text of the Hebrew Old Testament. Their intention was not to interpret the meaning of the Scriptures but to transmit to future generations the authentic Word of God. To this end they gathered manuscripts and whatever oral traditions were available to them."*[87]  To continue on the Maso-

---

84    Masorete - Any of the Jewish scholars of the 6th to 10th centuries AD who contributed to the establishment of a recognized text of the Hebrew Bible, and to the compilation of the Masorah. (Oxford Dictionary Online)

85    A Greek version of the Hebrew Bible (or Old Testament), including the Apocrypha, made for Greek-speaking Jews in Egypt in the 3rd and 2nd centuries BC and adopted by the early Christian Churches. (Oxford Dictionary Online)

86    (T. E. Britannica, Septuagint)

87    (T. E. Britannica, Masoretic Text)

retic, *"The best-known of these are the Qumran manuscripts (the "Dead Sea Scrolls"), though there are others such as the relics from the Cairo Genizah. With only a handful of exceptions, such as the Qumran Isaiah scroll, these manuscripts are damaged and difficult to read, and the portions of the OT they contain are limited."*[88]

## Specific Textual References

After reading the works of Professor Bart Ehrman, I placed full preterism on the back burner. Now that I had begun to understand that the bible was not preserved in its original form, that there was a wealth of copies, it became clear that to hold any position on eschatology was untenable. I began to look at specific textual references. The study of St. Paul in the New Testament was particularly interesting. Many Christians and perhaps others, do not realize just how much Christianity was influenced by Paul's writings. Paul's writings make up the majority of the New Testament. According to Ian Lyall, *"It has come into widespread use among non-Christian scholars, and depends on the claim that the form of the faith found in the writings of Paul is different from that found elsewhere in the New Testament, but also that his influence came to predominate."*[89]

Outside of Jesus, Paul is the most important person in Christianity. Paul's writings account for most of the New Testament, and it is his writings that provided a great deal of terminology and a foundation for church leadership.[90] With-

---

88    (Elliott)
89    (Lyall)
90    (Graber)

out the writings of Paul, there is no church in a sense. Jesus' words in the gospels were not concerned with the setting up and daily maintenance of an on-going church. What's interesting is that though Paul established churches and provided maintenance on some level, that maintenance was only for a time, and not as long as some may think. Harding observes of Paul's writings, *"... the 'oldest written testimonies of Christianity'"91*

It was to my surprise to find out that as early as 1807, the idea of the infallibility and inerrancy of the Bible was no longer taken seriously. The German scholar Friedrich Schleiermacher[92] was one of the most important Christian theologians of the 19th Century and was famous for defending the Christian faith against its "cultured despisers." He also was known for developing distinct theological views that influenced theologians well into the 20th Century.

Today, scholars still specialize in studying the works and teaching of Schleiermacher. Among his many writings is an open letter sent to a pastor in 1807 in which he tried to demonstrate that 1 Timothy was not written by Paul, because it used words and ideas that were at odds with the

---

91　(Harding, Disputed and Undisputed Letters of Paul 129) "Republished with permission of Brill, from The Pauline Canon, Stanley E. Porter, Volume I, 2004; permission conveyed through Copyright Clearance Center, Inc. "

92　Friedrich Schleiermacher, (born Nov. 21, 1768, Breslau, Silesia—died Feb. 12, 1834, Berlin), German theologian, preacher, and classical philologist, generally recognized as the founder of modern Protestant theology. His major work, Der christliche Glaube (1821–22; 2nd ed. 1831; The Christian Faith), is a systematic interpretation of Christian dogmatics. (Scharlemann)

other letters.[93] The vocabulary and writings styles were different from the 'undisputed letters' of Paul. The discussion of Paul concerning works and faith were very different. The ideas concerning marriage were different. The approach to the end times was very different. Jesus, Paul, and the others, as demonstrated above, all taught the nearness of the end. It was clear that they all expected the eschaton[94] to take place before all of them would die. None of the pastorals, I Timothy, II Timothy, and Titus, have that expectancy of a near end. They appear to be preparing their readers and listeners for a long haul, or at least a longer haul than the other New Testament writers anticipated. The pastorals also gave church structure a hierarchy, whereas there is none of that in the other New Testament writers, or at least the same way. It appears that everyone within the church was considered equal in the other New Testament writings, except for the writers of the letters themselves. I later realized that it was not just the pastorals at question regarding Paul's authorship, but also books like II Thessalonians, Ephesians, and Colossians. I came to understand that there was an entire discussion that had taken place within the last two hundred years concerning the disputed and undisputed letters of Paul, that is still going on currently.

Because in church many, including myself, learned that the Bible is the infallible, inerrant word of God that was authored by the Holy Spirit by forty (40) authors, the subject of textual criticism can be difficult to even consider.[95]

---

93      (Ehrman, Chapter 3: Forgeries in the name of Paul 95)

94      Eschaton - The final event in the divine plan; the end of the world. (Oxford University Press)

95      (Bibleinfo.com)

Many of us were never taught to read the Bible critically. We were guided by the philosophy that was handed to us, delivered by documents such as Article X of The Chicago Statement on Biblical Inerrancy. We were told that the Bible was straight from heaven, with no errors, and was to be taken as the most authoritative group of writings above all else. There were even ancient witnesses who contributed to this belief. *"Tertullian argued for the authority of the Hebrew Scriptures and the entire collection of apostolic writings (Gospels and Epistles) on the basis of their divine origin, ancient dignity, and unity."*[96]

When demonstrated by the various scholars involved within Biblical textual studies, these issues make it clear that the common understanding of the Bible that we have today is clearly erroneous, that perspective is unable to stand up to proper scrutiny. Our Bible was written in Hebrew for the Old Testament and Greek for the New Testament. These texts were translated to English. If we want to really understand them, we must study the original languages or we may never come to know their proper meaning. In general, we approach the Bible as though what we are seeing is exactly as it was written. I am afraid that we are incorrect in that assessment.

Personally, I have heard over the years how things didn't make sense here and there within the New Testament. I have also recognized that based on the indoctrination of the individual, one could not discuss these things. There are such things as sentence structure and basic rules of English. To be fair, as previously stated, these documents are ancient

---

96    (Olson 92)

and they were not written in English.  So, the rules of Hebrew and Greek are different, and you cannot use modern methods of established writing principles to foist them back into the past.  However, people in ancient times did write in a somewhat incoherent manner at times.  Scholars have found through several analyses that many of the ancient documents were interpolated and changed in other ways.  At times, you find documents merged together or harmonized as if to appear as the same document.  Generally, when someone is talking or writing, they stick to a particular subject matter.  So, it is not a stretch to question, at the very least, that when the reader sees the subject matter has changed within a paragraph or even within the same sentence, that may indicate a later change, or a change made within the same timeframe that the document was written.

After I had seen enough of what textual criticism had to offer, it became important for me to begin to approach Christianity from a broader contextual position.  I had learned my studies of eschatology and textual criticism would not be complete without approaching the study of what is known as Early Christianity.   My Christian studies had to go beyond the Bible, and they had to go to the period leading up to and the subsequent period(s) after the timeframe that has been "fixed" and known as the historical period in which the New Testament was written.

# 5 EARLY CHRISTIANITY

After having learned about eschatology and textual criticism, it occurred to me to take a more historical approach to the world of the Bible. I had reasoned that buying into a belief or ideology without knowing the origin of the belief or ideal was not a good position to take. I concluded that all ideas have a history, a starting point. Over time, the ideas were added to by others which often culminated into an ideological framework. A cluster of similar or even opposing ideas. The ideological framework could and often would turn into something altogether different after a while. Later people took a new approach to the older ideas through re-interpretation for their own times. With this understanding, I opined that while many take the approach that they have original thought or that their ideals are going to be realized within observable reality, this is not a safe position to take when you fail to account for history—history in the sense of knowing what ideas were already evident before the ideas entered into one's own consciousness. This helped me to consider that others were unaware that those ideas did not work before and that there was no guarantee that they would work at a later time.

The subject of Early Christianity encompasses more than just what the bible has to offer. It has to do with the Ante-Nicene period, which is the time from the inception of Christianity leading to the Council of Nicaea. The Deutero-canonical Apocryphal writings cover much of the history in between the writing of the prophet Malachi and the writing of the Book of Matthew. For this study, I relied heavily upon the works of Professor Bart D. Ehrman and Professor Philip Harland.[97] Professor Harland hosts one of the best podcasts that I have ever witnessed, which I listened to extensively while attending university.[98] The New Testament includes the Book of Acts, or Acts of the Apostles, which is said to be the earliest history written on the Christian church. Delbert Burkett tells us that the Book of Acts, *"... supplies a sequel to the Third Gospel. Both were written by the same person, traditionally identified as "Luke." Acts, or "Acts of the Apostles," recounts the founding of the church and the spread of its message to the Roman Empire."[99]*

One of the main things that is known from the study of early Christianity regards two theories related to the sequence of orthodoxy and diversity within the early church and when the theories first appeared in Christian history.

97    Harland's Bio / CV http://people.laps.yorku.ca/people.nsf/researcherprofile?readform&shortname=pharland
98    (Harland)
99    (Burkett 263)

One theory is that there was unity within the church first and diversity later. The other theory is that there was diversity within the church first and unity later. The former theory is taken from Eusebius of Caesarea[100] as recounted in his writings entitled "Ecclesiastical History" or "Church History."[ii]

Modern Christianity has been approached through textual criticism, as was discussed above in Chapter 4. After some time, I found out that it was just a question of the different Biblical criticisms.[101,102] My studies of Biblical criticism is what led to my studies of early Christianity.

The history of criticism in relation to Christianity and the Bible was summed up quite well in an excursus done by Richard I, Pervo in his work, *Dating Acts – Between the Evangelists and the Apologists*.[iii] The history of criticism within biblical studies is where the Bible and science converges. Biblical and historical criticism have become methods to study the Bible outside of the systemized faith-alone model that pervaded Christian studies for a good portion of Christian history. In another work, *Orthodoxy and Heresy in Earliest Christianity* by a modern yet late scholar, Walter Bauer[iv] argues against the notion that Orthodoxy preceded heresy.[103] Bauer argues from the opposite position that Christianity in its inception was first full of heresy, hence

---

100    Eusebius of Caesarea, also called Eusebius Pamphili, (flourished 4th century, Caesarea Palestinae, Palestine), bishop, exegete, polemicist, and historian whose account of the first centuries of Christianity, in his Ecclesiastical History, is a landmark in Christian historiography. (T. E. Britannica, Eusebius of Caesarea)

101    (Wikipedia, Criticism of Christianity)

102    (B. A. Robinson)

103    Heresy, a theological doctrine or system rejected as false by

diversity, and that orthodoxy came afterwards. Bauer's work was first published in 1934, but in German. It was later published in 1964 by Georg Strecker, to include minor additions and corrections, plus two supplementary essays. It was later printed in English by Fortress Press, in 1971, edited by Robert Kraft and Gerhard Krodel. For a more detailed discussion on Walter Bauer, please see below in the footnotes, read Professor Ehrman's "The Challenge: Walter Bauer" beginning on page 7 of "Orthodox Corruption of Scripture," and of course, read "Orthodoxy and Heresy in Earliest Christianity" by Walter Bauer, himself.

As stated earlier, the book of Acts is known as the earliest document to give a "history" on early Christianity, or as stated at other times, Christian origins. As stated by Delbert Burkett, *"The book of Acts supplies a sequel to the Third Gospel. Both were written by the same person, traditionally identified as 'Luke.' Acts, or 'Acts of the Apostles,' recounts the founding of the church and the spread of its message to the Roman Empire."*

*"The central theme of Luke-Acts is that the message of salvation was sent to the Gentiles because the Jews rejected it. We can infer the centrality of this theme not only because it appears so frequently in Luke-Acts, but also because it*

---

ecclesiastical authority. Heresy differs from schism in that the heretic sometimes remains in the church despite his doctrinal errors, whereas the schismatic may be doctrinally orthodox but severs himself from the church. The Greek word hairesis (from which heresy is derived) was originally a neutral term that signified merely the holding of a particular set of philosophical opinions. Once appropriated by Christianity, however, the term heresy began to convey a note of disapproval. (T. E. Britannica, Heresy)

*appears at all the high points of the story.* "[104]

The earliest mention in the available external sources and/or witnesses, to mention the book of Acts, was St. Irenaeus.[v] The time of St. Irenaeus was circa 180 CE.[105] Theophilus[106] was around the same time of St. Irenaeus, a man of the same name is mentioned within the Gospel of Luke and at the beginning of the Book of Acts,

*"....most excellent Theophilus,"*

*Luke 1:3 KJV*

*"The former treatise have I made, O Theophilus,"*

*Acts 1:1 KJV*

---

104    (Burkett)

105    See http://www.earlychristianwritings.com/ for a annual timeline of the Early Christian writings.

106    Theophilus Of Antioch, (born, near Tigris and Euphrates rivers, modern Iraq—died April 180, Antioch, modern Antakya, Tur.), Syrian saint, sixth bishop of Antioch, and Christian apologist.

Educated in the Greek tradition, Theophilus became a Christian as an adult, after extended deliberation, and by 170 was elected bishop of Antioch. His sole surviving work consists of three apologetic tracts To Autolycus, a pagan friend whose derision of the Christian faith prompted the defense.

His multifaceted literary activity, often rhetorical, was at first popular among Christian theologians, but by the 5th century it was largely forgotten. (T. E. Britannica, Theophilus Of Antioch)

Some scholars explain this Theophilus this way, *"lover of God, a Christian, probably a Roman, to whom Luke dedicated both his Gospel ( Luke 1:3 ) and the Acts of the Apostles ( 1:1 )."*[107]

This explanation by Easton and others seemed untenable. If the Theophilus to whom Luke was writing to, instead of a "lover of God" which was probably a Roman, then this Theophilus is said to have died around the same year that St. Irenaeus was writing.  That makes Acts later than the consensus agreements amongst some scholars.[vi]  Another major issue with the book of Acts is the content in comparison to some of the other letters within the New Testament corpus. The book of Acts shows Peter and Paul as on the same team, never in any disagreement.[108]  In the letter to the Galatians, we see Paul and Peter in disagreement to the point where he confronted Peter publicly for being a hypocrite, not eating with the Gentiles when his Jewish brothers were not present.[vii]  We only have Paul's side of this discussion, and none from Peter.[109]

It appears from the very beginning that there was a diversity of opinions and beliefs within the New Testament itself. That diversity, or as some call it, heresy, is from the New Testament moving forward.  The above was not a demonstration of heresy, but a matter of differences of opinion. The above was also to demonstrate how the book of Acts does not always include material from Paul's own letters. One final demonstration comes from comparing Paul's story

107    (M.G. Easton M.A.)
108    (Ehrman, Chapter 2 Forgeries in the Name of Peter 63)
109    (Ehrman, Chapter 6 Forgeries in Conflicts with False Teachers 189)

of conversion as is recounted in Acts 9:1-31; 22:6-21; and 26:9-23 with Galatians 1:17-24.  I had come across where some scholars posit that the divisions and heresies were said to have come in after the apostolic age, or when the apostles had all died. *"Influence of the 'pagan' religions on Christianity is not very perceptible in the 1st century."*[110]

While Mr. Easton may not perceive the influence of "pagans," the notice of diversity and heresy within the New Testament is quite clear to others.  The New Testament is nowhere near as cohesive as many believe and others proclaim.  Diversity and heresy lasted quite a while during the New Testament period, as well as the Ante-Nicene period.  It was such an issue that there were several Church Fathers[111] writing on the subject as recounted within the Patristic Literature,[112] and many others that denote details of the Church as recounted by them after the New Testament period.  These documents are included in the corpora entitled the "Apostolic Fathers" and the "Nicene Fathers Series."  A term was given to the early church fathers who wrote so much on those who were creators and spreaders of heresy.  That term was heresiologist.[113]

Diversity and heresy were both clearly within Christian

---

110     (Easton)

111     Church Father, any of the great bishops and other eminent Christian teachers of the early centuries whose writings remained as a court of appeal for their successors, especially in reference to controverted points of faith or practice.  (T. E. Britannica, Church Father)

112     Patristic literature, body of literature that comprises those works, excluding the New Testament, written by Christians before the 8th century.  (Kelly)

113     Heresiologist - a writer against heresies. (Merriam-Webster)

Origins from day one. Not only is diversity and heresy within the New Testament, but it is also evident within the patristic writings which were developed after the period of the New Testament. The issues with dating these documents, the New Testament and the Patristic literature, have been described and discussed extensively by many a scholar and researcher.

It was now evident that non-scholars, meaning non-PhD scholars, and those who have not gone to university for religious studies of any form, at times added more clarity than even those who had attended university or some other formal religious training, including non-accredited seminary schools. With philosophies developed and given to people to guide their understanding, this makes it quite difficult for a person to see beyond what they've been taught. Authorities, if you will, in religion are to be believed for knowing the matters of spirituality more than the lay person. This is true in general, but coming to understand the esoteric is not limited to those who have had formal training. A person with enough will, self-discipline, and determination can go very far, if not farther than, those who have become authorities in matters of esoteric-related subjects. During my research into Early Christianity, I would learn later that many of the learned ones, (i.e., scholars), knew and discussed many things amongst their community of which the average lay person would have no clue. This is not unheard of, there are many other fields of study in which the same thing is done. Language is key within the learned circles. The lay people are unaware of the power of language. It is one of the things that separates the learned from the unlearned. Regarding esoteric matters, with something as important as a faith that is to be shared and demonstrated in a public way to be the main religion that is to be believed as the standard, or at least a standard of morality, a passage of Isaiah within the Old Testament comes to mind:

*"11 And the vision of all is become unto you as the words of a book that is sealed, which men deliver to one that is learned, saying, Read this, I pray thee: and he saith, I cannot; for it is sealed:*

*12 And the book is delivered to him that is not learned, saying, Read this, I pray thee: and he saith, I am not learned.*

*13 Wherefore the Lord said, Forasmuch as this people draw near me with their mouth, and with their lips do honour me, but have removed their heart far from me, and their fear toward me is taught by the precept of men:*

*14 Therefore, behold, I will proceed to do a marvellous work among this people, even a marvellous work and a wonder: for the wisdom of their wise men shall perish, and the understanding of their prudent men shall be hid.*

*15 Woe unto them that seek deep to hide their counsel from the LORD, and their works are in the dark, and they say, Who seeth us? and who knoweth us?*

*16 Surely your turning of things upside down shall*

*be esteemed as the potter's clay: for shall the work say of him that made it, He made me not? or shall the thing framed say of him that framed it, He had no understanding?*

*[17] Is it not yet a very little while, and Lebanon shall be turned into a fruitful field, and the fruitful field shall be esteemed as a forest?*

*[18] And in that day shall the deaf hear the words of the book, and the eyes of the blind shall see out of obscurity, and out of darkness."*

*Isaiah 29:11-18 KJV*

After some time, I began to come across other authors, authors who would not be taken seriously by the vast majority of those who are believers and perhaps by some amongst the modern secular population, such as Craig Lyons Ms.D., D.D., M.Div., Acharya S. a.k.a. D. M. Murdock (R.I.P.), Earl Doherty, Timothy Freke and Peter Gandy, the late John Marco Allegro, Tony Bushby, Thomas L. Thompson Professor Emeritus, Martin A. Larson, Elaine Pagels, Robert M. Price, and Ahmed Osman. I would later learn about the earlier writers such as Flavius Josephus, Philo, Tacitus, Suetonius Tranquillus, Plutarch, Strabo. I also discovered a prominent, in my mind, YouTube personality, Michael C. Xoroaster. I learned that there were many who had begun to see what I saw and even saw much more than I saw. Some of these authors and their works will be discussed in the current chapter. Other authors listed above will be discussed in subsequent chapters. Beyond the diversity and heresy that is apparent in

# TRANSFORMATION

Early Christianity, I would then look into the actual sources of the mention of Christianity from other angles. I looked into eschatology again, as well as other subjects to include those mentioned external to the Bible and external to those who espoused to one degree or another Christianity itself.

Around this time, I was attending college courses towards a Bachelor's in Business Administration. Instead of focusing on my studies within college in an effort to obtain the highest possible G.P.A., I was unable to find a balance to align with my personal studies within Christianity. My entire faith had been shaken to the point where I put all of my belief on hold and approached my studies more academically. My circle of friends and acquaintances shrank significantly. I had already learned from the experiences of others who had studied similar subject matters that when one discusses these things with family, friends, etc., the responses, verbally and nonverbally, often took on rejection and distance. I decided to be proactive in my approach and utilize rejection and distance from the offense.

## Eschatology Again?

After looking into eschatology again in general, it was clear that the New Testament writers unanimously believed that they were living during the days that the Old Testament writers had been describing or foretelling. They made it clear to their readers and listeners that those were the "last days" and "end times." I had seen some scholars try to separate these, viz., the Partial Preterists. I had never personally seen a need or justification for doing so. Eschatology is a subject that is much more important than many realize. I was grateful to learn the importance of the works of Martin A. Larson regarding eschatology.  As mentioned above, eschatology has roots that go back to the Old Testament, as far back as Deuteronomy, with even hints of it in Genesis.  The ancient Hebrews typically believed that the dead went to a place that they called Sheol after death, whether they were good or evil.[114]

Some believe that during the Seleucid[115] and the Hasmonean[116] Periods a new eschatology appeared within the beliefs of the Jews while they were under Greek and Persian influence.[117]  One of the most important and significant books of the Old Testament that was quoted by the New Testament and the patristic writers was Isaiah.  Marvin A. Sweeney says of the book of Isaiah that it, *"... generally stands at the head of the major prophets in both the Jewish and Christian versions of the Bible, although one Talmudic*

114    (M. A. Larson 214)

115    Seleucid kingdom, (312–64 BC), an ancient empire that at its greatest extent stretched from Thrace in Europe to the border of India. It was carved out of the remains of Alexander the Great's Macedonian empire by its founder, Seleucus I Nicator. (T. E. Britannica, Seleucid kingdom)

116    Hasmonean Dynasty, also spelled Hasmonaean, dynasty of ancient Judaea, descendants of the Maccabee (q.v.) family. The name derived (according to Josephus, in The Antiquities of the Jews) from the name of their ancestor Hasmoneus (Hasmon), or Asamonaios. In 143 (or 142) BC Simon Maccabeus, son of Mattathias (and brother of Judas Maccabeus), succeeded his brother Jonathan as leader of the Maccabean revolt against the Seleucid dynasty. He soon became independent of the Seleucids as high priest, ruler, and ethnarch of Judaea; the offices were hereditary, and Simon thus became the first of the Hasmonean dynasty. (T. E. Britannica, Hasmonean Dynasty)

117    (M. A. Larson, Chapter 1 Judaism Section F. Eschatology 214-215)

*tradition places it as the third book of the prophets, following Jeremiah and Ezekiel (b. B. Bat. 14b)."*[118]

In light of eschatology within the Old Testament, in a part of Isaiah denoted by some scholars to be "The Little Apocalypse"[119], Isaiah states,

*"Thy dead men shall live, together with my dead body shall they arise. Awake and sing, ye that dwell in dust: for thy dew is as the dew of herbs, and the earth shall cast out the dead."*

*Isaiah 26:19 KJV*

This little apocalypse was important because it was said to be interpolated by later authors who seemed to incorporate material that is consistent with the Seleucid and Hasmonean Periods. The book of Isaiah overall is even said to be as many as three books in one.[120] There are other scholars and researchers who do not see the book of Isaiah as written by many authors. However, when following the timeline that consensus scholarship has formulated, and looking at the kings that Isaiah mentioned that his office coincided with,

*"The vision of Isaiah the son of Amoz, which he saw concerning Judah and Jerusalem in the days of Uzziah, Jotham, Ahaz, and Hezekiah, kings of Ju-*

---

118    (Sweeney, The Latter Prophets: Isaiah, Jeremiah, Ezekiel; III-The Book of Isaiah 75)

119    Isaiah Chapters 24-27 is titled, "The Little Apocalypse" by some critical scholars and is said to have been written at a later date.

120    (Sweeney, The Latter Prophets: Isaiah, Jeremiah, Ezekiel; III-The Book of Isaiah 76)

*dah."*

*Isaiah 1:1 KJV* [121]

There has to be a wide range of dating to account for in this book at some point. As far as Isaiah 26:19, it expresses a vague belief in a resurrection, as stated by Larson. Larson states that the book of Daniel is more definite in its declaration of a resurrection.[viii] There was also a comparison between the book of Daniel and the book of Revelation that I found.[ix]

The Sadducees[122] were said to have rejected the eschatological ideas that were reflected in Isaiah, Daniel, and others.[x] The Pharisees[123] were said to have accepted, to some degree, the ideas that said documents shadowed.[xi, xii]

Along with eschatology came the concept of a Messiah.[124] This Messiah concept played a central role within the eschatological frameworks involving the end of Jewish suf-

---

121     (B. Brasford)

122     Name given to the party representing views and practises of the Law and interests of Temple and priesthood directly opposite to those of the Pharisees. (Kohler, SADDUCEES (Hebrew, ; Greek, Σαδδου καῖοι))

123     Party representing the religious views, practises, and hopes of the kernel of the Jewish people in the time of the Second Temple and in opposition to the priestly Sadducees. They were accordingly scrupulous observers of the Law as interpreted by the Soferim, or Scribes, in accordance with tradition.
(Kohler, PHARISEES (Φαρισαῖοι; Aramaic, "Perishaya"; Hebr. "Perushim"))

124     Messiah, (from Hebrew mashia⊠, "anointed"), in Judaism,

fering and the establishment of a kingdom that would not end.[xiii] Flavius Josephus mentioned many "Messiahs" that had risen up during the timeframe of the New Testament under different Roman Emperors.[xiv] There were different concepts concerning this Messiah.[125] The more and more that I dove into this rabbit hole, the more it occurred to me that taking one position or another was untenable. I was fascinated by the amounts of information available and the time that was required in learning what all encompassed this altogether complicated subject. A group that I had come across which was not discussed, at least by name, within the New Testament tunneled me even deeper within the rabbit hole of loosing myself in order to find myself for the first time.

## The Essenes

In studying Early Christianity and the available sources, I came across the study of the Dead Sea Scrolls.[126] The group associated with this collection of writings were Jews called the Essenes.[127] They were spoken of by ancient writers who

the expected king of the Davidic line who would deliver Israel from foreign bondage and restore the glories of its golden age. The Greek New Testament's translation of the term, christos, became the accepted Christian designation and title of Jesus of Nazareth, indicative of the principal character and function of his ministry. More loosely, the term messiah denotes any redeemer figure; and the adjective messianic is used in a broad sense to refer to beliefs or theories about an eschatological improvement of the state of humanity or the world. (T. E. Britannica, Messiah)

125    (M. A. Larson, Chapter 1 Judaism Section F. Eschatology 217-218)

126    (Malkin)

127    ESSENES (etymology doubtful; probably two words are represented, "Essenes" and "Essæi": Essenes = Ἐσσηνοὶ = , "the modest,"

are well known today, including by Pliny the Elder.[128, xv] Some scholars believed that without studying the Essenes, that the study of Christian Origins would be incomplete.[129] *The discovery of the Dead Sea Scrolls casted new light on the relationship between Judaism and Christianity. The fact that the dates of the scrolls were around the time of the New Testament is far too important to ignore.[xvi]*

Josephus wrote on the Essenes in his "*Antiquities of the Jews*"[130] and his "*Jewish Wars*" or "*Wars of the Jews*". He mentioned that they were one of the three sects of the Jews during his time.[xvii]

The importance of the Essenes in relation to Early Christianity has to do with the similarities within their views with the early Christians. I also found that there were similarities between the Essenes and the views within the heresy side of Christianity, one set of eclectic views called Gnosticism. Josephus tells us that the Essenes believed, just as the Christians, in an afterlife and that bad men were to suffer punishment after death,[xviii, xix] in prophecy,[xx] fate,[xxi] and that they

"humble," or "pious ones" [so Josephus in most passages; A branch of the Pharisees who conformed to the most rigid rules of Levitical purity while aspiring to the highest degree of holiness. They lived solely by the work of their hands and in a state of communism, devoted their time to study and devotion and to the practise of benevolence, and refrained as far as feasible from conjugal intercourse and sensual pleasures, in order to be initiated into the highest mysteries of heaven and cause the expected Messianic time to come ('Ab. Zarah ix. 15; Luke ii. 25, 38; xxiii. 51). (Kohler, ESSENES)

128     (Elder, Book 5, Chapter 17 70)
129     (M. A. Larson, Chapter II The Essenes: The External Evidence 226)
130     Antiquities of the Jews is also called Antiquities.

were Pythagoreans.[xxii]  The mention of the Essenes being Pythagorean in thought seemed a direct reference to them being Gnostic.  Gnosticism will be discussed more later.

Concerning the documentation that is attributed by some to the hands of the Essenes,  Larson deals with The Damascus Document, the Habakkuk Commentary, The Manual of Discipline, The War of the Sons of Light, and the Thanksgiving Psalms.[131]  The historical setting for these documents is set within the Intertestamental period, much of which is chronicled within the writings of the Apocrypha[132] , specifically 1 and 2 Maccabees and Josephus.  The writers of these documents, while they did have liturgical writings among them, evidence of a poem, etc., they commentated on the Old Testament writings, interpreting history and modern life through them, utilizing them as though they foretold their own times, and they appeared convinced that they were in the last days, end times, near the end of the age, just as we see within the New Testament.[133]  These documents have been demonstrated by scholars to show the contextual and developmental tenets that the Essenes went through over a process of time, during the intertestamental period, and other documents, not referenced above, during the New Testament period.

---

131    See The Complete Dead Sea Scrolls in English by Geza Vermes

132    Apocrypha - Biblical or related writings not forming part of the accepted canon of Scripture. (Oxford Dictionary Online)

133    (Vermes, III. The History of the Community 49)

# 5 EARLY CHRISTIANITY
## Gnosticism

Gnosticism is another set of concepts and religious ideas that I came across, which I saw hints of within the New Testament and within the Ante Nicene Church Fathers. The ideals that became known as Gnosticism were in no way monolithic, any more than the ideas within Christianity. Even today Christianity is not monolithic. Gnosticism was a subject that was quite difficult for me to understand. I came across several scholars, researchers, and lay people who described it in their own terms and came from various angles, yet none of what I had read and observed was enough to bring to understand what Gnosticism really was. I saw hints of this understanding later when I began to study ancient history from the historians themselves.

As stated above, the various Ante Nicene church fathers wrote about various heresies. Gnosticism was considered a heresy, probably more accurately, a set of heresies. The ideological and philosophical wars during Early Christianity leading up to the Nicene Council were many. Unfortunately, these wars continued for many years after the council at Nice, especially after the establishment of the Catholic church when later councils were held and recorded. Many, like myself, were unaware of the fact that the history of Christianity as was commonly told, left much of the differences of opinion and philosophies out of the equation.

Like the findings of the Dead Sea scrolls that began in 1947 at the Qumran site near the Dead Sea, there were other writings found at a site in Upper Egypt, whose governate is Qena named Nag Hammadi, located *"40 miles (64km) from*

*Luxor, southern Egypt's biggest city, "[134]* in 1945 by, "*... two brothers, Muhammad and Khalifah 'All of the al-Samman clan."[135]* These texts were translated, each, from Greek to Coptic. These texts became known as the Nag Hammadi Library.[136] It has been stated that the priests that translated them from Greek to Coptic were not always capable of grasping the profundity or sublimity of what they sought to translate. In other words, what I took from this is that the process of transmission, translation, and copying of the Nag Hammadi documents revealed no difference regarding profundity and sublimity as was evidenced of what was transmitted, translated, and copied from the Old and New Testaments. This more than likely can be argued for any ancient text.

The Dead Sea Scrolls discovery should be taken much more seriously. In the eyes of some, the Dead Sea Scrolls has a link to the Old and New Testaments. The Nag Hammadi Library was not discussed as much as the Dead Sea Scrolls and was seen largely, from what I can surmise, as a load of garbage to not be taken seriously. We have the

---

134    (BBC News)

135    (J. M. Robinson, Introduction: 3. The Discovery 22)

136    The Nag Hammadi library consists of twelve books, plus eight leaves removed from a thirteenth book in late antiquity and tucked inside the front cover of the sixth. These eight leaves comprise a complete text, an independent treatise taken out of a book of collected essays. In fact, each of the books, except the tenth, consists of a collection of relatively brief works. Thus there is a total of fifty-two tractates. Since a single book usually contains several tractates, one may suspect that, like the books of the Bible, the texts were composed with a small format in mind, but that a larger format had come into use by the time these extant copies were made. This can be explained in terms of the history of the manufacture of books. (J. M. Robinson, Introduction 10)

Ante Nicene church fathers to thank for that, as well as the enigmatic writing itself. It seemed that many would have a problem with linking the Nag Hammadi documents to either the Old or New Testaments. After hearing many a podcast, reading many a book, and perusing extensively online, I decided to take a different approach to the texts of the Nag Hammadi Library. I looked at what some of the Ante Nicene church fathers stated as far as the beliefs of many of the Gnostic sects, and I decided to focus on what Josephus stated about the Essenes. Josephus stated that the Essenes were Pythagoreans. I saw where some have stated that the Gnostics were Platonic in their doctrines and beliefs. I had found a link between Pythagorean and Platonic doctrine and beliefs. If this "link" was true, then I would need to go back into the ancient Greek texts to see if I could find evidence between the Essenes, Pythagoras, Plato, and Gnosticism.

Another major thing that I began to realize, and had gleaned from writers such as Horace Butler[137] whether directly or implied, was that names are not always so strict in regard to people as well as names of geographical locations. There are times when the beliefs and practices take precedence over the names of a group as well as descriptions in regards to geographical locations. Sometimes a group adopted the name of a person or another group based strictly on belief and practice. The differences are not always so easy

137    Horace Butler - Stone River Publishing (First Edition 2001/Second Edition 2009) - The #1 Dallas Morning News regional nonfiction bestseller now throws open its earth shattering secrets for the entire world to see! Gripping from its opening page, WHEN ROCKS CRY OUT pulls you into a real-life deadly chase that uncovers the 'Forbidden Histories' of a 16th century friar who followed Columbus into the Americas. (Butler)

to find. But at the end of the day, belief and practice seemed much more important depending upon what the chosen focus of the particular study was at the time.

After having found a link between the Pythagorean doctrine and beliefs with the Platonic ideas, something that I had read before came into view. It appeared that some of the concepts found in Pythagoras, Plato, and others went to a much earlier time, as some of them even say themselves. That earlier time led me to Ancient Egypt.

About this time is when things between my wife, Conflict and I, began to tank significantly. I tried to work my way back to a place where she and I had some harmony. Nothing that I did worked. This was also about the time when Conflict and her friend from childhood, Bridge, had gone from having a peaceful reunion after many years of separation, to not talking much at all. The reason why they were not talking much at all is because Bridge and I were talking practically all of the time.

Bridge and I had a connection like I had never had with another person. I felt as if she was my friend. The best that I had ever had. We talked about anything and everything. We talked daily over the phone, and when we could not talk over the phone, we would e-mail each other. Eventually, Bridge and I would even text one another. We developed a romantic element over time and even shared our feelings for one another. We talked about how there was no one that saw the world the way that we did together. Our relationship seemed inseparable for a while. We looked forward until the next time that we could talk. We would talk early and even late.  We had such a strong connection that neither one of us wanted to let go.  We might have even experienced a type of love bond, though fate would never allow us to live that out.  For she was married and so was I.  And after a while, our romantic connection, as well as our friendship, dissolved altogether.  I suppose that when people get too comfortable and allow things that they really do not want to happen to take place, they grow irritated and desire to move on.  Bridge was forceful at times, mouthy, pushy, and dominant.  She had some of the same attributes as Conflict, but for different reasons.  She did come from a different place than Conflict.  I do believe that Bridge genuinely cared for me.  But I misread her and grew very distant and angry with her because I did not understand why she came off so domineering.  I am grateful for all that I learned from her and the fact that she was able to show me that I could love.  I had never experienced the feelings that I experienced before meeting her.  But some things are not meant to last.

First, my marriage ended, and then my relationship with Bridge.  I decided to go it alone for a time.  Those two women, Conflict and Bridge, had some of the greatest impacts on me.  For a while, I placed my anger on those two.  It would take me some time to realize that I was at fault as well.  I could no longer blame them entirely for the things that they did.  I decided to do what I found many others not doing.  I looked in the mirror and realized that I was fucked up.  I concluded that most of my issues stemmed from my childhood.  I was an adult in age but still a child in thought.  I saw the world the way I believed it to be instead of understanding observable reality.  I was unable to see things for what they were. I did not understand myself.  As a result, I landed myself in situations with people.  Some of the relationships began quite well and lasted for a time.  But over time, they would turn toxic.

Talking with Bridge made the subjects such as Gnosticism, Ancient Egypt, and the mysteries a lot easier.  She was involved in metaphysics and the occult world.  She introduced me to Tarot, Runes, Reiki, Astrology, etc.  While I was diving into the study of Gnosticism in relation to Pythagoras, Plato, and Ancient Egypt, whether the connections were correct or not, I could see them.  I began to stop reading scholars, researchers, etc., and go straight to the ancient texts as I had the Bible, the Dead Sea Scrolls, and the Nag Hammadi Library.  Little did I know that this would cause me to take even more time from Conflict and our children.  I was consumed.  I could not get enough of study.  I took breaks from time to time.  I would then dive right back into my studies.

## Ancient Egyptian Connection?

A sadly damaged stone[138] stands in the British Museum, which James Henry Breasted[139] opined to contain the oldest

---

138     (Breasted, The Philosophy of a Memphite Priest. With a Reproduction of the Memphite Slab. 458)

139     James Henry Breasted, (born August 27, 1865, Rockford, Illinois, U.S.—died December 2, 1935, New York City, New York), American Egyptologist, archaeologist, and historian who promoted research on ancient Egypt and the ancient civilizations of western Asia. (T. E. Britannica, James Henry Breasted)

The  first American whose profession was ancient history. (Wilson) ....He brought to America the realization that our cultural ancestry

known formulation of a philosophical "weltanschauung."[140] *"It is a rectangular slab of black granite, 0,92X1,375 m, and the inscribed surface is considerably smaller, being o,688x i)32 m, thus occupying only the upper three quarters of the stone, as it lies upon the long edge."[141]*

The major aim of this document seemed that certain concepts that Ancient Greece may have taken from Ancient Egypt came from it.[142]

This inscription suggests that heart would be better understood as mind, where thoughts and ideas came from, and that tongue would be the vehicle or channel used to express the thoughts and ideas that the mind conceived. Heart within this document would not be meant to be taken as the organ that pumps one's blood, but to be seen as the seat of the mind. It seems as though suggestions and guidance issues from the mind. Perhaps the more accurate understanding of *"Keep thy heart with all diligence; for out of it are the issues of life,"* Proverbs 4:23 KJV is that the issues are ideas and thoughts that are created or that issue from the mind should be kept with diligence or should be attended to, above all else. This would seem what the later concept of forms as spoken of by Plato, under that specific nomenclature, came

is rooted in the distant past and made European scholars aware of the peculiar contribution which American scholarship might make to humanistic research.

140    Weltanschauung - A particular philosophy or view of life; the world view of an individual or group. (Oxford Dictionary Online)

141    (Breasted, The Philosophy of a Memphite Priest. With a Reproduction of the Memphite Slab. 458)

142    (Breasted, The Philosophy of a Memphite Priest. With a Reproduction of the Memphite Slab. 464)

from.  Just as Plato and some of the others believed, physical things first existed within the realm of thought and became concrete in the form of words and physical objects that man manufactured.[143]

## Ancient Greek Connection?

I had seen where some had suggested that the Ancient Greeks stole their philosophy from ancient Egypt.[144]   I had also seen where others stated that some ideas Ancient Greeks brought forth had no Ancient Egyptian origin, especially in regards to philosophy.  Breasted discussed how Ancient Egypt had dealt with abstract subjects of people and things, how Ancient Greece had written that they owed their philosophical origin to Ancient Egypt, and Ancient Greece adopted Ancient Egypt's method of philosophical interpretation of their gods.[145]

I concluded from this that the ideas as found on the Memphite stone were built upon later by Pythagoras and others. I would even find that an Ancient Greek historian showed the connection between Ancient Greece and Ancient Egypt, and that the ideas and philosophy being stolen from Ancient Egypt did not seem to hold much weight. Herodotus[146] states,

---

143     (Breasted, The Philosophy of a Memphite Priest. With a Reproduction of the Memphite Slab. 471)

144     (James)

145     (Breasted, The Philosophy of a Memphite Priest. With a Reproduction of the Memphite Slab. 475)

146     It is impossible to give certain and undisputed dates for the lifetime of Herodotus. But if we are to believe Aulus Gellius, he was born in 484 B.C. ; and the internal evidence of his History proves that he was alive during some part of the Peloponnesian war, as he alludes

*"These customs, then, and others besides, which I shall in-dicate, were taken by the Greeks from the Egyptians."[xxiii]*

Of course, one would need to look further into exact-ly what customs Herodotus was talking about.[xxiv] Even amongst the Pythagorean writers, there are those who state that Pythagoras himself, *"...was in Egypt when Polycrates sent him a letter of introduction to Amasis; he learnt the Egyptian language, so we learn from Antiphon in his book On Men of Outstanding Merit,... he also entered the Egyp-tian sanctuaries,3 and was told their secret lore concerning the gods."[147]*

---

to incidents which occurred in its earlier years. He may therefore be safely said to have been a contemporary of the two great wars which respectively founded and ended the brief and brilliant pre-eminence of Athens in Hellas. He belongs in the fullest sense to the "great" period of Greek history.

Herodotus was (it is agreed on all hands) a native of Halicarnassus in Caria ; and if his birth fell in 484, he was born a subject of the Great King. His early life was spent, apparently, in his native town, or possi-bly in the island of Samos, of which he shows an intimate knowledge. Tradition asserts that after a visit to Samos he " returned to Halicar-nassus and expelled the tyrant " (Lygdamis) ; " but when later he saw himself disliked by his countrymen, he went as a volunteer to Thur-ium, when it was being colonized by the Athenians. There he died and lies buried in the market-place." 1 This is supported by good evidence, and there seems to be no reason for doubting it. It is also stated that he visited Athens and there recited some part of his history ; this may have happened, as alleged, about the year 445. It is evident from his constant allusions to Athens that he knew it well, and must have lived there. (Herodotus)

147    (Laertius 323)

# TRANSFORMATION

There was also a link established between Pythagoras and Plato that I found.[148]

This Philolaus[149] spoken of by Socrates, was a Pythagorean from Crotona.  This indicates that the ideas from Pythagoras related by a later follower, agreed with ideas that Socrates, himself, had come to adopt as his own.  So, the concept that the body was a prison and that to die is better than to live was spoken of by Socrates.  Further, since it was understood that the gods took care of men, so death is not up to the individual man but to the gods.[xxv]  Socrates, within the dialogue of Phaedo, would continue to speak the conceptual ideas of the body alone being the hindrance from what is,[150] that being wisdom and knowledge.  He would even speak on duality, reminiscence (or being reminded of previous knowledge), and philosophy "herself" as in terms of "she" and "her."[151]  Also, within Phaedo, Socrates mentions abstract[152] in relation to equality and beauty.  These same concepts, cleverly nuanced, are found in the writings of Apostle Paul, the Nag Hammadi writings, and others.  Many of the ideas laid out in certain of Plato's writings were gleaned from Pythagoras and perhaps other ancient philosophers.

---

148    (Plato, Phaedo or The Immortality of the Soul 58)

149    Philolaus, (flourished c. 475 BC), philosopher of the Pythagorean school, named after the Greek thinker Pythagoras (fl. c. 530 BC). (T. E. Britannica, Philolaus)

150    What is meant what exists, whether in the realm of "spirit" or within the realm of observable reality.

151    The book of Proverbs in the Old Testament mentions wisdom as she and her, as demonstrated in Proverbs chapter 1 verse 20, "Wisdom crieth without; she uttereth her voice in the streets:"

152    Abstract - Existing in thought or as an idea but not having a physical or concrete existence. (Oxford Dictionary Online)

After much study, I took the approach to let the writings speak for themselves and to take seriously the people who were much closer to the events and people of their own time and even earlier. After having studied, for a time, Preterism, Textual Criticism, and Early Christianity, I concluded that what I had learned growing up was not good enough to hold on to anymore. I never stopped learning though. I had decided to look into other subjects as well. I came across a book by a gentlemen named, A. J. Deus.[153] His work entitled, *The Great Leap-Fraud–Social Economics of Religious Terrorism*,[xxvi] written in two volumes, had taken me for yet another loop, or deeper into the rabbit hole. This time, I had begun to consider that which some might think inconceivable.[154] The idea that perhaps the greatest example of mankind having never been a part of our human family and community was coming into view.

---

153    A. J. Deus is an economist specializing in the history of religious organizations and systemic poverty. He is an expert in the history of comparative religions, economics of religion, religious fraud, terrorism, and poverty. He earned an economics degree from the University of Applied Sciences in Economics and Business Administration, Zürich, Switzerland, and a master's degree from the University of Ottawa, Canada.

In his investigations over a period of two decades, the author has conducted field research throughout Europe, from England to Portugal, Spain, France, Italy, and Bulgaria, as well as in North Africa and in South Asia. (A. J. Deus)

154    Inconceivable - Not capable of being imagined or grasped mentally; unbelievable. (Oxford Dictionary Online)

# 6 DID JESUS CHRIST EVER EXIST?

After learning about Textual Criticism and Early Christianity in general, something became quite clear. I had to look at Eschatology in general, and Preterism in particular, a different way. Preterism now seemed to be an erroneous attempt to rescue the New Testament from prophetic failure. I understand the implications and the seeming outright disrespect in that statement. I would like to make it clear that I have much respect for the Bible. Perhaps even more than most since I actually took the time to read and focus on what many may have not—at least those that I have come across over the years. It also seemed that the Bible was not a book authored by the Holy Spirit and recorded by forty (40) writers. It appeared, rather, that the Bible was a book of human history and the experiences that they had with the deity, other entities, and perhaps divine things. It actually made me feel much better to know that those that lived long ago were just as human as people are today.  But just as I had learned over time and from a specific person that I truly respect and honor, "Humans do, what Humans do."

By this time I did not know what to think.  My family was falling apart.  I did just enough to pass my college courses.  I had really good classmates.  We studied together and compared our notes.  I was older than most of the other students. I was near thirty years old, while many of my classmates were either in their late teens or early to mid-twenties. While at college, in between classes, I would find secluded areas and rooms where I was alone to dive into the studies of eschatology, textual criticism, early Christianity, and other subjects.  By this time, I no longer cared about belief.  I had become very much information-focused.  I only put in time for college study when it came to projects, mid-terms, and final exams.  Now looking back, I wish I had balanced my college, family, and personal studies much better.

From the beginning of my journey, I truly believed in God.  When I gave my life to Jesus Christ, I did it genuinely.  I truly believed that all of my troubles were over.  I had many insecurities.  I had felt inadequate and out of place my entire life.  I had little to no confidence and felt like an alien.  I desired death but was afraid of laying a hand on myself.  I wanted God to do it.  I never really told anyone about what I felt over the years.  I would hint at it from time to time to those who were close, but it seemed like no one understood the little that I did share.  So, becoming a Christian meant very much.  It meant the world.  I did my best to use it to clean up the negative aspects of my nature.  If such a thing is possible.

Here I was after having gotten married based on false promises and a belief that that is what God wanted me to do, now facing something that tore me apart inwardly. How could I now be at a place where I would even remotely contemplate letting my faith go? I had begun to rely far more on logic and less on emotion when it came to study. I learned to follow the evidence and not devotion. I had gone too far to accept a belief. I cried like a baby for nights. I was afraid. I thought that God was going to harm me. After years of asking God to take my life from me, I was now afraid that he would. The one thing that I believed to be the crowning moment of life, I was about to let go of. My heart pounded with pain. My joints ached. I sweated often. I began to experience anxiety. I could not sleep. I was afraid to talk to anyone. When I shared my beliefs on eschatology with others, I scared them away. There was no way that I was about to share with others that I had now accepted that Jesus never existed.

Having come across the Great Leap-Fraud series, authored by A. J. Deus, I was introduced to a deeper and at first, seemingly more skeptical approach to Textual Criticism and the social, economic, and religio-historical process in general. I had already begun to realize that reason, intellect, and logic were spiritual—at least the ancients thought so. I had seen where some believed that using your logic and so called, "head" was relying on the ego. That is not how the ancients understood it. Back to this discussion at a later time.

Deus' work was quite influential in me changing my position about church and Christianity in general. From his work moving forward, my religious foundation was shattered. Over a process of time, though, I had successfully worked to re-lay my foundation. One thing that I had learned about the mind though, is when you answer one question, new questions come. Until I was able to get my mind right, I had to keep searching. Nothing else mattered. I was told once that if you are not right, you can do nothing for anyone else. I was effectively hit with what is termed "instinctive elaboration."[155]  This went in line with what I had heard from a prominent preacher once, "It is difficult to unlearn what you first learned." I wholeheartedly agree with this statement.

Deus' work is about people and their underlying religious thought process and how it influences their economic and social behavior.[156] He made quite a profound statement, among many in the book, *"Refusing to believe does not help one escape a cultural heritage. We just don't seem to be able to cope without our share of superstitions. Even in the twenty-first century, religious activists still perform their rituals, prayers, and readings in a self-enforcing mechanism: the more they engage in it, the narrower their thought process."* I cannot disagree with that assessment. I would come to realize that even the ancients had their fair share of superstitions as well.

---

155    Instinctive Elaboration - When a question is posed, it takes over the brain's thought process. And when your brain is thinking about the answer to a question, it can't contemplate anything else. (Hoffeld)

156    (A. J. Deus, Leap of Faith : A Cultural Heritage 9)

While diving into the studies that led me to accept that Jesus never existed, there was a sort of natural progression that took place. There were different aspects of study within Christianity and Judaism that I came across. Some of the material was studied and debated for more than 200 years. The same studies and debates ensue today. The studies included whether Moses wrote the first five books of the bible, Biblical Archaeology, the three main Biblical schools of thought, a long and still disputed statement concerning Jesus made by Flavius Josephus, a different look at the Gospels, a closer look at the Apostle Paul, and finally a closer look at the Essenes.

## Did Moses Write the Pentateuch?

One of the main things that stuck out during the study of Early Christianity, was that many believers were saying that Moses wrote the first five books of the bible. Within the texts of the Old and New Testaments there is no specific reference that states that Moses wrote the first five books of the bible. There are references to the Law of Moses.

*"And Moses wrote this law, and delivered it unto the priests the sons of Levi, which bare the ark of the covenant of the LORD, and unto all the elders of Israel."*

*Deuteronomy 31:9 KJV*

I would eventually find one of the earliest references to the first five books of the Old Testament having been written by Moses. Josephus tells us, *"For we have not an in-*

*numerable multitude of books among us, disagreeing from and contradicting one another, [as the Greeks have,] but only twenty-two books, (8) which contain the records of all the past times; which are justly believed to be divine; and of them five belong to Moses, which contain his laws and the traditions of the origin of mankind till his death.* "[xxvii]

Philo is probably the earliest reference to Moses writing the first few books, which he alludes to in "On the Creation" and other writings. Later on, this would stir up quite a bit of confusion. Some of this confusion led to the German school of higher-biblical criticism which would come from Julius Wellhausen and his Documentary Hypothesis. There were stages of development that culminated into the development of this historical process that Wellhausen played a role in. He utilized the works of those who preceded him. Having taken their works, he compiled them, made some of his own additions, and presented the Documentary Hypothesis in a clear, organized, and connected whole or synthesis.[157]

*"...modern literary analysis and criticism of the texts has pointed up significant differences in style, vocabulary, and content, apparently indicating a variety of original sources for the first four books, as well as an independent origin for Deuteronomy."*[158]

The Documentary Hypothesis, among other things, has caused the conflict or opposition to the critical examination of the Bible to diminish not only amongst the Catholics, but also the Protestants. The J document was presented to be

---

157     (R. E. Friedman 26)
158     (Emilie T. Sander)

associated with the Yahweh or Jehovah name(s) for God within the Old Testament. The E document was presented to be associated with the Elohim name for God. The third document which was P, and the largest of all of them, was the document that included mostly legal and priestly information. The D source was for Deuteronomy. The main purpose, it seemed, for formulating the Documentary Hypothesis was to investigate and present why there were different sources that were later pieced together, who wrote the sources and finally why.

| Source | Name of God | Stage |
| --- | --- | --- |
| J | Yahweh | Nature and/or Fertility |
| E | Elohim | Nature and/or Fertility |
| P | Priestly | Legal and/or Priestly |
| D | Deuteronomy | Spiritual and/or Ethical |

These sources are what made up various portions of the Pentateuch, that were woven together by a later scribe which is brilliantly displayed by Richard Elliott Friedman.[159] The oldest of the sources are believed to be the J and E sources, while the P and D sources are the youngest of the four, with P believed to be older than the D source.

*"Genesis, Exodus, and Numbers are considered compilations of J, E, and P, with Leviticus assigned to P and Deuteronomy to D."*

---

159    (R. E. Friedman 26)

# 6 DID JESUS CHRIST EVER EXIST?

*... "The Bible begins with the account of the Priestly Code of the creation of the world."*[160]

I, personally found Wellhausen's work, as well as Friedman's explanation of the Documentary Hypothesis to be most relevant in helping me understand some things about the sources utilized within the first five books of the Old Testament.  One example is why are there two creation stories that don't agree?  Another example is why are there two flood stories that don't agree?  Friedman demonstrated side by side comparison and even showed differences within the same paragraphs of texts.  His work entitled, *The Bible with Sources Revealed* is a must for bible students.

## Biblical Archaeology

After diving into the Documentary Hypothesis, the next step was to approach the subject of Biblical Archaeology. Deus' work mentions an archaeologist named Ze'ev Herzog.[161],[162]  I, personally, was not aware that, *"The archaeology of Palestine developed as a science at a relatively late date, in the late 19th and early 20th century, in tandem with the archaeology of the imperial cultures of Egypt, Mesopo-*

---

160    (Emilie T. Sander)

161    Ze'ev Herzog. Professor of Archaeology. herzog@post.tau.ac.il. Ph.D. 1977, Tel Aviv University: The City-Gate in Eretz Israel and Its Neighboring Countries. Took part in the excavations of Hazor and Megiddo with Yigael Yadin and in digs at Tel Arad and Tel Beer Sheba with Yohanan Aharoni. Directed the excavations at Tel Michal and Tel Gerisa and in 1997 has begun a new exploration project at Tel Yafo (ancient Jaffa). (University)

162    (A. J. Deus, Leap of Faith : David Kills Goliath 76)

*tamia, Greece and Rome.* *[163]*

Herzog mentioned that the archaeology of Palestine was founded upon religious motives rather than the actual finding of monuments that would have spoken for themselves that Palestine was in fact Ancient Israel. The early excavators among the places in Palestine happened to be biblical researchers who utilized the Bible to find the remains of cities. William Foxwell Albright[164] was a very important person in that he was the initiator of the archaeological excavations, the history and the study of language for Israel and the ancient Near East. Albright went through great lengths to dismiss the claims of the Wellhausen school's Documentary Hypothesis. In the end, Herzog states, *"Following 70 years of intensive excavations in the Land of Israel, archaeologists have found out: The patriarchs' acts are legendary, the Israelites did not sojourn in Egypt or make an exodus, they did not conquer the land. Neither is there any mention of the empire of David and Solomon, nor of the source of belief in the God of Israel.*

*These facts have been known for years, but Israel is a stubborn people and nobody wants to hear about it."*

This was huge for me. From the words of an Israeli Archaeologist, the physical remains to back up the Bible as evidence, were not adding up. I later come across Margreet

---

163    (Herzog)

164    W.F. Albright, in full William Foxwell Albright, (born May 24, 1891, Coquimbo, Chile—died Sept. 19, 1971, Baltimore, Md., U.S.), American biblical archaeologist and Middle Eastern scholar, noted especially for his excavations of biblical sites. (T. E. Britannica, W.F. Albright)

Steiner,[165] after having read "When Rocks Cry Out" by Horace Butler. Steiner states, *"The history of Jerusalem is going to have to be rewritten. As we gradually assimilate the archaeological record, we are finding more and more evidence that calls into question long-held assumptions about the city's past."[166]*

For the purposes of demonstrating a historical finding in relation to archaeology, Richard Elliott Friedman is able to provide us with just such instance. When discussing Assyria under Sennacherib when they invaded Judah during the reign of Hezekiah,[xxviii] after demonstrating the records from the Bible as well as the "Prism Inscription of Sennacherib",[xxix] Friedman states, *"The showdown between the Assyrians and Judeans (or Jews) at Jerusalem is of special interest because it is one of the very rare cases in which we have both biblical and archeological witness to the same event."[167]*

That was monumental in helping me realize that I had quite a bit of homework to do. I had seen where some stated

---

165    Margreet Steiner. I am a Near Eastern archaeologist with a special interest the archaeology of the Southern Levant. My research has focussed on the archaeology of Jerusalem, stratigraphical analysis, Iron Age pottery, Islamic glass bracelets, field work and the management of archaeological projects. (Steiner)

166    (Steiner, It's Not There: Archaeology Proves a Negative 26) Steiner, Margreet. "It's Not There: Archaeology Proves a Negative," Biblical Archaeology Review 24.4 (1998): 26. Reprinted with permission from the Biblical Archaeology Review.

167    (R. E. Friedman 93) From WHO WROTE THE BIBLE? by Richard Elliott Friedman. Copyright © 1987 by Richard Friedman. Reprinted with the permission of Simon & Schuster, Inc. All rights reserved.

that God did not want anyone to find anything. How would such an individual explain God allowing all of the human remains of other civilizations to still be extant? Faith is a good thing to have, though faith alone is not. Even Proverbs 13:12 reads, *"Hope deferred maketh the heart sick: but when the desire cometh, it is a tree of life."* It did not make any sense that faith would not be expected to at some point be realized. People live, people die, and something remains as evidence that those people lived. I find it hard to believe that God would hide something and have later people fighting and dying over lack of evidence. There is, however, an explanation for the lack of evidence. Either the things written never happened, those things happened differently, or perhaps they happened in another place. More on this later.

## Biblical Schools of Thought

The lack of archaeological evidence to back up the biblical record was quite devastating for me at the time, in conjunction with Deus' work. I would then come to realize that there were differing schools of biblical thought. There are three main biblical schools of thought that developed as a reaction to the lack of archaeological evidence. I had come across the works of Israel Finkelstein,[168] Niels Peter Lem-

---

168    Israel Finkelstein is the Jacob Alkow Professor of the Archaeology of Israel in the Bronze and Iron Ages at Tel Aviv University. He is a member of the Israel Academy of Sciences and Humanities and a 'correspondant étranger' of the French Académie des Inscriptions et Belles Lettres. (Finkelstein)

che,[169] Thomas L. Thompson,[170] and Philip R. Davies.[171]

Two schools of thought in relation to biblical archaeology and criticism were evident; the conservative approach, and the higher-critical approach. Later another school came into view which was the minimalist school, in the 1990s. The minimalist school was said to have, *"... rejected altogether the value of biblical history for the study of the history of Canaan/Israel in the Iron Age."[172]*

Some others, to include Finkelstein, describe the pros and cons of both the conservative and the minimalists schools, and later turns introduces their own view which is from the middle.[173] So, Finkelstein and others decided to take a middle view, or a more neutral one.

The biblical schools of thought showed me that for cen-

---

169     Niels Peter Lemche, Professor Emeritus. Section of Biblical Exegesis. Karen Blixens Plads 16. 2300 København S. npl@teol.ku.dk (Copenhagen, Faculty of Theology Niels Peter Lemche)

170     Thomas L. Thompson. Professor emeritus. Department of Biblical Exegesis. Faculty of Theology. University of Copenhagen. Mail: tlt@teol.ku.dk Mobile: + 45 29 62 06 89 (Copenhagen, Palestine History and Heritage Project)

171     Philip R. Davies is a British biblical scholar and archaeologist. He is Professor Emeritus of biblical studies at the University of Sheffield, England. (Wikipedia, Philip R. Davies)

172     (Finkelstein, Digging For The Truth: Archaeology And The Bible 9) "Republished with permission of Israel Finkelstein, from The Quest for the Historical Israel : Debating Archaeology and the History of Early Israel, Israel Finkelstein, First Edition and 2007; permission conveyed through Copyright Clearance Center, Inc. "

173     (Finkelstein, Digging for the Truth: Archaeology and the Bible : The Rise and Fall of the Conservative Camp 9)

turies there has been debate on how to approach the Bible. Even within the different schools there was and still is wide disagreement. Scholars are able to read and translate from other languages into English. The layperson is unaware of this largely. Most laypeople only approach the Bible from a devotional standpoint. The scholarly world goes far deeper in their approach. The scholars have an entirely different conversation than the general public. Many people may not care about this and decide to remain in their particular view point. For me, to remain in any particular view point and not be aware of the intricate details was no longer an option.

Deus' take on the Bible was quite different and very influential in my learning at the time while I was transitioning from Christianity. I remember in a conversation with him that I stated that I would die a Christian. Months later after having digested both volumes of his work, I could no longer hold my Christian views. I read other things around the same time that helped me see how my position as a Christian was no longer tenable. It was through Deus' work that I learned that the archaeological record did not establish the Bible historically. The Biblical history is quite enigmatic while fascinating at the same time. When one thinks that they understand what the Bible has to offer, if they decide to go deeper, they will find that they are in fact mistaken regardless of position taken. Some researchers believe that the Bible was pieced together from scratch much later than the period(s) have been fixed for the history to have occurred. Others believe that the Bible is very early. I would recommend that regardless of historicity one should read the Bible and get what they can from it. I have gained far more respect for the Bible and history in general during my study over the years.

## Implications for Christianity

After having studied for a time, archaeology, and the biblical schools of thought in relation to archaeology, I would then come to the New Testament yet again. If the Old Testament was questionable, then the New Testament, by default, had to be questionable as well. If B rests on A, and A is not solid, then that would make B shaky. It benefits the Christian religion to have Judaism[174] seen in a way that is validated by the Old Testament texts. Without Judaism being firmly established, then that leaves Christianity in question, since its very foundation is from the concept of the Old Testament and Judaism, in general, as many of us have come to understand it.

I would later learn, after having no longer been Christian philosophically nor in religious practice, that there were many who had questioned the existence, not just of the Old Testament people, but even the New Testament people. This included Jesus Christ, himself.

Early on, the Patristic writers were combating others who questioned the Christian religion. There were many writings as stated above, that were written against those who

174    Judaism, monotheistic religion developed among the ancient Hebrews. Judaism is characterized by a belief in one transcendent God who revealed himself to Abraham, Moses, and the Hebrew prophets and by a religious life in accordance with Scriptures and rabbinic traditions. Judaism is the complex phenomenon of a total way of life for the Jewish people, comprising theology, law, and innumerable cultural traditions. (Shlomo Pines)

were involved in heresy.  Justin Martyr is one such Patristic writer who fought the views of others who did not hold his own view(s).[xxx]  Justin Martyr gives us our first document outside of the New Testament that names Jesus Christ as the Word.  In Chapter 21 of his Apology, he compares Jesus Christ with the sons of Jupiter.  If the sons of Jupiter are fictional, then according to Justin Martyr, Jesus, too, is fictional.  It appeared that Justin and others were trying to replace the mythical figures with Jesus.  Justin also went as far as to say that the things that the sons of Jupiter and other gods performed prior to Jesus were to be imitated by the devil, having foreseen the prophecies of Jacob as recorded by Moses and others concerning Jesus Christ.[xxxi]

I had seen the arguments where some stated that Justin Martyr quoted the gospels, and where others said that he had not quoted any of them.  And to reiterate what was stated above, Justin Martyr never states that these sons of Jupiter, nor the others stated above, nor even Jupiter himself, as being fictional, mythical or otherwise, ever actually lived as human beings.  An indication of how Justin Martyr may have seen those sons of Jupiter, to include Jupiter,  may be, *"And we have learned that those only are deified who have lived near to God in holiness and virtue;"* What Justin Martyr seems to be a proponent of here, as many were before him, is called euhemerism.[175]

---

175    Euhemerism - : interpretation of myths as traditional accounts of historical persons and events. (Merriam-Webster Online)

Euhemerus, also spelled Euemeros, or Evemerus, (flourished c. 300 BC, Messene? [now Messina, Sicily, Italy]), author of a utopian work that was popular in the ancient world; his name was given to the theory that gods are great men worshipped after their death (i.e., Euhemer-

Another interesting thing to point out that Justin Martyr refers to is the Word, or Logos, that Philo also spoke of.  I have seen much controversy over this term throughout the years.[xxxii]  Some scholars believe that there is no connection between the Logos of Philo and the Logos of the Book of John within the New Testament.[176]  I had seen where some state this Logos concept goes back to Plato, and where others state that it does not.  What was interesting concerning Philo is that while he lived in the first century, he never mentioned Jesus Christ or even Christians.  He did mention, though, the Essenes and the Therapeutae.[xxxiii]  Josephus himself comes very close to mentioning Christians, with perhaps subtle nuances, as some have demonstrated.  There is an interesting passage in his Antiquities, where he seems, or not, to mention Jesus Christ.

## Testimonium Flavianum

*"Now there was about this time Jesus, a wise man, if it be lawful to call him a man; for he was a doer of wonderful works, a teacher of such men as receive the truth with pleasure. He drew over to him both many of the Jews and many*

---

ism). His most important work was Hiera Anagraphe (probably early 3rd century BC; "The Sacred Inscription"), which was translated into Latin by the poet Ennius (239–169 BC). Only fragments survive of both the original Greek and the Latin translation. (T. E. Britannica, Euhemerus)

The philosophy attributed to and named for Euhemerus, euhemerism, holds that many mythological tales can be attributed to historical persons and events, the accounts of which have become altered and exaggerated over time. (Wikipedia, Euhemerus)

176    (Frederick Copleston 459)

*of the Gentiles. He was [the] Christ. And when Pilate, at the suggestion of the principal men amongst us, had condemned him to the cross, (9) those that loved him at the first did not forsake him; for he appeared to them alive again the third day; (10) as the divine prophets had foretold these and ten thousand other wonderful things concerning him. And the tribe of Christians, so named from him, are not extinct at this day.* "*xxxiv*

Deus and D. M. Murdock a.k.a Acharya S. are the two main writers that I focused on in order to properly understand the authenticity of the above passage attributed to Josephus. *In Suns of God, Krishna, Buddha, and Christ Unveiled*, the late D. M. Murdock a.k.a. Acharya S. states, *"The Testimonium Flavianum has been demonstrated repeatedly over the centuries to be a forgery, likely interpolated by Church historian Eusebius in the fourth century. So thorough and universal has been this debunking that very few scholars of any repute continued to cite it after the turn of the last century. Indeed, it was rarely mentioned, except to note that it was a forgery. In reality, numerous books by a variety of authorities over a period of a couple centuries basically took it for granted that the Testimonium Flavianum in its entirety was spurious, an interpolation and a forgery.*"[177]

I would come to learn that this passage in Josephus' Antiquities was not quoted by any church father or otherwise, prior to Eusebius in the fourth century C.E. Acharya S. continues, *"... not only do several Church fathers from the second, third and early fourth centuries have no apparent knowledge of the TF, but even after Eusebius suddenly*

---

177    (Sanning, 12. The "Historical Jesus?" 381)

*'found' it in the first half of the fourth century, several other fathers into the fifth 'often cite Josephus, but not this passage.'"[178]*

Acharya S. continues further with a very good list of those that preceded Eusebius, and some that succeeded him, that did not quote the above written passage by Josephus in his Antiquities.[179]  After reading A. J. Deus, Acharya S., and others who cited various previous people coming to the conclusion that the *"Testimonium Flavianum"* was a fake, I too had accepted this conclusion.

## The Gospels

Later, while reading Deus' work, I was surprised to see that he, too, noticed that the end of the world or age was to culminate in 70 A.D or C.E.[180]  This implies that the New Testament, or at least parts of it, were written well after the fact.  It is easier to write prophesy after the events have already taken place.  I realized later that parts of the Old Testament were written after the fact as well.  Source material was available for the authors of the Matthew, Mark, and Luke documents as has been shown through synopsis.  The truth is that it can be demonstrated very easily that much of the New Testament was obviously written from sources, primarily written and perhaps many oral.  The prominent YouTube personality mentioned above, Michael C. Xoroaster,[181] in my opinion, nailed it when he demonstrated how

178    (Sanning, 12. The "Historical Jesus?" 384)

179    (Sanning, 12. The "Historical Jesus?" 385)

180    (A. J. Deus, THE POORHOUSE : Keys to Eternal Life 252-253)

181    Revelation Raw Exploration (Old Series)

Revelation was written after the fact and that it is primarily about the Jewish Roman War that culminated in 70 C.E., as well as the Bar Kokhba Revolt in 135 C.E.[182] The point concerning the book of Revelation is the reading of "*Jewish Wars*" or "*Wars of the Jews*" by Josephus, and seeing that it records those major events. Some may be so caught up in nomenclature and due to wrongful teaching from those who never truly understood the book, may fail to make the connections.

As stated above, I had seen the arguments where some stated that Justin Martyr quoted the gospels, and where others stated that he had not quoted any of them. It appears that he quoted nuances and perhaps pieces of them. He definitely quoted the Old Testament and the New Testament Apocrypha. He never mentioned the New Testament gospels by name.[183]

The first time in literary history that the gospels come into view is during the time of St. Irenaeus.[xxxv] St. Irenaeus did not attribute to God or the Holy Spirit the reasons why there had to be four gospels. Instead, he gives a very bizarre

url: https://www.youtube.com/watch?v=JGRR14TWC-JE&list=PLDB59F2D746F648CF

Book of Revelation url: https://www.youtube.com/watch?v=cG3DB-w6Gscg&list=PL4335742F56DEC203

182    Bar Kokhba, original name Simeon Bar Kosba, Kosba also spelled Koseba, Kosiba, or Kochba, also called Bar Koziba, (died 135 CE), Jewish leader who led a bitter but unsuccessful revolt (132–135 CE) against Roman dominion in Judaea. (T. E. Britannica, Bar Kokhba)

183    (Sanning, 12. The "Historical Jesus?" 419-420)

explanation for their necessity, which I have never seen any serious scholar or otherwise take seriously.[184]

I would later learn of the work of one Earl Doherty, which was quite influential in my quest for the understanding of Jesus Christ from a different perspective. Once the texts were in question, and the history as presented was not what was portrayed by the early patristic writers, the characters had to be revisited. Earl Doherty, along with Acharya S. and others, introduced me to a term entitled, *" 'Jesus mythicism'—the theory that no historical Jesus worthy of the name existed, that Christianity began with a belief in a spiritual, mythical figure, that the Gospels are essentially allegory and fiction, and that no single identifiable person lay at the root of the Galilean preaching tradition."[185]* This study was at first strange but by this time in my studies it was not too far reaching. I subsequently found that this was nowhere near new and that even during the days surrounding the New Testament time period, some believed that Jesus was never a human being.

## Did the Apostle Paul Preach a Historical Jesus?

Apostle Paul is very important to Christianity, more so than many may even care to be aware of. The majority of the letters of the New Testament were attributed to him, though as was demonstrated above, only seven of those letters were shown to be from his hand, or from the same author. The modern Christian church follows Paul's writings primarily for their beliefs, and not the gospels. It has been well known

---

184    (Sanning, 12. The "Historical Jesus?" 408-409)

185    (Doherty, "Preface" vii-viii)

for some time that Paul did not teach the same things as Jesus as shown in the gospels. Paul did things differently from the twelve apostles as well. He was more of a lone ranger. He possibly fought Jewish Gnostics as is displayed in II Corinthians chapter 11 and other places. Yet Paul, himself, seemed quite Gnostic, at least in some of the six letters that were deemed to not be written by him. There are even some Gnostic tendencies in the Corinthian letters, Philippians, and possibly even in Romans. The end of the world or age was seen by him to be near in his own lifetime. In my own view, Paul took liberty, just as much as Matthew and others, with the Old Testament scriptures, to give his own ministry and writings validity, often taking things out of context and applying them to what he, himself, was relaying to his audience. Walter Bauer demonstrated that many of the places Paul preached at were very Gnostic following his visits and would have been deemed heretical. This struck me as quite odd since Paul is seen as the apostle par excellence for the gospel message. Gnostics even deemed Paul as their apostle and performed commentaries on his works.

## Marcion of Sinope and the Apostle Paul

Marcion[186] is a very important early person within Christian history. The first patristic writer to mention Marcion, was St. Irenaeus.[xxxvi]   Thanks to Michael C. Xoroaster,

---

186    Marcion of Pontus, (flourished 2nd century CE), , Christian heretic. Although Marcion is known only through reports and quotations from his orthodox opponents, especially Tertullian's Adversus Marcionem ("Against Marcion"), the principal outlines of his teaching seem clear. His teaching made a radical distinction between the God of the Old Testament (the Creator) and the Father of Jesus Christ(the God of Love). (T. E. Britannica, Marcion of Pontus)

I came to find an interesting take on the apostle Paul that was given by Tertullian in his writings against Marcion.[xxxvii] What makes Tertullian's take so interesting is the fact that Marcion is the first person to compile a list of books, those of apostle Paul mainly, which was said to be the first canon of New Testament writings.[187]  Since Marcion was the first to have a collection of Paul's writings, claimed Paul to be the greatest apostle, and he lived before Tertullian, how can we then conclude that he didn't know Paul based solely on Tertullian's word?  Tertullian says that he doesn't know Marcion's Paul, but according to the literary record, he is the first one who knew of Paul outside of the New Testament writings, with exception of perhaps St. Clement,[188] St. Ignatius, and Polycarp.  It seemed that Tertullian tried to claim Paul based on the "*Acts of the Apostles*" as the only Paul— though the Book of Acts is the only document that Tertullian had that recorded the career of Paul. What about the letters that were said to have been written by Paul's own hand?  So, are there two Pauls' or is there just Marcion's or just Tertullian's?  We've already seen above that scholars have found out that only seven letters were "authentically" Paul's.  The <u>remainders</u> were declared deutero-.[189] This would mean that

187     (Salamis, Anacephalaeosis : Against Marcionites 302)

188     Saint Clement I, byname Clement Of Rome, Latin Clemens Romanus, (born, Rome?—died 1st century AD, Rome; feast day November 23), first Apostolic Father, pope from 88 to 97, or from 92 to 101, supposed third successor of St. Peter. According to the early Christian writer Tertullian, he was consecrated by Peter. Bishop St. Irenaeus of Lyon lists him as a contemporary of the Apostles and witness of their preaching. Bishop Eusebius of Caesarea dates his pontificate from 92 to 101. His martyrdom is legendary, and he has been hypothetically identified with the Clement mentioned in Phil. 4:3. (T. E. Britannica, Saint Clement I)

189     Deutero – 1. Second 1.1 Secondary. (Oxford Dictionary On-

they were written by someone else, perhaps after Paul.  Were these letters written by Marcion or his followers?  Epiphanius states, *"This man has only Luke as a Gospel, mutilated at the beginning because of the Savior's conception and his incarnation.32 (2) But this person who harmed himself < rather > than the Gospel did not cut just the beginning off. He also cut off many words of the truth both at the end and in the middle, and he has added other things besides, beyond what had been written. And he uses only this (Gospel) canon, the Gospel according to Luke."[190]*

Marcion was said to have not only rejected the Old Testament, but to also reject the Old Testament God altogether. Concerning Jesus, Irenaeus states, *"But Jesus being derived from that father who is above the God that made the world, and coming into Judaea in the times of Pontius Pilate the governor, who was the procurator of Tiberius Caesar, was manifested in the form of a man to those who were in Judaea, abolishing the prophets and the law, and all the works of that God who made the world, whom also he calls Cosmocrator."[xxxviii]*  This appears to be the first instance outside of the New Testament corpus, where Jesus is mentioned as, *"... manifested in the form of a man to those who were in Judaea, ..."* instead of an actual man.  Yet this does not seem so far off from what Paul, himself, states,

---

line)

190    (Salamis, Anacephalaeosis : Against Marcionites 302) "Republished with permission of Brill, from The Panarion of Epiphanius of Salamis A Treatise Against Eighty Sects in Three Books Book I, Frank Williams,2009; permission conveyed through Copyright Clearance Center, Inc. "

*"⁶ Who, being in the form of God, thought it not robbery to be equal with God:*

*⁷ But made himself of no reputation, and took upon him the form of a servant, and was made in the likeness of men:*

*⁸ And being found in fashion as a man, he humbled himself, and became obedient unto death, even the death of the cross."*

*Philippians 2:6-8 KJV*

*"In the form of God," "took upon him the form of a servant," "was made in the likeness of men,"* and *"being fashioned as a man."* It appears as though it might have been better to just state, Jesus came as a man. Marcion was termed by scholars to be a Docetist.[191] A New Testament author of the first book of John wrote, concerning those that held such a view,

*"¹ Beloved, believe not every spirit, but try the spirits whether they are of God: because many false prophets are gone out into the world.*

*² Hereby know ye the Spirit of God: Every spirit that confesseth that Jesus Christ is come in the flesh is of God:*

---

191     Docetism, (from Greek dokein, "to seem"), Christian heresy and one of the earliest Christian sectarian doctrines, affirming that Christ did not have a real or natural body during his life on earth but only an apparent or phantom one. (T. E. Britannica, Docetism)

# TRANSFORMATION



*<sup></sup> And every spirit that confesseth not that Jesus
Christ is come in the flesh is not of God: and this is
that spirit of antichrist, whereof ye have heard that
it should come; and even now already is it in the
world."*

*1 John 4:1-3 KJV*

People who did not believe that Jesus Christ had come in the flesh were to be seen as antichrists.  Already during the days of the New Testament, antichrists were amongst the church.  This belief continued, if one accepts the consensus or even the traditional dating of the New Testament.  There was an instance, dated prior to Marcion, that stated the belief that Jesus was God and man outside of the New Testament.  This instance is from the writings of St. Ignatius.[xxxix] Apparently, St. Ignatius was fighting those in his lifetime against the belief that Jesus was not human.  He is the first author outside of the New Testament to mention Jesus being both God and man.  St. Irenaeus and other writers mention how others saw Jesus as a man, but a man only.  Those that saw Jesus as a man only was one Cerinthus[192] and a group named the Ebionites.[xl]

It has been demonstrated, then, that there were those who saw Jesus as a man, some saw him as God and man, while others saw that Jesus was only God.  After reading authors from the Mythicists camp,[193] and then going back to see what the patristic writers had to say about the matter, it became

192    Cerinthus, (flourished c. AD 100), Christian heretic whose errors, according to the theologian Irenaeus, led the apostle John to write his New Testament Gospel. (T. E. Britannica, Cerinthus)

193    Those that write on the subject of Jesus Mythicism.

clear that the writings of apostle Paul had to be re-visited.

I had found one of the best modern studies on the apostle Paul in Earl Doherty, as mentioned above. While Doherty's primary focus is on the apostle Paul, he also gives us a lot of useful insight in regard to Jesus. From Doherty's material, I had gleaned that the New Testament, outside of the gospels, did not give any real indication that Jesus was understood to be a human being.[194]

Concerning the apostle Paul himself, he never attributes his message to the apostles who were in their offices before him, nor does he ever give you an indication of a human Jesus by discussing anything specific about his earthly life. Galatians 1:11-12 states,

> *[11] But I certify you, brethren, that the gospel which was preached of me is not after man.*

> *[12] For I neither received it of man, neither was I taught it, but by the revelation of Jesus Christ.*

Apostle Paul received his message from Jesus by revelation and not instruction of any kind by a man. After having already preached to the Galatians at a time before, the apostle was surprised that they had listened and accepted a message from another group after he visited them. The apostle believed that his gospel from the revelation that he had received was the right message so much so that he called those who had a different message accursed. The importance of this, though, is that the apostle received his message by rev-

______________

194    (Doherty, "Part Two: a Life in Eclipse : Chapter Six: From Bethlehem to Jerusalem" 63)

elation and not by man. *"immediately I conferred not with flesh and blood"[xli]* God revealed his Son in the apostle and *"Neither went I up to Jerusalem to them which were apostles before me; but I went into Arabia, and returned again unto Damascus."* Finally, after three years he went *"up to Jerusalem to see Peter, and abode with him fifteen days."* The apostle Paul attributes his ministry to a revelation of Jesus, not having received any instruction from those that walked and lived with Jesus. So, the humanity of Jesus is never in the apostle's focus. When the apostle discusses the resurrection of Jesus, he explains that according to a revelation of an event that he did not witness personally, but perceived, perhaps through his intellect as Plato and Philo discussed, from the scriptures.

*"³ For I delivered unto you first of all that which
I also received, how that Christ died for our sins
according to the scriptures;*

*⁴ And that he was buried, and that he rose again
the third day according to the scriptures"*

*I Corinthians 15:3-4 KJV*

Later within the same passage, he discusses how Cephas, the twelve, above five hundred, James, and then all of the apostles had perceived this burial and resurrection on the same par as he did—according to the scriptures through revelation. He placed himself on the same level as the *"... very chiefest apostles."[xlii]* Those chiefest apostles were perhaps the twelve, which is interesting since they supposedly experienced something that he, himself, did not—the humanity of Jesus.  The humanity of Jesus is never the focal point of the apostle Paul's message.  He was more concerned with Christ being inside of his listeners.  As far as how some try to claim that the apostle did take the humanity of Jesus seriously by appealing to Romans 1:3, *"...which was made of the seed of David according to the flesh..."* this position is demonstrably untenable.[195]  I had accepted that the apostle Paul did in fact preach a different Jesus than the one that is presented to us in the gospels.

## The Essenes Again?

During the time of Jonathan called Apphus,[xliii] who later became High Priest,[xliv]

*"At this time there were three sects among the Jews, who had different opinions concerning human actions; the one was called the sect of the Pharisees, another the sect of the Sadducees, and the other the sect of the Essens."*[xlv]

Josephus mentioned in his *"Life,"* that he had studied under all three sects, but chose the office of the Pharisees ultimately.[xlvi]

*"Then came there vnto him a company of Assideans, who were mightie men of Israel, euen all such as were voluntarily deuoted vnto the Lawe."*

*1 Maccabees 2:42 KJV*

---

195    (Doherty, "Part Three: The Gospel of the Son : Chapter Eight: The Word of God in the Holy Book" 88)

These Assideans or Hasideans/Chasideans in other translations, were speculated by some to be where the Sadducees, Pharisees, and Essenes had derived from, depending upon the author/scholar. In The Manual of Discipline, or the Community Rule of the Covenant, referenced above, a title is mentioned, "*Sons of Zadok*",[196] that received quite a bit of attention within the study of the DSS.[197, 198]

The Essenes were understood to be the New Israel. This new Israel, as did the old Israel, consisted of both priests and laymen, "*... a House of holiness for Aaron, in order that the supreme holiness be united, and a House of Community for Israel (for) those who walk in perfection.*"[199] The priests belonging to the community were described as '*Sons of Aaron*', believing like all priests that they descended from Aaron. They were also said to be '*Sons of Zadok*'.[200] The Essenes even called themselves the elect or chosen of Israel.[201] The name Zadok appears approximately thirty times within the Old Testament.

The title '*the sons of Zadok*' seems to have first been applied to the priests and later was applied to the entire sect. It is stated by some that the title 'Sadducees' came from the

196    ZADOK (Heb. ▨▨▨▨▨, "righteous"), priest in the time of king *David. Zadok established a high priestly dynasty which continued until approximately 171 B.C.E., both in the First and Second Temple periods. He first appears, together with *Abiathar, as the priest in charge of the Ark at the time of Absalom's revolt (II Sam. 15:24–37). (Library)

197    DSS = Dead Sea Scrolls.

198    (Dupont-Sommer 67)

199    (Dupont-Sommer 67)

200    (M. A. Larson, Chapter Four Preparation: 195-145 47)

201    (Dupont-Sommer 69)

name Zadok.  There may have been a schism at some point in time where there was a split between these 'sons of Zadok' where it resulted in one being the Sadducees and the other being the Essenes.  Dupont-Sommer, in his view, saw that *"... the new Party thus combined both the priests who left the Sadduccaean sect and the Assidaeans or 'the pious' of the period of Judas Maccabaeus."[202]*   Others saw the Pharisees and the Essenes being split.  We are well aware now that the Essenes lived leading up to the period and during the period of the writing of the New Testament.  The apex[203] of their writings involved a character titled *"The Teacher of Righteousness," "the Lawgiver," "the Star," "the Interpreter of the Law,"* and others.  They also wrote documents such as what "The Damascus Document" alludes to entitled, the "Book of Remembrance" or the "Book of Meditations," some of the book of Enoch, The Testament of the Twelve Patriarchs to include the "interpolations",[204]  and commentated on other writings.  They called themselves the "New Israel" and established a "New Covenant."  They looked for their "Star" to return in the future to vanquish their enemies and free them.


What is further interesting, is that the other order of Essenes mentioned by Josephus,[xlvii] could in fact be the Therapeutae that was mentioned by Philo.[xlviii] In Eusebius' Church History  or  Ecclesiastical  History,  while  recounting  what Philo stated in his writings in "On The Contemplative Life or Suppliants", Eusebius compares these Therapeutae to the

202    (Dupont-Sommer 70)
203    Apex - The top or highest part of something, especially one forming a point. (Oxford University Press)
204    Interpolation – 1 mass noun The insertion of something of a different nature into something else. (Oxford Dictionary Online)

Christians.[xlix] Philo's mention of churches, something also mentioned by Eusebius of Caesarea, was quite interesting concerning these Therapeuts.[l]

Regardless if one takes this passage seriously, the very fact that you have the "Father of Church History" stating that these Therapeuts having writings that are highly probable "... *the works of the ancients, which he says they had, were the Gospels and the writings of the apostles, and probably some expositions of the ancient prophets, such as are contained in the Epistle to the Hebrews, and in many others of Paul's Epistles* ",[205] is huge. It is huge due to the fact that Q has not been found.[206] It is also interesting due to the allegorizing that was done by these Therapeuts, since the Essenes not only allegorized,[li] but they also provided commentaries on the Old Testament writings that demonstrates how the later ones utilized the earlier writings within the explanation of the events that were taking place in their own times. The New Testament writers also used the Old Testament writings in their own documents for various reasons, even providing commentaries, or even showing that the Old Testament prophecies were being and to be fulfilled during their time.[lii] More to follow on this subject later in another

---

205    Eusebius, Church History or Ecclesiastical History, Book 2, Chapter 17. Philo's Account of the Ascetics of Egypt. (Eusebius) http://www.newadvent.org/fathers/250102.htm

206    The symbol (said to have been adopted as being the initial letter of the German Quelle, source) for that material common to both Matthew and Luke of about 230 verses, mostly sayings of Jesus, which is not from Mark. (Oxford University Press)

For a layout for the Q document, see: The Lost Sayings Gospel Q (Kirby, The Lost Sayings Gospel Q.)

work.

After having covered the subjects of biblical archaeology, the biblical schools of thought, and realizing the gaps and inconsistencies in the historical record that I had found at that time, it became apparent that either Jesus was the 'Teacher of Righteousness' that lived perhaps in the first century B.C.E., or perhaps like some of the earlier Christians and non-Christians were right in their understanding that Jesus never existed at all. I took the latter option since there just wasn't enough human history devoid of mythological tenants that I could stomach. Even the euhemerist model didn't work when it came to Jesus for me at that time.

## 7 WAKING UP TO SLEEP AGAIN

During my studies, just before diving into metaphysics, I later stopped going to church and began taking inventory of my life. I realized that if I continuously allowed myself to get into the same situations, then perhaps it wasn't the fault of the churches. Perhaps the problem was my own. So, I no longer attended church regularly. I finally decided to study the subjects that were taboo to study. After a while, and when things were turning even more so for the worse between Conflict and I, an unexpected person came into view. This was the help.

Conflict and the help spent some time reconciling after having not spoken to one another for many years. After some time during their reconciliation, the help and I began to talk. The help was very knowledgeable and seemed genuinely helpful. Let's call her Bridge. For she was a bridge from trouble, that unfortunately led to another kind of trouble - trouble that was not from a malicious place, but from a place of selfishness. Selfishness that still led to deep concerns of mistrust in people, in general, for me moving forward. Conflict and Bridge would no longer really speak anymore after a while. In time, Bridge and I would talk quite often.

The conversations between us would eventually leave from discussing history, politics, religion, and metaphysics, to discussing specific things about my marriage and some of Conflict's past. During this time, Conflict received a temporary relocation from the army. This is the time when Bridge and I began to get to know each other very well. We became friends.

At first, the information concerning Conflict's past that Bridge provided seemed liberating and troubling at the same time. Her and I would talk for hours about this and occasionally about metaphysical subjects. We would e-mail and phone each other daily for a number of years. After a while though, I began to get quite irritated discussing Conflict and the issues surrounding her. It would appear that Bridge would go too far at times concerning Conflict. The truth is, since I was the one in the situation, I too would go too far at times as well. In time, the friendship between us was severed. Bridge was a very confident, outspoken and semi-possessive woman. She is the type that cares deeply - perhaps too much.

I decided to go under her wing for a time for instruction in metaphysics. Metaphysics would encompass subjects related to astrology, reiki, spell work, psychic work, tarot readings, chakra balancing, and even the use of runes. Learning all of this exciting knowledge, while I was still learning through my own personal studies, fascinated me. At first I yielded willingly to her instruction, since she was so knowledgeable. She even provided emotional support since she was the only friend I had during one of the worst times of my life. The severing of my relationship with Conflict was in progress. Conflict would be a different person on a regular basis. During this time, Bridge and I got even stronger in our friendship. In time, my personal studies were placed upon the back burner due to my constant talks with Bridge and the related stress between Conflict and I. Things got so bad, that at one point, the old experience that I experienced as spoken of while at Soul's Last Stop, in Chapter IV – Clouds, Rain, Acid, Pain of Volume I of the Work, reared its ugly head again, though minor in comparison to the first time.[207]  It was as if someone worked roots on me that I might experience that horrible ordeal yet again. I had my suspicions as to who, but I knew that whomever was behind it, were well aware of what was actually going on with me years earlier. Could this have made that same individual a spiritual accomplice many years earlier?

After a while, Conflict and I split for good and never got back together. We also got divorced and split the children. I managed to be allowed to get the two oldest boys, who were nearing adulthood, and Conflict got the youngest boy.

Now Bridge was married also. She would spend a significant amount of time on the phone and would e-mail me back and forth for quite a while. I even visited her and her hus-

---

207    (Brasford)

band's home a few times. After some time, I felt bad about what I was feeling. I felt smothered, though Bridge meant well. This ordeal with Conflict was a shroud of darkness that needed to pass. After all, Bridge did so much to help me, yet at the same time, she stifled me in my growth and kept me focused on the past - focused on what Conflict was doing. I eventually made up my mind, to take responsibility for my own life, and live my own life on my own terms.

After some time, Bridge offered me services through others that were in similar fields as she was in, viz. metaphysics. I received every reading that I could get from tarot, to runes, to psychic, to other readings that I couldn't even name. I even got reiki treatments from practitioners. After the various readings, I came to the conclusion that Bridge and I needed to part ways. That it would be best for the both of us. I was so conflicted though. We had been friends and had had a mentor/mentee relationship for a few years. I made the decision anyway. I decided to do it as I had broken relationships with others in the past. Coward or not, I would just drop off the radar. Some now commonly call this a ghosting, meaning that you cut off all contact and move on.

My encounter with the metaphysical world was much like my encounter with the Christian world. They both had their benefits, but they both indeed had their detriments. I had already began my journey of discovery before I met Bridge through Conflict. This journey would entail me stripping down what I thought I knew in order to rebuild a new foundation. A foundation that I would lay on my own, through countless hours of study, and meticulous research. After having severed ties with Bridge, I returned to my studies. In my studies I began to learn more about metaphysics. I even began to learn about the subjects of sociology, psychology, and intersexual dynamics. I became a sponge to knowledge, which I believed was the only thing that could save myself at this point. After all, you can only do what you know - whether that knowing is intuitive, or intellectual.

# 8 THE REALM OF MODERN METAPHYSICS

Over time, I had come to the realization that Christianity in its inception consisted of various groups that shared some tenants while being widely divergent amongst others. It was not one thing, formulated and maintained on common beliefs across the board. One will not come to the formulation of a more cohesive attempt at a common understanding until the fourth century C.E. from the likes of Eusebius of Caesarea and others like Epiphanius of Salamis. It is from these gentlemen and others that you finally start seeing Christianity becoming a more organized religion. So, I decided to expand my studies in an effort to find out what happened if not before the "biblical" world, what did and was taking place outside of it.

I had learned some time along the way in my studies the subject of metaphysics. I had my earliest encounter with what is termed "New Age", though many may disagree you will find all of what is termed "metaphysics" also within "New Age", within the websites of Dr. Craig Lyons.[208] After much research, and coming to the knowledge of others who were much more versed[209] than I, I had come to the conclusion that any belief and/or spiritual system that one espouses that has no practical application should be jettisoned[210] and relegated[211] to the trash heap. This is not to say that metaphysics should be ignored. Like many other things in regards to subjects, I found that everything has a level of value. The problem comes in with things that we cannot realize in our daily lives. Life is for the living and living requires action and human beings need results that can be measured for the purposes of tracking progression, stagnation, and regression. I did find some metaphysicians who took a more practical approach. That is what caused me to approach this subject from my own personal study with much more respect. Like many other subjects and movements, New Age itself is just as eclectic[212] as others.

---

208     (Lyons)

209     Versed - Experienced or skilled in; knowledgeable about. (Oxford Dictionary Online)

210     Jettison - Abandon or discard (someone or something that is no longer wanted). (Oxford Dictionary Online)

211     Relegate - Assign an inferior rank or position to. (Oxford Dictionary Online)

212     Eclectic – 1 Deriving ideas, style, or taste from a broad and diverse range of sources. 2 Philosophy
Denoting or belonging to a class of ancient philosophers who did not belong to or found any recognized school of thought but selected doctrines from various schools of thought. (Oxford Dictionary Online)

# 8 THE REALM OF MODERN METAPHYSICS

One of the major themes that I got from Dr. Lyons' websites regarding the Old Testament, the documents from Qumran, the New Testament, and the overall understanding of Ancient Egypt was that it was for the most part "mystical metaphysical."[213]

While I do agree to some degree that not all of the Ancient Egyptian documents contain so-called literal and historical information only, it is also important to not deny the so-called literal and historical information that said documents demonstrably, categorically, and verifiably contain. It appears as though some rationalists deny spirituality, and on the other hand, some spiritualists deny the physical and visible reality.[liii]  I, over time, had found that being in the middle is a far safer position to take.  The major issues come in with the pre-conceived inherited beliefs that Dr. Lyons has mentioned.  The best approach that I have found is to let the authors of those documents state what they mean and if you find value in the modern authors that support what those earlier authors had to say, by way of clarity, then you are much closer to the "truth".  Since the Renaissance Era, there has been a re-learning, and learning for the first time effort that is still in progress.  With the decipherment of the hieroglyphs, which took place in the early 19th century—1800s—there was much knowledge and information published that did not take into account what Ancient Egypt said about themselves.  Once I came to this realization, relying solely on the so-called "classical"[214] writers, Neoplatonists,[215] and others concerning Ancient Egypt, left many with gross mis-

213     (Lyons)
214     Classical - Relating to ancient Greek or Latin literature, art, or culture. (Oxford Dictionary Online)
215     Neoplatonism - A philosophical and religious system devel-

representations and misunderstandings. If you are utilizing something that came from a civilization that you don't understand, how do you know if you are utilizing it properly? This was a dilemma for me. So I went looking.

Meta-physics or New Age was quite a difficult subject to tackle for me.[liv] It has no unification and the way that it is practiced among many today has to do with the self. Not many scholars touch this subject, or these subjects, but as I kept searching, I began to find some answers from across various directions.[lv]

I am in agreement with Dr. Lyons that all roads lead to Ancient Egypt. So, the modern understanding of meta-physics according to many derive from some understanding, or misunderstanding as we will soon see, of Ancient Egypt.[216]

I, too, found that authors like John Anthony West believed that some of the modern tenants of New Age, though many of them don't explain it this way, goes back to Ancient Egypt. There appears to be some truth to this, though many fail in their demonstrations of such truth. If it is true that there is *"...no perceived difference between sacred and mundane,..."* then it is important to still approach them with caution so that we can see how those ancients themselves explained things. Moving forward, "modern meta-physics" and "New Age" will be used interchangeably.

---

oped by the followers of Plotinus in the 3rd century AD. (Oxford Dictionary Online)

216     (Lyons)

# 8 THE REALM OF MODERN METAPHYSICS

## Whipping Excursion into Atheism

For a period of time, post Jesus Mysticism, I had travelled down the road of Atheism. I figured that since archaeology couldn't prove either Jesus' existence or any other ancient person's existence, and that relying on the texts for matter of faith was a misnomer, why even bother with the so-called spirit realm?

I had learned about Bertrand Russell, Sam Harris, Richard Dawkins, Richard Carrier, and even John Loftus. These are just a few authors that I had come across during my detour from "God." By this time, I had begun to travel down the more rational, and less emotional, road. Much of what I had come across made "sense." Many atheists relied more so on the scientific method and answered questions from the more natural science[217] approach. I still, to this day, hold to some atheistic concepts. The late Acharya S. observes, *"The difference between theism and atheism is also very slight. Indeed, it is evident that the human mind has the capacity to be monotheistic, polytheistic, pantheistic and atheistic all at the same time."[218]*

At the end of the day, though, because of the encounters that I had lived from the "spiritual" side of things, and how I had heard "God's" voice many times, and even had seen some things that I had heard actually happen in my life and within the lives of others, I could not hold to an all-atheis-

217    Natural Science - any of the sciences (such as physics, chemistry, or biology) that deal with matter, energy, and their interrelations and transformations or with objectively measurable phenomena. (Merriam-Webster Dictionary Online)

218    (Sanning, Introduction 4)

tic approach. But the rational cognitive process began to become much more important in my life. After some time, through reason, I had successfully overcome a lot of issues—emotional and otherwise—and utilized the rational cognitive process to rebuild my life.[lvi]

## On Ancient Greece and Egypt

Two very important things in regards to the "origins" of modern meta-physics seemed extremely important after reading a book by Mary Lefkowitz.[219] It seemed paramount to properly approach the Corpus Hermeticum[220] and the decipherment of the ancient Egyptian hieroglyphs.[221] The importance of these two submissions in regards to modern meta-physics is whether or not the understanding of modern meta-physics came from ideas prior to these two subjects or afterwards. One of the very important realizations that I received from reading *Not Out of Africa* was the importance of the Renaissance, the Reformation, and the Enlightenment

219    "Not out of Africa: How Afrocentrism Became an Excuse to Teach Myth as History" by Mary Lefkowitz

220    Hermetic writings, also called Hermetica, works of revelation on occult, theological, and philosophical subjects ascribed to the Egyptian god Thoth (Greek Hermes Trismegistos [Hermes the Thrice-Greatest]), who was believed to be the inventor of writing and the patron of all the arts dependent on writing. (T. E. Britannica, Hermetic writings)

221    Champollion's decipherment - This task of complete decipherment was first accomplished by the Frenchman Jean-François Champollion (1790–1832) in 1822, after long years of intensive work and many setbacks. His success was due to the recognition that hieroglyphic writing, exactly like the hieratic and demotic scripts derived from it, did not constitute a writing system of symbols but rather a phonetic script. (Brunner)

Eras in relation to Europe in its learning of all things ancient Egypt. Another question later came to mind regarding these three periods of Europe and the notion of modern meta-physics. I had learned that "New Age" was a rehashing of old ideas. How old those ideas actually were became a quest for me within this study. If those ideas did not go back to a more accurate understanding of ancient Egypt, then perhaps the movement or, as some state, the notion of the "Age of Aquarius", was not quite as valid as many would like to believe.

According to Copenhaver, concerning the Corpus Hermeticum, *"In Egypt, in the midst of this cultural and spiritual turmoil, over the course of several centuries when the Ptolemies, the Romans and the Byzantines ruled the Nile valley, other persons unknown to us produced the writings that we call the Hermetica."*[222]

I had seen where some thought that the Hermetic writings go back to Hermes Trismegistus (Thrice Great)[223] whom was said to be the grandson of the god Hermes. The god Hermes was said to be the equivalent of the ancient Egyp-

---

222    (Copenhaver xxiv)

223    HERMES TRISMEGISTUS ("the thrice greatest Hermes"), an honorific designation of the Egyptian Hermes, i.e. Thoth (q.v.), the god of wisdom. In late hieroglyphic the name of Thoth often has the epithet "the twice very great," sometimes "the thrice very great"; in the popular language (demotic) the corresponding epithet is "the five times very great," found as early as the 3rd century B.C. Greek translations give ὁ μέγας καὶ μέγας and μέγιστος: τρίσμεγας occurs in a late magical text, ὁ τρισμέγιστος has not yet been found earlier than the 2nd century A.D., but there can now be no doubt of its origin in the above Egyptian epithets. (Company)

tian god Thoth,[224] who was called the scribe of the gods.[225] Aside from the fact that there were different approaches to "Hermes" as well as Thoth during different timeframes as well as who the author was and how they referred to said "Hermes", there is no definitive literary or other evidence that the Corpus Hermeticum goes back to "Hermes". Rather than one author, like many other ancient texts, the Corpus was written by many hands. According to Copenhaver, *"From Hellenistic times forward, the theologies of the eastern Mediterranean were complicated by the tangle of correspondences between the traditional Greek pantheon and the newfound gods of nations subjugated by Alexander and later conquerors."[226]*

From those Hellenistic times moving forward, there were quite a few changes in matters related to philosophy and theology, one of which was syncretism. At some point Hermes,[227] Hermes Trismegistus, and Thoth appeared to have been merged. It became apparent that with dealing with ancient civilizations, ancient Egypt in particular, the further you get away from their timeframe, the more confusion

224 (Copenhaver xiii)

225 (Heinrich Karl Brugsch)

226 (Copenhaver xxvi)

227 HERMES, a Greek god, identified by the Romans with Mercury. The derivation of his name and his primitive character are very uncertain. The earliest centres of his cult were Arcadia, where Mt. Cyllene was reputed to be his birthplace, the islands of Lemnos, Imbros and Samothrace, in which he was associated with the Cabeiri and Attica. In Arcadia he was specially worshipped as the god of fertility, and his images were ithyphallic, as also were the "Hermae" at Athens. Herodotus (ii. 51) states that the Athenians borrowed this type from the Pelasgians, thus testifying to the great antiquity of the phallic Hermes. (The Encyclopedia Britannica Company, Hermes)

comes into the mix, perhaps due to the later ones misunderstanding and/or misrepresenting the earlier philosophical, theological, etc. of earlier peoples and civilizations. Concerning the Corpus or Hermetica or even discourses of Hermes, Iamblichus, a Neoplatonist who lived from the third to fourth centuries C.E., reported to have learned from other authors that the discourses of Hermes numbered among 20,000, and even up to 36,525. They were written in Greek well after the timeframe of the ancient Greek philosophers that they were attributed too. The style and vocabulary of these writings do not jibe with that which was developed by the fourth century BCE philosophers.[228]

It was not uncommon in ancient times for authors to pretend as though their writings were written by earlier peoples. Some would even claim to have found hidden documents from earlier languages.[229] There are several modern scholars that can attest to ancient "forgery" or pseudepigrapha. In other words, some ancient ones placed words in the mouths of "gods", or even earlier people to give their own writings credence.[230] I would later come to realize that even some of our dearest writings were done in a similar way. One must do their homework, though, to be careful to still find value in those pseudepigraphic writings as to not throw out the baby with the bathwater.

During my study on this, I was very fortunate to learn of one Rabbi Isaac Casaubon, whom was mentioned by Lef-

228    (Lefkowitz, The Myth of the Egyptian Mystery System 100-101)

229    (Lefkowitz, The Myth of the Egyptian Mystery System 101)

230    Credence - The likelihood of something being true; plausibility. [Oxford University Press]

kowitz. Prior to his discovery, one Marsilio Ficino translated the *"the dialogues of the Hermetic Corpus into Latin."*[231] Grafton and Weinberg continues, *"From then on, most Western readers believed that Thrice-Wise Hermes, an Egyptian sage, really composed these dialogues, with their detailed description of the creation of the world and the life of the soul.[104]"*[232] Later, during the fifteenth and sixteenth centuries, Hermes was honored as a pagan prophet. Afterwards Cesare Baronio cited Ficino honorably within his church history, which through demonstration, Casaubon began showing that the dialogues of Hermes had to have been written later. As Grafton and Weinberg recounts, *"The style of this book could not be farther from the language that the Greek contemporaries of Hermes used. For the old language had many words, phrases, and a general style very different from that of the later Greeks. Here is no trace of antiquity, no crust, none of that patina of age that the best ancient critics found even in Plato, and even more in Hippocrates, Herodotus, and other older writers. On the contrary, there are many words here that do not belong to any Greek earlier than that of the time of Christ's birth."*[112], [233]

To sum up the masterful work by Casaubon, Grafton and Weinberg conclude, *"So Casaubon demolished Hermes— but with the further twist that he revealed not only the text's flaws, but also the author's conscious effort at deception.[119] A number of Catholic scholars tried to rebut Casaubon's* <u>*critique in the course of defending Baronio against him, and*</u>

231     (Grafton & Weinberg, "I have always loved the Holy Tongue" : Isaac Casaubon, the Jews, and a Forgotten Chapter in Renaissance Scholarship. 30)
232     (Anthony Grafton 30)
233     (Anthony Grafton 31)

*Protestants as well as Catholics did their best to prove that the treatises contained Egyptian elements even if their language, in this version, was Greek.[120] From the 1990s on, the view that these texts contain fragmentary but real elements of Egyptian belief and ritual has gained favor. But the core of Casaubon's arguments about the transmitted text itself remains unshaken.[121] The demolition of Hermes was a masterpiece of iconoclastic classical scholarship, and it helped to unleash a wave of destructive criticism that would eventually reach the Bible itself: "the advent of the critical philology of Joseph Scaliger's and Isaac Casaubon's generation, which engaged in a search for classical forgeries, initiated a massive process of realignment of authority."[234]*

With no definitive "proof" that these writings go back to Thoth, this revelation lays to rest the ancient Egyptian origin of the Corpus Hermeticum.  Lastly, and secondarily, the statement *"The demolition of Hermes was a masterpiece of iconoclastic classical scholarship, and it helped to unleash a wave of destructive criticism that would eventually reach the Bible itself"* is interesting as this period led straight into the Enlightenment Era[lvii], and correlates with earlier chapters within this work.

## Freemasonry Early or Late?

Along with dealing with Hermeticism, the subject of Freemasonry is nearby and should be explored for consideration.  Lefkowitz does a masterful job demonstrating that the modern Freemasonic movement has its origins in the seventeenth century, with an imaginative approach to

---

234    (Anthony Grafton 34)

ancient Egypt rooted primarily in European ideas, redis-covered during the Renaissance, having created a mystical Egypt.[235]  Giordano Bruno,[236] a Dominican monk, taught that Christianity was a corruption of Hermeticism.  It was through Hermeticism that Freemasonry approached ancient Egypt, and in this way pushed their ideals.  At that time, Horapollo was utilized to understand the ancient Egyptian hieroglyphs.  Later Horapollo was shown to be erroneous in being utilized to properly understand the ancient Egyptian hieroglyphs.  The fundamental notions of Egypt expressed in the Corpus Hermeticum, Horapollo's interpretations of the ancient Egyptian hieroglyphs, and from the philosophy of the Renaissance concerning said works, were preserved in Freemasonry.  So, Freemasonry, as it is understood in modern times, is based on a misrepresentation and misun-derstanding of ancient Egypt.

Despite the fact that the ancient Egyptian hieroglyphs were deciphered in 1822, there were during that time, and afterwards, those that challenged that decipherment, just as there are some during modern times.  One of the arguments against the decipherment of the hieroglyphs that I had come

235      (Lefkowitz, The Myth of the Egyptian Mystery System 106-107)

236      Giordano Bruno The most notable of these were his theories of the infinite universe and the multiplicity of worlds, in which he re-jected the traditional geocentric (Earth-centred) astronomy and intui-tively went beyond the Copernican heliocentric (Sun-centred) theory, which still maintained a finite universe with a sphere of fixed stars. Bruno is, perhaps, chiefly remembered for the tragic death he suffered at the stake because of the tenacity with which he maintained his un-orthodox ideas at a time when both the Roman Catholic and Reformed churches were reaffirming rigid Aristotelian and Scholastic principles in their struggle for the evangelization of Europe. (Aquilecchia)

across was by Walter Williams,[237] who believed that they had never been deciphered.[238]  In the Appendix of The Historical Origin of Christianity, Williams gives his argument as to why they haven't been.  He cites a very important statement by Carol A. R. Andrews from the book *The Rosetta Stone*, that is summed up by Andrews stating that you cannot compile an alphabet of hieroglyphic signs, though certain unilateral hieroglyphics were chosen to form a sort of alphabet which is universally used.[239]

There are many who have chronicled the history of that decipherment.  A good start for me was Sir Ernest Alfred Thompson Wallis Budge,[240] as well as others.  One of the early ones that countered Champollion's decipherment was Gustav Seyffarth.  Gustav Seyffarth was a noted Egyptol-

237    Walter Williams, Historian and Research Analyst of Ancient History.  Author of "The Historical Origin of Christianity, and "The Historical Origin of Islam."  "They would have been taught the meaning of the Medu-Netcher (Hieroglyphic) symbols which never have been deciphered (read revised edition of The Historical Origin of Christianity appendix);" (Williams)
238    (Williams, Appendix : Why The Medu-Netcher-Hieroglyphics Have Never Been Deciphered 146)
239    (Williams, Appendix : Why The Medu-Netcher-Hieroglyphics Have Never Been Deciphered 150)
240    Sir Wallis Budge, in full Sir Ernest Alfred Thompson Wallis Budge, (born July 27, 1857, Cornwall, Eng.—died Nov. 23, 1934, London), curator (1894–1924) of Egyptian and Assyrian antiquities at the British Museum, London, for which he collected vast numbers of cuneiform tablets, Egyptian papyri, and Greek, Coptic, Arabic, Syriac, and Ethiopic manuscripts. He entered the museum's service in 1883 and subsequently made many trips to Mesopotamia, Egypt, and the Sudan to conduct archaeological excavations. He published many works, including translations of ancient texts such as the Egyptian Book of the Dead. He was knighted in 1920. (T. E. Britannica, Sir Wallis Budge)

ogist,[lviii] who presented his own system that never gained enough academic followers of distinction.[241]

Without the decipherment of ancient Egypt, what would we refer to or consult to understand ancient Egypt? Why go see monuments that have information carved on them that you cannot understand? If ancient Egypt was as connected to the ancient world as the ancient writings of the various nation states, why wouldn't it be important enough for us in modern times to try to understand them? As Williams, himself, asserts, *"Find your way back to ancient Egypt."* How could this be done if we are unable to read what they wrote? Regardless of the rejection that took place during Champollion's life and even later, the decipherment that he and others performed has been widely accepted.[242] As a side note, I found something else interesting. While reading through the source material provided by Horace Butler in his book "When Rocks Cry Out", I found, *"How we came to know about this history is one of the greatest stories of archaeology. The adventure began with an eccentric nineteenth-century naturalist of dubious renown named Constantine Rafinesque. A man who seemed to just miss fame throughout his lifetime (he almost went on the Lewis and Clark expedition), Rafinesque became interested in the strange writing from Mexico that had been published in the reports of Humboldt's and Antonio del Rio's journeys through the region now known as Chiapas. After deciding this odd writing was Mayan and deducing how to read the numbers, he published the first modern decipherments in the Saturday Evening Post of January 13, 1827, and June 21, 1828. In a*

---

241   (Encyclopedia Britannica)

242   (Budge)

*wonderful historical irony, Rafinesque sent letters describing his discoveries about Maya writing to Champolion, who was already famous for his decipherment of Egyptian hieroglyphic writing. ⁷"*[243] More on this correspondence and the implications in a later work.

While I, personally, am not against a mystical, meta-physical component within the hieroglyphs, I think it best to hold what the ancient Egyptians, themselves, held about their own writing.  I also think it best to focus more so on what the early ancient Greeks stated about said writing system.  Over time in my studies, it seemed that the further you get away from the earlier period, even of the ancient Greeks, though there are some later ones who did hold fast to earlier understandings, the more distorted in their understandings the Greeks and others become.  Erik Iversen in his *The Myth of Egypt and Its Hieroglyphs In European Tradition*, demonstrates how some of the ancient Greeks, at a later period, understood the hieroglyphs.  Iversen discusses Plutarch, Diodorus, Clement of Alexandria, and others.

Iversen showed how the Greeks were ignorant, at least leading up to the time of Plotinus, concerning the true nature of the ancient Egyptian hieroglyphs.  They were in awe over the symbols but never truly came to what they meant.  The hieroglyphs were discussed in many debates and Plotinus[244] at a later time presented his method of approach and under-

243    (Linda Schele 46)

244    Plotinus, (born 205 CE, Lyco, or Lycopolis, Egypt?—died 270, Campania), ancient philosopher, the centre of an influential circle of intellectuals and men of letters in 3rd-century Rome, who is regarded by modern scholars as the founder of the Neoplatonic school of philosophy. (Armstrong)

standing to them. Neoplatonism is attributed to Plotinus. It is from Neoplatonism that the Renaissance and other periods derive their understanding of Ancient Egypt as Lefkowitz observed.[245]

Iversen observed how there was a metaphysical application to the hieroglyphs that formed the understanding of the philosophical discussions which were very important up until Neoplatonism ceased to exist mainstream. After Plotinus, quite a bit of literature on the hieroglyphs was produced in the Greek language. About this time the Hermetic writing came about, even Iamblichus' treatise on the ancient Egyptian mysteries. This shows that ancient Egypt had only been understood from a Hellenistic standpoint, rather than ancient Egypt itself. Finally, Iversen submits that there was a syncretism of ancient Egyptian wisdom, Neoplatonism, humanism, and Christianity which formed the backdrop of the knowledge of God as it came to be understood from the time of the Renaissance.[246] Iversen does chronicle in his work how there are surviving writings that were indeed useful in the later decipherment and understanding of the hieroglyphs.

Despite the Neo-Platonists' influence, the ancient Egyptian hieroglyphs and the history of their decipherment are too important to leave out of the discussion of the origins of the modern meta-physical movement.[247] The humanists that Iversen spoke of were more influential than many realize in the formulation of many of the ideas that were incorpo-

---

245    (Iversen, II. The Classical Tradition 45)
246    (Iversen, II. The Classical Tradition 46)
247    (Iversen, III. The Middle Ages and The Renaissance' 60)

rated within "New Age" philosophy. The absolution of the universal Christian beliefs and truth that the humanists held is what fueled and drove the humanists in their approach in said matters. When you approach life like there is only one truth, instead of seeing that there are many truths, there is no wonder why 'errors' and 'mistakes' abound. So, the Renaissance and later periods were rife with such 'errors' and 'mistakes' that were founded upon an ancient Egypt of a later creation, built upon a foundation laid from those that lacked the fundamental understanding and so-called 'initiation' into what constituted those earlier truths.

And it is the eighteenth century that now comes into view concerning the "New Age" movement and how it is, in my opinion, to be more accurately understood.

## Why Discuss Gerald Massey?

Some have observed that the "New Age" does have *"antecedents that stretch back to southern Europe in late antiquity."*[248] Continuing, *"Following the Age of Enlightenment in 18th century Europe, new esoteric ideas developed in response to the development of scientific rationality. Scholars call this new esoteric trend occultism, and this occultism was a key factor in the development of the worldview from which the New Age emerged."* New ideas that go back to a period where those ideas failed to reach ancient Egypt, itself, but to a later period of inaccurate approaches. Since the Corpus Hermetica is late, and the ancient Egyptian hieroglyphs were deciphered in 1822 and the understanding of ancient Egypt was already crafted "mystically" and not based on

---

248    (Wikipedia, New Age)

sound information, it is indeed necessary to study, at least to some degree, to know when the modern movement began and some of what was incorporated into the ideology(ies).

Gerald Massey is important within the discussion of the "New Age" movement, at least in how some "New Agers" saw/see him. During my research on Massey, I came across a website (www.masseiana.org), maintained by Jon Lange and others. After some time, the website went down. I was disappointed by this but kept looking. I eventually stumbled upon a website which discussed how Jon Lange had closed down www.masseiana.org and was able to be followed on Twitter. I found his twitter account. I realized that he was in the process of making all of the website material available via book form. I was very happy to know this. I eventually purchased the book material on Massey. Jon Lange is important, in fact paramount, in studying Gerald Massey. He has provided the most balanced and detailed account of Massey's works in modern times that I have ever seen. I, personally do not utilize Massey as an "authority" so to speak on studying ancient history. The reason being is what I had already learned about Massey through others and from what Lange, while going through quite a bit of explanation on behalf of, has demonstrated in Volume I of his "Masseiana" series.[249] In this section, I will not be delving into Massey's works but will deal with some of the explanation of the source material that Massey utilized within his corpus as laid out by Lange. As Lange, himself, observes, works

249    Masseiana is a 17 volume work made from the material that was developed by Jon Lange and others from their previous, now no longer operational, website www.masseiana.org. Information and explanation available via Jon Lange's twitter handle: https://twitter.com/JonLange93?lang=en.

should be *"... fully referenced, with citations that can be traced to their source, as all books should be."*[250]  I could not agree more with Lange in this statement.

Lange also gives a very balanced and honest critique of Massey in regards to how he dealt with his source material, while at the same time demonstrating the obvious brilliance that Massey displayed throughout his writings.  Massey seemed to have a habit of utilizing sources that he failed to give proper credit.  Lange states, *"Massey likewise samples texts from other works (usually wholesale quotations) and introduces them into the text as if he has consulted the work himself, whereas in reality he has relied on another scholar to provide it for him."*[251]

As a result of how Massey utilized his source material, he has been accused of making things up by some and out-right plagiarism by others.  Over time, I began to realize that people in general have flaws.  That might be simple and even nonsensical in a way, and one may respond, "Duh." None of us are above them.  The problem comes in when they are pointed out.  Some dismiss them for the good and fail to realize that they do matter.  Others take them too far and dismiss the good altogether.  I respect that while Lange obviously revered Massey, having devoted so many years to the study of Massey's works, he was still able to be honest enough to point out his errors.  Errors that caused many to not take him seriously and dismiss his corpus to its entirety. Lange observes, *"Massey displays all the characteristics of the standard model in that his poor referencing demon-*

---

250     (Lange 35)
251     (Lange 33)

*strates laziness; he simply couldn't be bothered to cite properly. And this is evident through his whole attitude toward his work: laziness pervades his books; also demonstrable in the arrangement of his points, the divisions of his chapters—entirely arbitrary in most cases as he discusses the same points in different chapters, showing no sign of logical progression—illustrations taken from other books without acknowledgement, Latin and Greek quotes not translated (not so inexcusable for his time since even Thomas Taylor, writing over fifty years prior to Massey, always translates his foreign quotes for his readers), etc., although his talent as a perceptive thinker is undeniable and his originality in the field of typology is without doubt."*[252]

Before leaving this section, I will show what Lange found concerning Massey's source material specifically. Some of the major works that Massey relied upon tentatively, according to Lange, were from John Brand (Observations on Popular Antiquities), Thomas Firminger Thiselton-Dyer (British Popular Customs Present and Past), Samuel Birch and Archibald Henry Sayce (Records of the Past – first and second series, respectively according to the authors), Edward Davies (Mythology and Rites of the British Druids), William Forbes Skene (Four Ancient Books of Wales), Edward Burnett Tylor (Primitive Culture: Researches Into the Development of Mythology, Philosophy, Religion, Language, Art and Custom and Researches Into the Early History of Mankind and the Development of Civilization), and John Lubbock, 1st Baron Avebury (The origin of civilisation and the primitive condition of man). Lange helps us understand that we can know that he borrowed from by simply *"… reading the*

---

252    (Lange 34)

*books he read. You will then find most of the quotes he used and be staggered, no doubt, by how much of his material is really not of his own making.* "[253] So, others did the work for Massey which made Massey able to rely on them for much of his research. There is no problem with relying on others peoples' works, so long as you get permission from them and give them credit for providing those works. Researching and writing takes a considerable amount of money and time. It is a huge sacrifice to make in writing books, articles, etc., especially depending upon the subject matter. So, after one has done the long hours, days, and spent the money to provide the public or private with what they have obtained, to have one utilize your work without giving you proper respect and credit by letting it be known that they got it from you, is like a slap in your face. If the work wasn't important to enough to cite, then why would the person not citing the work utilize it then? Especially for the purposes of making money?

## Scholars within New Age

According to Wouter J. Hanegraaff,[254] *"Most of the beliefs which characterise the New Age were already present by the end of the 19th century, even to such an extent that one may legitimately wonder whether the New Age brings anything new at all."*[255] Even Hanegraaff rightly demonstrates that "New Age" doesn't really bring anything new. Yet, as

253    (Lange 35)
254    Wouter J. Hanegraaff is a full professor of History of Hermetic Philosophy and related currents at the University of Amsterdam, the Netherlands. (Amsterdam)
255    (Hanegraaff, Chapter Fifteen. The Mirror of Secular Thought : 4. The Psychologization of Esotericism 482-483)

stated above, the two older discoveries already discussed show that it still is perhaps not as old as many want to think. Hanegraaff does an excellent work in the above referenced book, making known different aspects of the modern "New Age" movement and the tenets of the philosophy(ies) that are incorporated within it. In his introduction, Hanegraaff writes, *"During the 1980s, and continuing into the 1990s, there has been much talk in western society about the New Age movement. The term "New Age" has entered the standard vocabulary in discussions about ideas and practices regarded as alternative vis a vis dominant cultural trends, especially if these ideas and practices seem to be concerned with "spirituality". In spite of the popularity of the term, its actual content remains extremely vague. This is largely due to the fact that the New Age is not an organization, which could be unambiguously identified or defined on the basis of self-proclaimed leaders, official doctrines, standard religious practices, and the like. The initial fact about the "New Age" is that it concerns a label attached indiscriminately to whatever seems to fit it, on the basis of what are essentially pre-reflective intuitions. As a result, the New Age means very different things to different people. This observation provides the proper—if sobering—starting point of the present study. My purpose will be to characterize and delineate the New Age movement on the basis of an analysis and interpretation of its implicit structure of beliefs. This seems to presuppose, however, that we already know in advance what it is and, even more importantly, what it is not. In other words, defining the term "New Age" is a necessary condition for finding out how it may be understood. That this apparent paradox is not insurmountable will be discussed-*

*below.* "[256]

Hanegraaff charts within the above referenced work many other scholars that are of the "New Age" persuasion. While studying the "New Age" from the scholarly perspective, I came across Dr. Sean Creaven, the Senior Lecturer in Sociology and Criminology at the University of the West of England.[257] Creaven, in his work entitled "*Against the Spiritual Turn: Marxism, Realism, and Critical Theory*", is writing for the purpose of arguing against what was "*... the recent 'spiritual' trajectory of Roy Bhaskar's work, upon which he first embarked with the publication of his From East to West, undermines the fundamental achievements of his earlier work. The problem with Bhaskar's new philosophical system (transcendental dialectical critical realism, or simply meta-reality), from the critical-realist Marxist perspective endorsed here, is that it marks both a departure from and a negation of the earlier concerns of Bhaskar to develop a realist philosophy of science and under-labour for an emancipatory materialist socio-historical science.*"[258]    While perusing this work, I found a section entitled, "New ageism and reincarnation." Apparently "New Age" has been applied to science and politics. Science and politics in this regard is not my aim in this section. In this section, there are some profound statements made by Creaven. I had learned earlier, that "New Age" was a push back against secular rationalism, and other things. Creaven states, "*Secular rationalism is a target of New Age and so too is scientific reason. Expert secular knowledge is distrusted as well as traditional reli-*

---

256    (Hanegraaff, Introduction 1)

257    (University of the West of England)

258    (Creaven, Preface viii)

*gious claims for moral authority. Spiritual self-discovery is championed as a surer route to knowledge than both. Occult arts and practices (magic, paganism, witchcraft, astrology, etc.) are emphasized as alternative routes to self-knowledge. The task is to explore oneself rather than the external world of social relations. This move parallels the 'postmodern' decentering of the notion of objective truth (as correspondence of beliefs and the world). Truth is a property of the subject, not of the relationship of subject and object, and each individual has his or her own inner truth to discover.[112] For these reasons, New Age eschews a rational theorization of the ills of capitalist modernity. Social ills are personalized as ills of the self-alienated individual. Consequently, New Age is fundamentally incompatible with a critical social science of modern social forms."[259]*

Over time, I had begun to understand that this statement holds true, at least in regards to what I had found. Creaven continues, *"Despite its diversity and eclecticism, the New Age movement is collectively wedded to what Paul Heelas describes as 'self-spirituality'. This is a narcissistic deification of the individual subject. The self is, from this viewpoint, a self-alienated god or goddess, which can become knowledgeable of its own 'true' nature through involvement in a range of practices—including meditation, arcane arts, music, playing sports, psychotherapy, listening to music, drug-consumption, and so on.[113] In this sense, New Age spiritualism marks the highest stage of bourgeois individualism. No longer is individualism defined simply as the right of every person to act as he or she wishes, so long as this does not infringe the civil liberties of others. Instead it is defined*

---

259    (Creaven 33-34)

*as the power of the individual to arbitrate between what is true and what is false on the basis of his or her own intuitive self-judgement. This narcissistic individualism, whereby knowledge is just one's point of view, is the basis of New Age's decentring of enlightenment rationality, scientific expertise and traditional religious authority. In New Age too, we see something resembling (the source of) Bhaskar's Promethean voluntarist idealism. For New Age insists that individuals have the power to chart their own lives and make of themselves what they wish, irrespective of constraining ills or unfavourable circumstances. The subject has the power to hammer 'outsider reality' into conformity with 'insider reality'."[260]*

I had begun to recognize this individualism that Creaven speaks of among many "New Agers". It can indeed lead to narcissism.[261] I had, personally, a few "New Age" mentors along the way, and found that some of them only had empathy as long as you were in agreement with them. As soon as you had your own mind about things, well, it seemed that that empathy went right out the window. I found that, like many people, some just like to be right regardless of what you have to bring to the table. I say, "Be right. Let's go our separate ways, shall we?"

---

260    (Creaven 34)

261    Narcissism – 1. Excessive interest in or admiration of oneself and one's physical appearance. 1.1 Psychology Selfishness, involving a sense of entitlement, a lack of empathy, and a need for admiration, as characterizing a personality type. 1.2 Psychoanalysis Self-centredness [sic.] arising from failure to distinguish the self from external objects, either in very young babies or as a feature of mental disorder. [Oxford University Press]

# TRANSFORMATION

I had noticed much of this, *"Spiritual self-discovery is championed as a surer route to knowledge than both. Occult arts and practices (magic, paganism, witchcraft, astrology, etc.) are emphasized as alternative routes to self-knowledge. The task is to explore oneself rather than the external world of social relations."*, as stated above. I had studied the social environment via sociology for different periods of history. I had also studied how the earlier ones saw things utilizing their methods of spirituality. Social relations seemed to not matter to some of the "New Agers" that I had come across. Another thing that I noticed was how "truth" was approached. As quoted above, *"Instead it is defined as the power of the individual to arbitrate between what is true and what is false on the basis of his or her own intuitive self-judgement."* Terms such as self-enlightenment, inner-knowing, and others pervaded the speech of some of those that I had read and others that I actually met in person. The key focus that I could not grasp was the fact that *"For New Age insists that individuals have the power to chart their own lives and make of themselves what they wish, irrespective of constraining ills or unfavourable circumstances. The subject has the power to hammer 'outsider reality' into conformity with 'insider reality.'"* I had seen where some actually believed that you could change the outer environment from your inner environment. There is some truth in this, changing one's own life and circumstances is very important. But to disregard the aspects of reality that you cannot change could be catastrophic. There are many things you can do in regards to taking responsibility for your own life by making changes. As Rollo Tomassi rightly stated in *The Rational Male*, you can make modifications to your personality.[lix] It is not as static as many would like to think.

However, one must know their own limitations. And at the end of the day, many of the earlier ones found themselves just as pillaged, plundered, driven away, and even murdered as everyone else who may or may not have held their beliefs. In order for a society to function, you do need some commonality. In order for relationships to work, you must agree on more than what you disagree on. Everything and everyone is not for everyone. I did find much useful within the "New Age" philosophy(ies). I came to the conclusion that that was not the path for me to take wholeheartedly, nor primarily. I decided to use it as other things. At my convenience.

Finally, after delving more into science in general, it became evident how science and spiritual phenomena have had a long process of development through ideals with many people being on different sides of the spectrum. I began to read Carroll Quigley, and saw where he stated, *"The one major difference between the natural sciences and the social sciences is the assumption, made in the former, that human thoughts cannot influence what happens. This is an assumption, justified by the rule of simplicity, although few persons recognize that it is. There is a considerable body of evidence that human thoughts can influence the physical world, but this evidence, segregated into such fields as parapsychology or the psychic world, is not acceptable to the natural sciences. As a result, phenomena such as poltergeist manifestations (largely because they cannot be repeated on request) go unexplained and are generally ignored by the natural sciences. The latter continue to assume that physical processes are immune to spiritual influences.*

*In the social sciences, on the other hand, it is perfectly clear that human thoughts can influence what happens; and, accordingly, the social scientist must face the more complicated situation created by this admission.* "[262]

After a while, I wanted to see if there was a way to merge science with spiritual phenomena, like some others had thought. I was happy to see how Quigley explained this. "... *the natural sciences are concerned with phenomena where we do not expect subjective factors to influence what happens, while the social sciences are concerned with phenomena where subjective factors may affect the outcome.* "[263] It was from this premise that I had endeavored to continue my studies. But first, I had to get to know more about science if such a thing were possible.

---

262    (Quigley, 1. Scientific Method and the Social Sciences 46)
263    (Quigley, 1. Scientific Method and the Social Sciences 47)

# 9 TRUTH-SEEKER

Having studied some aspects of the spirit world, the rational world, then coming to grips with the choices that I made moving forward, I decided that I wanted to learn about mankind's origins. I could no longer accept the book of Genesis nor the other creation stories as a doorway into understanding how the world came about or how mankind was "created" and how they passed on their genes. Science, though, had a different position to take, whether a school of scientists agreed or disagreed. Going deeper into science seemed inevitable in this regard.

Since I had found the explanations that we have not changed as a human species within the past 100,000+ years, it became clear that studying the past would be extremely helpful in understanding who we are today. Behavioral psychology is another field that was quite useful in this regard. I even learned that the cultural and social environments take part in the dictation of politics, religion, male and female relationships, economics, business, etc. What the population wants in general, regardless if they were guided to certain conclusions via government or otherwise, or they came to those conclusions on their own as a collective, those conclusions are the direction that the world will go. There are always exceptions to every rule. Rules are made by the majority or those in power. The exceptions do not disprove the rule, though some believe that they do. A minority, or smaller group, does not determine what the larger group does, unless they have the position, wealth, and influence to do so. So, unless a minority controls a resource that the whole cannot afford to live and flourish without, then the exception can only prove the rule that the majority has already set.

Finding the field of genetics, anthropology—including archaeology—and tracing historical events as written by previous civilizations became my quest. I learned about the out-of-Africa hypothesis as well as the Multi-Regional hypothesis.[264] A report published in 1987, said to be ground-

---

264    The out-of-Africa theory postu¬lates that humans with modern traits left Africa from 50,000 to 60,000 years ago to settle the world. Along the way, they replaced archaic hominids, such as Homo erectus, that left Africa as early as 1.8 million years ago. The competing multi-regional theory holds that modern characteristics evolved not just in Africa but in archaic hominid populations in Asia and Europe. Interbreeding among all these groups ensured that they remained a single species. (Stix 60)

# 9 TRUTH-SEEKER

breaking, explained how mtDNA[265] had been utilized to add value to our knowledge in relation to the history of the human gene pool. Approximately 147 people from different geographical locations were studied for this experiment. Except for the African population, the remaining populations were of many different origins which implies that they each were colonized separately. The DNA taken from these individuals was theorized to have come from one woman that perhaps lived 200,000 years ago, maybe in Africa.[266]

Continuing this type of study, I came across L. Luca Cavilla-Sforza,[267] who wrote one of the most important works on human history related to human genes. He explained that while those that are studying human evolution are developing better methods for understanding it, some of the remains of identification for the aboriginal people are being decimated. There is then an urgency to preserve as much as possible for studying the past in light of this decimation. Cavilla-Sforza believed that genetic data alone is not enough to provide satisfactory evidence for studying human history. It is important to bring in other disciplines, along with genetic data, such as history, linguistics, anthropology, and archaeology whereby we can have a more complete picture of our past.

---

265    MITOCHONDRIAL DNA - an extranuclear double-stranded DNA found exclusively in mitochondria that in most eukaryotes is a circular molecule and is maternally inherited —abbreviation mtDNA. (Merriam-Webster Dictionary Online)

266    (Rebecca L. Cann 31)

267    Luigi Luca Cavilla-Sforza born 25 January 1922) is an Italian-born population geneticist, who has been a professor (now emeritus) at Stanford University since 1970. (Wikipedia, Luigi Luca Cavalli-Sforza)

It was from him and others that I learned about the different theories of human origins in relation to geography. The out-of-Africa hypothesis seemed plausible just as the Multi-Regional hypothesis. I had come across Lefkowitz' as well as the arguments of others against the out-of-Africa hypothesis. I had stumbled upon an article concerning the movement of some of our early ancestors, from the Scientific American magazine entitled, *Traces of a Distant Past.* In it I found that a small group of Africans, roughly fifty or sixty thousand years ago, sailed away from Africa and never returned.[268]

There were not a few debates concerning this out-of-Africa issue. Perhaps some of it was racially motivated, perhaps not. An African origin, or possible one, does not necessarily yield to the idea of everyone being "black," "dark," or "melanated." Regardless of the modern concept of race, a group of the Africans that left, along with evidence that they were characterized just as modern as we are, found their way to Tierra del Fuego. After a while, I began to realize that all people on the continent of Africa, and those who left, did not have to necessarily be "black."

Science seemed to carefully, and at many times not so carefully, weave together different disciplines in an attempt to explain in a more cohesive manner, how people came into being and moved about the planet.

Later Stix discusses two reports, one on Science and the other on Nature, that were deemed to be the largest surveys

---

268    (Stix 56)

to that time, 2008, that discussed human diversity. Two research teams completed the studies, the Human Genome Diversity Panel and the Center for the study of Human Polymorphisms in Paris. After the findings of both of these groups *"jibed with previous research from anthropology, archaeology, linguistics and biology (including previous mitochondrial and Y DNA studies), also provided a broader statistical foundation for the out-of-Africa hypothesis..."*[269] I decided to stick with the out-of-Africa hypothesis..

I am not against the Multi-Regional Hypothesis or any other. None of us, scientists or otherwise, really know where we all originated from. This is why we are studying this, whether we are scientists or not. It is still very important that we start somewhere and realize that beliefs should be held loosely. When searching for truths, we cannot become rigid in a belief or set of beliefs, especially since we don't have enough information to stake a claim on at times. I had learned that the scientific method involved the gathering of evidence, developing a hypothesis, and testing that hypothesis. Carroll Quigley does an excellent job of explaining the details of the scientific method in his "The Evolution of Civilizations." What I really began to appreciate about Quigley was his use, explanation, and adequate demonstration of culture and environment. As quoted above, *"...the natural sciences are concerned with phenomena where we do not expect subjective factors to influence what happens, while the social sciences are concerned with phenomena where subjective factors may affect the outcome."*[270] Quigley focused on the social science of culture and its relation to en-

---

269    (Stix 60)
270    (Quigley, 1. Scientific Method and the Social Sciences 47)

vironment. In a very detailed discussion of the development of humans in comparison with turtles within an environment as part of Quigley's definition of culture, he states, *"All of these things, patterns of action, feeling, and thought, as well as concrete objects used in these activities, are known in the social sciences as culture. This culture forms the environment in which a child grows up..."*[271] The natural environment surrounds animals and has caused them to evolve differently from humans, especially on the instinctual level. For animal development, some are not in need of culture. Mankind is different in this regard. Though mankind is surrounded by the natural environment, it is the cultural environment that *"...intervenes as a kind of insulation between him and his natural environment. In fact, the surrounding environment of culture penetrates both into him as a person and into his natural environment, changing both. His neurological reactions in behavior, in feeling, and in thought are largely determined by his cultural environment, and at the same time this cultural environment modifies his natural environment by such activities as heating his home, cooking his food, cutting down forests, draining swamps, killing off animals, and generally modifying the face of the earth."*[272]

It was through Quigley that I was able to put many ancient documents that I had read into perspective. That perspective was even more strengthened when I began to learn about human behavior through the study of psychology, with a peek into psychiatry as well. As mentioned elsewhere within this work, the instinctual, emotional, and rational cognitive processes that I was introduced to by Rollo Tomassi became

---

271    (Quigley, 2. Man and Culture 52)
272    (Quigley, 2. Man and Culture 52)

paramount in helping me understand that human beings, whether we come from a common ancestor as mentioned by Cann and others, from Africa or some other region or territory, we have not changed as long as we have been in the form that we are in from what I have seen. It is our cultural environment that matters, which Quigley brilliantly explains. The physical remains and the writings that aid us in peeking into the window of the minds of those before us were definitely a bonus in this process. In order to get a more complete picture of who we were and are, weaving, carefully, all of these things together is what will explain the common human experience, as well as what we have the potential to be, and finally what the outcome is of what we actually will be. This was and still remains the quest for the truths of why we are here, what our capabilities are, and what we will become in the future through the passing on of not just genes but our cultural tenets as well.

## Regarding my Approach to "Race"

Race has been and still is an extremely controversial, emotional, and political, for some, issue. Many things have been attributed to ethnicity and skin tones. Yet what I found interesting is that modern scholars for the most part agree that we come from either a single common or multiple common ancestors. After having read Charles Darwin,[273] I came across information that solidified a conclusion that I had <u>come to quite</u> some time ago. In Volume I of The Descent of

273    Charles Darwin, in full Charles Robert Darwin, (born February 12, 1809, Shrewsbury, Shropshire, England—died April 19, 1882, Downe, Kent), English naturalist whose scientific theory of evolution by natural selection became the foundation of modern evolutionary studies. (Desmond)

Man, Darwin observes, *"Man has been studied more carefully than any other organic being, and yet there is the greatest possible diversity amongst capable judges whether he should be classed as a single species or race,.."* [274]

As much as mankind has been studied, the variation that Darwin mentions is due to, *"...long habit the term "race" will perhaps always be employed. The choice of terms is only so far important as it is highly desirable to use, as far as that may be possible, the same terms for the same degrees of difference. Unfortunately this is rarely possible; ..."* [275] The concept of race as has come down to us in modern times was altogether too familiar and convenient for some naturalists and others. But as Darwin and some others rightly concluded, this position is untenable. Darwin observes, *"But the most weighty of all the arguments against treating the races of man as distinct species, is that they graduate into each other, independently in many cases, as far as we can judge, of their having intercrossed."* [276]

The diversities of opinions on the matters of race were clearly evident in Darwin's day, yet mankind was the most carefully studied than any other organic being. It is clear that the concept of race in the minds of the so-called learned at that time was clouding their judgment. Darwin did not believe that the races of man could all be treated as distinct species. He saw that we were far more connected than many, even those of his day, may have or wanted to have realized. Darwin continues, *"When the races of man diverged at an extremely remote epoch from their common progenitor, they*

---

274    (Darwin 226)
275    (Darwin 228)
276    (Darwin 226)

*will have differed but little from each other, and been few in number; consequently they will then, as far as their distinguishing characters are concerned, have had less claim to rank as distinct species, than the existing so-called races. Nevertheless such early races would perhaps have been ranked by some naturalists as distinct species, so arbitrary is the term, if their differences, although extremely slight, had been more constant than at present, and had not graduated into each other."[277]* ... *"We have now seen that the characteristic differences between the races of man cannot be accounted for in a satisfactory manner by the direct action of the conditions of life, nor by the effects of the continued use of parts, nor through the principle of correlation. We are therefore led to inquire whether slight individual differences, to which man is eminently liable, may not have been preserved and augmented during a long series of generations through natural selection."[278]* ... *"It can further be shewn that the differences between the races of man, as in colour, hairyness, form of features, &c., are of the nature which it might have been expected would have been acted on by sexual selection."[279]*

I have seen where many thought that Darwin was a racist. Maybe. But what was just quoted above doesn't seem to indicate such a position. Sexual selection must be accounted for as opposed to a blanket racial argument that is based on specific distinctness or specific species. A better explanation can be considered for racial evolution. It could be that, whether the Out-of-Africa Hypothesis, or the Multi-Region-

---

277    (Darwin 230)

278    (Darwin 248)

279    (Darwin 250)

al Hypothesis holds true, what part of the world by way of climate people inhabited over long periods of time is what determined their physiognomy, physiology, traits, and overall habits.

The word race was not used in ancient times as we have come to understand it today. Herodotus used the word race to imply humankind as a whole. He also utilized the word race to refer to a specific people or group of people, such as the Pelasgians. Herodotus would at times also use the word race to imply a people that go back to a common ancestor. Race was also translated from Herodotus' works as stock.

*"When he heard these verses, Croesus was pleased with them above all, for he thought that a mule would never be king of the Medes instead of a man, and therefore that he and his posterity would never lose his empire. Then he sought very carefully to discover who the mightiest of the Greeks were, whom he should make his friends. [2] He found by inquiry that the chief peoples were the Lacedaemonians among those of Doric, and the Athenians among those of Ionic stock. These races, Ionian and Dorian, were the foremost in ancient time, the first a Pelasgian and the second a Hellenic people. The Pelasgian race has never yet left its home; the Hellenic has wandered often and far."[280]*

The Pelasgian is said by some to be prehistoric Greek people.

*"[4] In the smith's two bellows he found the winds, hammer and anvil were blow upon blow, and the forging of iron*

---

280    (Herodotus, Book 1. Chapter 56. Section 1-2. 63)

*was woe upon woe, since he figured that iron was discovered as an evil for the human race.*"[281]

Diodorus Siculus or Diodorus the Sicilian, utilized race within the same manner as Herodotus. He utilized it as human race or the human population of people.

*"In general, then, it is because of that commemoration of goodly deeds which history accords men that some of them have been induced to become the founders of cities, that others have been led to introduce laws which encompass man's social life with security, and that many have aspired to discover new sciences and arts in order to benefit the race of men.*"[282]

While Massey and many others came to the conclusion that the "black" race was a much more major part of civilization than those such as Breasted mentioned above, whether or not the Afrocentrists went too far in their arguments, I hold that you cannot exclude the "blacks" from the argument, any more than you can exclude the other "colors." It would probably be more accurate to state that "color" didn't hold the weight that it does today in the ancient world. I cared about getting as close to the truth(s) as possible in my findings. No matter how uncomfortable those truths may have been. Even Darwin noticed negro features amongst a statue of Amenhotep III, *"Again, whilst looking in the British Museum with two competent judges, officers of the establishment, at the statue of Amunoph III., we agreed that he had a strongly negro cast of features.; but Messrs. Nott and*

---

281    (Herodotus, Book 1. Chapter 68. Section 4. 83)
282    (Siculus 9)

*Gliddon (ibid. p. 146, fig. 53) describe him as a hybrid, but not of negro intermixture.""*[283]

## Most Accurate Approach to Historical Matters

During my search, I came across a book at a time when my faith and beliefs were shaking. After the religious aspects and even while other schools of thought pervaded my mind, they still seemed to fail me as if there were missing pieces. *When Rocks Cry Out* came into focus. In this book, Horace Butler gives many direct sources. What was interesting about this study book is that while he gave very good direct sources, the indirect sources that you can only pick up on by reading the book and studying it several times, were equally as important as the direct sources. It amazed me how someone could interweave so many sources, packed into such a small book. The 2009 edition of *When Rocks Cry Out*, only 194 pages of reading, I had obtained early on. I later acquired the 2002 edition, which is 234 pages. From Butler, I learned how to take the ancient witnesses seriously, even down to their explanations of geography. Many will take a skeptical approach to his works. You should be skeptical towards anyone's works. Some of what I had heard over the years was the argument of consensus and what people had been taught and believed for several years. What many fail to understand is that the period of the Renaissance and the later periods were periods of learning just as now. They did not get everything right, and to be fair they were not wrong about everything. What Butler shows is that getting as close to the eye witness is your best bet. Compare the an-

---

283    (Darwin 217-218)

cient writings with other ancient writings and take seriously the geographical references, the beliefs and practices, and do not leave the "black" part of the historical contribution to society out of the equation like many "Europeans" and others have. The reason why I believe that the "black" part of the argument became so important is due to a statement by Breasted, where he said that black Africans contributed nothing appreciable to civilization.[284]

Breasted, like many scholars and others during his day and the days that preceded, published that the "blacks" were insignificant in any relation to the contribution to civilization. Over the years, Massey, and many others, found that this just was not the case. Later, the Afrocentric[285] movement cropped up as a push back against this which was said to go back to Marcus Garvey and later George G. M. James.[286]

Horace Butler brilliantly showed that the "blacks" had a much more important contribution to civilization, Western civilization in particular. There were many "black" authors who labored to demonstrate the "black" contribution. In my opinion, no one demonstrated it more accurately and

---

284    (Breasted, Chapter II The Food-producers and the Neolithic Age : The Quarter of the Globe Where Civilization 44-45)

285    Afrocentrism, also called Africentrism, cultural and political movement whose mainly African American adherents regard themselves and all other blacks as syncretic Africans and believe that their worldview should positively reflect traditional African values. The terms Afrocentrism, Afrocology, and Afrocentricity were coined in the 1980s by the African American scholar and activist Molefi Asante. (Early)

286    (Lefkowitz, Introduction 10)

unassailably than Horace Butler.  Butler was able to find the pieces in the ancient Egyptian, Greek ("Classical"), Roman, Hebrew, Assyrian, and various other sources that not only hinted at the "blacks", but also the different geographical orientation that we have been taught, partly from the Roman period, and later periods, such as the "Middle Ages", moving forward.  One of the common things that I kept noticing in the writings of many Egyptologists, was the constant comparison of ancient Egypt with Oriental nations.  It was as if they tried their best to divorce ancient Egypt from all things African, yet ancient Egypt is very much a part of the continent of Africa.  While many an Afrocentric were publishing and lecturing that all of the ancient Egyptians were "black", much earlier, those like George Rawlinson stated, *"Though Egypt really belongs to the continent of Africa, the inhabitants were certainly of Asiatic origin; and the whole of the valley of the Nile has been peopled by the primeval immigration of a Caucasian race."*[287]

Others were focusing on the geographical delineation and re-orientation such as, "Edward Gibbon, inspired by the works of great writers of antiquity such as Pliny or Sallust, did not hesitate to make Egypt Asian: *"By its situation that celebrated kingdom is included within the immense peninsula of Africa; but it is accessible only on the side of Asia, whose revolutions, in almost every period of history, Egypt has humbly obeyed."*[24]"[288]

Ancient Egypt is important in the argument of early civilization because of their ancient remains.  They are also

---

287    (Herodotus, The Nile-Causes of the inundation 21)
288    (Foliard 59)

important in the fact that many of the early civilizations wrote about them, traded with them, warred with them, and utilized their ideas for various reasons.  So, a "race" driven or focused individual has a vested interest in making the ancient Egyptians their particular "color."  Butler addresses this argument, beginning with the Spanish exploration of the Americas, utilizing the writings from the Spanish Friars, as well as other primary, and even secondary sources.  Prior to him, Dr. Ivan Van Sertima addressed the "black" contribution to the Americas, extending the works of Professor Leo Wiener and Professor Alexander von Wuthenau, where Sertima says, *"Here were visible witnesses of a vanished time and they were telling us a remarkable new story.  Wiener and von Wuthenau, two ostracized German-American scholars, fifty years apart, their works unknown to each other, joined forces that day in my mind to establish a base for the hypothesis that Africans were here in the Americas before Columbus."*[289]

As we can see, there were some "Europeans" that even saw the African connection, not just in Africa, but also here in America.  Butler's works demonstrate the back-and-forth movements of Africans to the Americas, as well as how some of whom we had not known before were more connected to Africa than we would have ever thought.  It is from his model that I began to read ancient history in general, while also taking things that I had learned from the various schools of thought that I had adopted over the years, some of which I still utilize, while others I no longer deem useful.

After many years of studying the past, the movements of

---

[289]    (Sertima xv)

people, the artifacts, the monuments, and relics, it all came down to one thing: human behavior, the best indicator of what is going on consciously, and unconsciously, whether past or present. It seemed that at the end of the day, I was studying us. I was studying myself the entire time. While I wore many a label, adopted many an ideology, embraced many a teaching, I took what I had learned that was necessary and left the rest on the plate. I realized that not everything is for everyone and that none of us have all of the answers. While I am indeed still in pursuit of answers, and will be for the rest of my days, I concluded that the past is too important to ignore in my estimation of things. Through studying the past, I have escaped many ills, saved much time and money, and have become a better person overall. The past records have everything concerning the lives of those who lived before us. It is not just about reading history. No. It is about learning what was important to those before us and why they went through all of the trouble to pass it down to us, even to the point of death. If someone was willing to give their life for me to know something, then I think it is more than admirable to see what they had to say. Especially if there is a chance that that person's or persons' blood has travelled over the ages and into my veins.

# 10 CONCLUSION

This has been a many year labor through research, contemplation, experience, and reflection. This began at a time when I could no longer accept the answers, or what appeared to be answers, that were given me by those who loved me, and others who desired to control me. I was at a place where I could move no further. I could move no further because after a pattern of experiences that I did not understand at the time, and I was partly to blame. I did not understand myself nor did I know who I was. Over time, I realized that the more ignorant that I was and remained, the more that I would have a hand in my own demise. I had become a part of something that I did not understand at a time when I was not mature enough to even know what I wanted out of life, where I wanted to go in life, neither could I truly grasp why I thought the way that I did, felt the way that I felt, and did not know my place in this world. M. Scott Peck sums my situation up quite nicely when he says, *"Whenever there is a major deficit in parental love, the child will, in all likelihood, respond to that deficit by assuming itself to be the cause of the deficit, thereby developing an unrealistically negative self-image."* (Peck 60)

Deep rooted and seated emotional issues that stems from ones' childhood that are not dealt with in sufficient time and dealt with effectively, causes that child to develop into an adult that is incomplete emotionally. It will take years for that adult to take an honest look at themselves, realize that they have emotional issues, and then begin to seek proper help. I believe that deep down, we all want a purpose and to understand why we are here. We want our lives to have meaning. I did not have it bad growing up, but ended up in a bad place in my formative adult years. It took quite some time for me to find a reason to live. Some say that knowledge is power. I would say that the right path to gain that knowledge and the right application of such would be the real power. We as people must live out what we know and see it work. That will give us the confidence to move forward, knowing that the knowledge was worth obtaining.

Studying mankind in the manner that I have laid out, caused me to understand people more. I had begun to better understand myself. This is why I left particular viewpoints while perusing these various schools of thought whether they were still within the rubric of Christianity or not. I do not believe that Christianity whether from its inception or its evolution is a negative thing at all. But I did decide to instead of remaining within Christianity, Metaphysics or another ideology that I had come to learn to whatever degree, seeking truth in general was the best roadmap for me. I had learned mankind, as much as they have achieved through knowledge, art, architecture, civilization, etc., is still learning. Still evolving. I see that we do yet not know our end. We strive to live and pass on our genes to ensure that when we die, we do not die. We are seeking, but do not always know what we seek. We gain, we enjoy, but it is never enough. We are satisfied, but then we become bored. We achieve, and then we are yet again, unhappy. We still move forward, though, despite our shortcomings, and deliberate wrongs that we do to one another. We are after all…human.

In the beginning of thinking and writing this book, I was primarily concerned with showing what I had learned over the years. I wanted to demonstrate it in detail hoping that the reader would see the importance of learning, not just for the sake of learning, but for the purpose of growing. However, I was missing the forest for the trees. I was so focused on the tools that I missed what I was building within the process. The tools that I had come across were just tenets within a guiding principle that I had come to understand that worked for me. My guiding principle involves seeking answers that leads to finding truth on terms that I am comfortable with utilizing. Instead of yielding to the methods of others alone, I wanted to learn and become my own person on my own terms through efforts that I had chosen to do so. Where those efforts would lead me, I ultimately had to become comfortable with even if it meant losing family, friends, and acquaintances.

# 10 CONCLUSION

My intention for this particular work is for the reader to see as I now do that regardless of the tool or method used, if the chosen tool(s) and/or method utilized causes one to come to a greater understanding of life and how to live it on their own terms, then that is what one should do. What is life about? I have found that life is about you. I believe that we are learning ourselves. It is why we have the relationships that we have. It is why we have the challenges and even successes that we have. This life is about experiencing it through living from our own perspective while respecting the perspectives of others so that we might live in relative harmony if we are to move forward as a species.

Human cooperation is key if we are to move forward in history. Despite wars, famine, plagues, booms, busts, poverty, wealth, we are still here. Though, in my opinion, we are still unsure of our origins and we are unsure of where we will end up, we are still here. While we are here, I believe that it is important to become the best that we can become and aid one another within the process. This is the message that I came to within all of my studies. It was not about becoming learned so that I could boast to others for the purposes of seeming intelligent. No. It was from a genuine place of finding a deeper meaning to life and to search for a way to get others to find that meaning for themselves.

Whether we agree or not on the chosen tool(s) and/or method, finding a deeper meaning and a way to move forward is key for our species' survival. I want us to survive. I appreciate all that I went through. It took me a long time to realize that it was all necessary. There were times that it hurt so badly that I wanted to die. I wanted to take my life but didn't have the courage to do so, if such a thing is even worthy of being aided by courage.  I wanted to give up on all things and everyone.  I wanted God to wipe my very existence and history away for good.  Something would not allow me to remain within that mindset.  Opportunities came for me to engage with different ways of seeing things.  I took those opportunities.  It was as if I was being guided by something or someone.  I am very glad that I took those opportunities.  I would not be able to share this with you at this time had I not done so.

# ABOUT THE AUTHOR

Benjamin Samuel Brasford lived a relatively normal life, though he went through some major changes and battles in the beginning stages of his adulthood. After having been involved in an arranged marriage for a long time, he finally was able to free himself and begin to live life on his own terms. During the latter five years of his marriage, he began doing research in an effort to learn about and understand life, beginning from where he was mentally at the time, Christianity. The Christian studies led to several others topics to include metaphysics, atheism, sociology, biology, anthropology, archaeology, ancient and modern history, economics, business, and cultural diversity. After the years of time, effort, situations, and application, Benjamin began writing about what he had learned with a desire to assist others in their journey. While "The Work Volume I" was in introduction, the current work was a broad sketch of the culmination of what he had come to know overall. Benjamin will continue learning, exploring and writing in the future on many of these same subject matters, as well as others not expressly stated within the current work. Please feel free to visit the following links, if you desire to follow Benjamin to remain aware of his current and future developments.

Blog: https://www.theworkseries.com/

Twitter: https://twitter.com/BenBrasford

Academic Website: https://independent.academia.edu/BenjaminBrasford

*This page intentionally left blank*

# ENDNOTES

i        Origen. Contra Celsus. Book II. Chapter XXVII. Kirby, Peter. "Historical Jesus Theories." Early Christian Writings. 2019. 10 Jan. 2019 <http://www.earlychristianwritings.com/text/1clement-hoole.html>.

ii        "7. In addition to these things the same man, while recounting the events of that period, records that the Church up to that time had remained a pure and uncorrupted virgin, since, if there were any that attempted to corrupt the sound norm of the preaching of salvation, they lay until then concealed in obscure darkness.

8. But when the sacred college of apostles had suffered death in various forms, and the generation of those that had been deemed worthy to hear the inspired wisdom with their own ears had passed away, then the league of godless error took its rise as a result of the folly of heretical teachers, who, because none of the apostles was still living, attempted henceforth, with a bold face, to proclaim, in opposition to the preaching of the truth, the 'knowledge which is falsely so-called.' (Caesarea, Ecclesiastical History or Church History, Book III, Chapter 32 164)

iii        "From the viewpoint of modernism, all scholarly labors prior to the time of the philosopher Emmanuel Kant (1724-1804) are "pre-critical." Broadly speaking, before Kant content dominated the academic world.  Of method there was no lack, but these methods were not "scientific."  (The German Wissenschaftlich is broader than "scientific" in that it applies not only to "the science", and means "methodologically appropriate and objective").  Critical observation is no modern invention.  The third century Christian theologian Origen, for example, can still impress readers with the acuity of his observations and his openness in the face certain problems and questions.  Method, however, was primarily theological in structure and pastoral in orientation.  The task of theologians was to systematize faith of the church and to exegetes went the responsibility of demonstrating that Scripture presented the same faith.  From the Reformation Era onward the production of complementary but competing systems and expositions had a destabilizing effect upon such "assured results."  The Wars of Religion (1618-1714) capsized these unsteady vessels and left substantial skepticism in their wake. In the nineteenth century critical tools had become, more often than not, handmaids to proclamation of the Christian faith. Postmodernism, which has done to the assuredness of critical method and consensus similar damage to that done by early criticism to the sureties of the faithful, has greatly reduced the distance between "pre-critical" and "critical." Moreover, much contemporary NT study, especially in the United States, has but tenuous links if any to Christian institutions and people." (Pervo, The Date of Acts and Some of its Souces Issues and Methods 2)

iv        The classical understanding of the relationship of orthodoxy and heresy met a devastating challenge in 1934 with the publication of Walter Bauer's Rechtgldubigkeit und Ketzerei im altesten Christentum, possibly the most significant book on early Christianity written in modern times. Bauer argued that the early Christian church in fact did not comprise a single orthodoxy from which emerged a variety of competing heretical minorities. Instead, early Christianity embodied a number of divergent forms, no one of which represented the clear and powerful majority of believers against all others. In some regions, what was later to be termed "heresy" was in fact the original and only form of Christianity. In other regions, views later deemed heretical co-existed with views that would come to be embraced by the church as a whole, with most believers not drawing hard and fast lines of demarcation between the competing views. To this extent, "orthodoxy," in the sense of a unified group advocating an apostolic doctrine accepted by the majority of Christians everywhere, did not exist in the second and third centuries. Nor was "heresy" secondarily derived from an original teaching through an infusion of Jewish ideas or pagan philosophy. Beliefs that were, at later times, embraced as orthodoxy and condemned as heresy were in fact competing interpretations of Christianity, one of which eventually (but not initially) acquired domination because of singular historical and social forces. Only when one social group had exerted itself sufficiently over the rest of Christendom did a "majority" opinion emerge; only then did the "right belief" represent the view of the Christian church at large. (Ehrman, The Challenge: Walter Bauer 7)

v        "… -they who wish may learn from the very words and acts of the apostles, and may contemplate the fact that this God is one, above whom is no other."

"… If, then, any one shall, from the Acts of the Apostles, carefully scrutinize the time concerning which it is written that he went up to Jerusalem on account of the forementioned question, he will find those years mentioned by Paul coinciding with it. Thus the statement of Paul harmonizes with, and is, as it were, identical with, the testimony of Luke regarding the apostles." (Kirby)

vi      For a more detailed explanation and visual of the many scholars who have broached the topic of dating the book of Acts, see "Dating Acts – Between the Evangelists and the Apologists" by Richard I. Pervo Appendix II Scholarly Estimates of the Date of Acts, page 359

Broach - Raise (a difficult subject) for discussion. (Press, broach, v.1)

vii     Galatians 2:11-21

viii    Daniel 12:2

ix      Daniel 12:4-13; Revelation 22:8-10

x       Acts 23:8

xi      Antiquities of the Jews, Book 18, Chapter 1, Sections 2 and 3 by Flavius Josephus

xii     Ibid. v

xiii    Maimonides – Laws Pertaining to the Messiah Chapter 11 Halacha 1 (Judaism)

xiv     Jewish Wars or Wars of the Jews, Book 2, Chapter 13, Section 5 and Book 5, Chapter 6, Sections 2 and 3.

xv      Pliny the Elder, Latin in full Gaius Plinius Secundus, (born AD 23, Novum Comum, Transpadane Gaul [now in Italy]—died Aug. 24, 79, Stabiae, near Mt. Vesuvius), Roman savant and author of the celebrated Natural History, an encyclopaedic work of uneven accuracy that was an authority on scientific matters up to the Middle Ages. (Stannard)

xvi     The archaeological case for connecting the scrolls with the community at Qumran was originally made by Roland de Vaux, the initial excavator of Khirbet Qumran. His conclusions have since been accepted by most researchers. De Vaux upheld the linkage by observing that the pottery in the caves can be dated to the same period as the abandoned site (I CE), and, moreover, that inscriptions on ostraca (potsherds) found at Qumran match the style of writing found in the scrolls.

The link between the scrolls and the Essenes has been ascertained through a comparison of the sectarian writings with descriptions of the Essenes found in the first-century writings of Philo, Josephus and Pliny the Elder. Although discrepancies exist between the accounts, the similarities are striking and have convinced most researchers that the Dead Sea sect and the Essenes are one and the same. (Binder)

xvii    Jewish Wars or Wars of the Jews, Book 2, Chapter 8, Section 14.

xviii   Ibid., xxii, Section 10.

xix     Ibid., xxii, entirety of Section 11.

xx      Ibid., xxii, Section 12 and See also Antiquities, Book 15, Chapter 10, Sections 4 and 5.

xxi     Antiquities, Book 13, Chapter 5, Section 9.

xxii    Antiquities, Book 15, Chapter 10, Section 4.

xxiii   Herodotus The Histories, Book II, Chapter 51. (Herodotus, Herodotus With An English Translation 339)

xxiv    Herodotus The Histories, Book II, Chapters 50 to 52. (Herodotus, Herodotus With An English Translation 337-341)

xxv     " I however speak only from hearsay ; what then I have heard I have no scruple in telling. And perhaps it is most becoming for one who is about to travel there, to enquire and speculate about the journey thither, what kind we think it is. What else can one do in the interval before sunset?"

" Why then, Socrates, do they say that it is not allowable to kill one's-self ? for I, as you asked just now, have heard both Philolaus, when he lived with us, and sevei'al others say that it was not right to do this ; but I never heard any thing clear upon the subject from any one." (Plato, Phaedo or The Immortality of the Soul 59)

xxvi    THE GREAT LEAP-FRAUD  Social Economics of Religious Terrorism

Religion is a difficult topic in social economics. Most authors avoid it altogether and by doing so probably miss the most important building blocks of economic and cultural life. If they do touch on it, they seem to rely on glorifying their own faith rather than asking the hard questions, or they follow the comfort of the conformists. Indeed, religion seems to be instinctively ingrained in humans, possibly as a means to bettering the chances for survival of any given group. Because religion is instinctual, it can easily be abused for power, and people can easily be misled.

The Great Leap-Fraud is but one piece in a puzzle of how economic growth and prosperity of nations work. It is an attempt to unlock a strategy to get the poorest nations of the world unto a path of positive societal evolution. The Great Leap-Fraud zeroes in on the Judaic religions and connects its doctrines to success and failure of economies through the eye of history. It shows how the religious messages have changed over time and how they influenced economic behavior and a propensity toward terrorism.

Religious ignorance is as dangerous for societal stability as religious extremism. In The Great Leap-Fraud, author A. J. Deus shows that only through the cowardly behavior of a majority that is uneducated in religious questions can sectarian extremism and terrorism take shape and overtake societies.

Based on a reassessment of primary documents from the beginning of Judaism through to the Reformation, The Great Leap-Fraud evaluates the Judaic scriptures of the Jews, the Christians, and the Muslims for their potential to stir hatred, violence, and terrorism. It searches for messages in the scriptures that may alter the economic behavior of societies.

While providing an overview of three major religions—Judaism, Christianity, and Islam—The Great Leap-Fraud uncovers a series of frauds and premeditated deployment of "prophets⊠? with the goal to establish or redeem the Jewish state of Israel. It also uncovers how the vested interest of Christian historians has pushed the rise of Christianity unto Roman Emperors. Deus shows that the way humans think and act are strongly influenced through a culture driven by the norms of religious organizations, both past and present. (A. J. Deus, The Great

Leap-Fraud Social Economics of Religious Terrorism)

xxvii    Josephus, Against Apion I, Section 8.

xxviii   II Kings 18-19

xxix     (1) From the Oriental Institute Prism of Sennacherib, which contains—as does the so-called Taylor Prism (cf. Rawlinson, Vol. 1, Pls. 37-42)—the final edition of the Annals of Sennacherib. Publication: D. D. Luckenbill, The Annals of Sennacherib ( O I P , 11, Chicago, 1924). Translation: ibid., and Luckenbill, AR, 11, §§233 ff. (Pritchard)

xxx      Justin Martyr, Apology, Chapter 21.

xxxi     Justin Martyr, Dialogue with Trypho, Chapter LXIX.

xxxii    Philo Judaeus or Philo of Alexandria, Allegorical Interpretation of Genesis Book III, Line 175. (Philo, Allegorical Interpretation, III (Legum Allegoriae, III) 70)

xxxiii   Philo Judaeus, On the Contemplative Life.

xxxiv    Josephus, Antiquities, Book 18, Chapter 3, Section 3.

xxxv     Against Heresies, Book 3, Chapter 11, Section 8. (Alexander Roberts)

xxxvi    Ibid., liii, Book 1, Chapter 27, Section 2.

xxxvii   Tertullian, The Five Books Against Marcion, Book V, Chapter 1.

xxxviii  St. Irenaeus, Against Heresies, Book I, Chapter 27.

xxxix    St. Ignatius, Letter to the Trallians, Chapter IX.-Reference to the History of Christ.

xl       St. Irenaeus, Against Heresies, Book I, Chapter 26.

xli      Galatians 1:16 KJV

xlii     II Corinthians 11:5 KJV

xliii    Josephus, Antiquities, Book 13, Chapter 1, Section 1.

xliv     Ibid., lxii, Antiquities, Book 13, Chapter 5, Section 8.

xlv      Ibid., lxiii, Josephus, Antiquities, Book 13, Chapter 5, Section 9.

xlvi     Josephus, The Life, Section 2.

xlvii    Josephus, Antiquities, Book 2, Chapter 8, Section 13.

xlviii   Philo, On The Contemplative Life or Suppliants. C. D. Yonge's Translation.

xlix     Eusebius, Church History or Ecclesiastical History, Book 2, Chapter 17. Philo's Account of the Ascetics of Egypt. (Eusebius)

l        Ibid., lxviii

li       Philo, Every Good Man Is Free, Section 12, Lines 82 & 83. (Philo, Every Good Man Is Free Section 12). Josephus, Antiquities, Book 2, Chapter 8, Section 6.

lii      [14] But Peter, standing up with the eleven, lifted up his voice, and said unto them, Ye men of Judaea, and all ye that dwell at Jerusalem, be this known unto you, and hearken to my words:

[15] For these are not drunken, as ye suppose, seeing it is but the third hour of the day.

[16] But this is that which was spoken by the prophet Joel;

Acts 2:14-16 KJV

liii     "Dr. Brown sees a coherent philosophy in all of the approaches: Human beings are the equivalent of gods, able to tap into the deepest powers in the universe. We can shape reality with our thoughts. Rational judgment of almost any kind is a bad thing." (Shea) Used with permission of The Chronicle of Higher Education Copyright© 2018. All rights reserved.

"Until recently the accepted 'science' about our emotional process has been based on a blank-slate equalist approach to emotion." "… In light of new technology and new research in a variety of interrelated disciplines we know this is old presumption is patently untrue." "… The rational process deals with the nuts and bolts of what we can understand of our reality. From there it can modify the other processes (instinctual and emotional) or it can serve to interpret stimuli on its own." 'Emphasis mine' (Tomassi, Demystifying intersexual dynamics : Instinct, Emotion and Reason)

liv      "Despite its influence, the New Age doesn't attract many researchers. "Most people I know who are thinking of studying the New Age decide not to," says Robert Wuthnow, a professor of sociology at Princeton University who writes frequently about religion. "It really isn't a coherent movement-even the term doesn't adequately describe it." (Shea) Used with permission of The Chronicle of Higher Education

lv      "Most academics despise the New Age. They find the loose conglomeration of spiritual views that goes by the name to be self-indulgent, anti-rational, and terribly middlebrow." (Shea) Used with permission of The Chronicle of Higher Education Copyright© 2018. All rights reserved.

lvi      For an explanation of the Instinctual, Emotional, and Rational Cognitive Processes, see the Behavioral Psychology Series on the Mental Processes by Rollo Tomassi at the Rational Male Blog.  (Tomassi, Instinct, Emotion and Reason)

lvii      "French historians traditionally place the Enlightenment between 1715 (the year that Louis XIV died) and 1789 (the beginning of the French Revolution). Some recent historians begin the period in the 1620s, with the start of the scientific revolution. Les philosophes (French for "the philosophers") of the period widely circulated their ideas through meetings at scientific academies, Masonic lodges, literary salons, coffee houses and in printed books and pamphlets. The ideas of the Enlightenment undermined the authority of the monarchy and the Church and paved the way for the political revolutions of the 18th and 19th centuries. A variety of 19th-century movements, including liberalism and neo-classicism, trace their intellectual heritage to the Enlightenment.[7]" (Wikipedia, Age of Enligtenment) (Cited by Wikipedia from "Movements, Currents, Trends: Aspects of European Thought in the Nineteenth and Twentieth Centuries" by Eugen Weber)

lviii      "His method of interpreting hieroglyphs was fundamentally different from that of Champollion. Seyffarth held that the hieroglyphs designated the consonant elements of a syllable ; e g., klil (sacrifice), might be designated by a basket (kalil), the image of an owl (mulak) could be read as melek (king), whereas Champollion taught that the hieroglyphs were symbols standing for definite letters of the alphabet. A few years after his tour, Seyffarth was made professor extraordinarius of archaeology (at Leipzig), and held this position from 1830 to 1854. He did not succeed, however, in gaining academic followers of distinction, for Lepsius, Brugsch, Miiller of Gottingen, Ebers, and others followed the system of Champollion. Uhlemann and Wuttke were the most noted of his own adherents. After 1840 he began to experience great difficulty in finding avenues for publication. Academic advancement also seemed to be cut off."

"… Vast as was the erudition of Seyffarth, these extreme chronological speculations and assertions, coupled with the abstruse and involved character of his presentation, as well as his uncompromising hostility to Champollion's system, tended to isolate him more and more from kindred scholars." (BRITANNICA)
lix     "However, one article that is agreed upon almost universally is that identity and personality are never static and are mailable and changeable due to influencing variables and conditions." (Tomassi, Unplugging: Dispelling the Magic 85)

# WORKS CITED

_Star_ The Star of Jews, who is the Antichrist? n.d. Website. 14 June 2018. <https://truelightoflife.com/star.php>.

Alexander Roberts, James Donaldson, and A. Cleveland Coxe, eds. Ante-Nicene Fathers. Trans. Alexander Roberts and William Rambaut. Vol. 1. Buffalo: Christian Literature Publishing Co., 1885. Book. 20 July 2018. <http://www.newadvent.org/fathers/0103311.htm>.

Amanat, Abbas. Imagining the End: Visions of Apocalypse from the Ancient Middle East to Modern America. London: I.B. Tauris. 2001. 165. Book

Anthony Grafton and Joanna Weinberg. "Rabbi Isaac Casaubon : A Hellenist Meets the Jews." Anthony Grafton, Joanna Weinberg. "I have always loved the Holy Tongue" : Isaac Casaubon, the Jews, and a Forgotten Chapter in Renaissance Scholarship. Cambridge, London: The Belknap Press of Harvard University Press, 2011. 1-59. Book.

Aquilecchia, Giovanni. "Giordano Bruno." 4 February 2018. Encyclopædia Britannica. Encyclopedia entry. 1 June 2018. <https://www.britannica.com/biography/Giordano-Bruno>.

Armstrong, A. Hilary. "Plotinus." 14 June 2017. Encyclopædia Britannica. Encyclopædia Britannica, inc. Encyclopedia Entry. 13 October 2018.

BBC News. "Egypt Copts killed in Christmas church attack." 10 January 2010. BBC News. Website. 17 March 2018. <https://www.bbc.com/news/world-middle-east-42511813>.

Bible Study Tools. 15.1.5. Representative of Seven Stages of Church History. n.d. Website. 13 November 2017. <https://www.biblestudytools.com/commentaries/revelation/related-topics/representative-of-seven-stages-of-church-history.html>.

Bieler, Ludwig G.J. "Saint Ignatius of Antioch." 20 July 1998. Encyclopædia Britannica. Encyclopedia entry. 14 June 2018. <https://www.britannica.com/biography/Saint-Ignatius-of-Antioch>.

Binder, Donald D. Qumran Overview. n.d. Website. 20 June 2018. <http://www.pohick.org/sts/qumran.html>.
Birks, Dr. Kelly Nelson. About Dr. Kelly Nelson Birks. 2008. 14 June 2018. <http://www.drkellynelsonbirks.com/about.php>.

Blue Letter Bible. Four Views of the Millenium - Study Resources. n.d. Website. 20 November 2017. <https://www.blueletterbible.org/faq/mill.cfm>.

Brasford, Benjamin Samuel. "Benjamin Brasford." March 2018. Academia.edu. Journal. 14 June 2018. <https://www.academia.edu/38307202/An_Internal_Examination_of_the_Multiple_Author_theory_in_the_book_of_Isaiah>.

Brasford, Benjamin Samuel. "Clouds, Rain, Acid, Pain." Brasford, Benjamin. The Life of Benjamin Samuel Brasford. Columbia: Intelligent Publishing, 2018. 18-24. Book.

Breasted, James Henry. "Chapter II The Food-producers and the Neolithic Age : The Quarter of the Globe Where Civilization." Breasted, James Henry. The Conquest of Civilization. New York and London: Harper & Brothers Publishers, 1926. 24-46. Book.

—. "The Philosophy of a Memphite Priest. With a Reproduction of the Memphite Slab." The Open Court: Vol. 1903 : Iss. 8 , Article 2. (1903): 458-479. Journal Article.

The British Museum. Sir Ernest A T Wallis Budge (Biographical details). n.d. Website. 18 June 2018. <http://www.britishmuseum.org/research/search_the_collection_database/term_details.aspx?bioId=93650>.

 Brown, Judith Anne. JOHN MARCO ALLEGRO SCROLLS SCHOLAR AND FREETHINKER A brief biography. 2005. Website. 16 June

2018. <http://www.johnallegro.org/>.

Brunner, Peter F. Dorman and Hellmut. "Hieroglyphic writing." 17 October 2017. Encyclopædia Britannica. Encyclopedia entry. 31 May 2018. <https://www.britannica.com/topic/hieroglyphic-writing>.

Budge, Sir Ernest Alfred Thompson Wallis. "Chapter V The Labours of J. F. Champollion." Budge, Sir Ernest Alfred Thompson Wallis. The decrees of Memphis and Canopus in Three Volumes - The Rosetta Stone Volume I. New York: Oxford University Press, 1904. 115-134. Book.

Burkett, Delbert. An Introduction to the New Testament and the Origins of Christianity. Cambridge: Cambridge University Press, 2002. Book.

Butler, Horace. When Rocks Cry Out (English Edition) 2nd Edition. n.d. Website. 18 March 2018. <https://www.amazon.com/When-Rocks-Cry-Out-English/dp/0615292658>.

Chadwick, Henry. "Origen." 17 June 2017. Encyclopædia Britannica. Website. 24 March 2018. <https://www.britannica.com/biography/Origen>.

—. "Origen." 14 June 2017. Encyclopaedia Britannica. Website. 14 November 2017. <https://www.britannica.com/biography/Origen>.

Chicago Statement on Biblical Inerrancy. "Chicago Statement on Biblical Inerrancy." Journal of the Evangelical Theological Society, vol. 21 no. 4 (December 1978), 289-96. (1978): 289-296. Journal.

Chilton, David. The Days of Vengeance: An Exposition of the Book of Revelation. Ft. Worth: Dominion Press, 1987, 1990. Book.

Collins, John J. "Part One General Topics: Current Issues in the Study of Daniel." Flint, John J. Collins and Peter. The Book of Daniel Composition and Reception. Leiden: Koninklijke Brill, 2001. 1-15. Book.

Copenhagen University of Applied Sciences. Copenhagen University of Applied Sciences. n.d. Website. 29 October 2018. <https://ucc.dk/sites/default/files/cohe_table_04.pdf>.

Copenhaver, Brian P. "Introduction." Copenhaver, Brian P. Hermetica : The Greek Corpus Hermeticum and the Latin Aslepius in a New English Translation, with Notes and Introduction. Cambridge: Cambridge University Press, 1992. xiii-lxi. Book.

Coty, Charles. About Us. n.d. Website. 14 June 2018. <http://www.charlescoty.com/AboutUs.html>.

Creaven, Sean. "1: Bhaskar's 'spiritual turn': logical and conceptual problems." Creaven, Sean. Against the Spiritual Turn: Marxism, Realism, and Critical Theory. 1st. Abingdon, New York: Routledge, 2010. 13-79. Book.

—. "Preface." Creaven, Sean. Against the Spiritual Turn: Marxism , realism and critical theory. Abingdon, New York: Routledge, 2010. viii-ix. Book.

Darwin, Charles. "Chapter VII. The Races of Man." Charles Darwin, M.A., F.R.S., &c. The Descent of Man and Selection in Relation to Sex in Two Volumes-Volume I. London: John Murray, Albermarle Street, 1871. 214-250. Book.

Davies, Philip R. "Dead Sea Scrolls." 26 December 2017. Encyclopædia Britannica. Website. 5 March 2018. <https://www.britannica.com/topic/Dead-Sea-Scrolls>.

Dennis, Todd. Sam Frost: Free Ebook: Why I Left Full Preterism (2017). n.d. 14 June 2018. <https://www.preteristarchive.com/frost-free-ebook-why-i-left-full-preterism/>.

Desmond, Adrian J. "Charles Darwin." 6 September 2018. Encyclopædia Britannica. Encyclopædia Britannica, inc. Encyclopedia

Entry. 14 October 2018. <https://www.britannica.com/biography/Charles-Darwin>.

Deus, A. J. "A Clan of Infiltrators." Deus, A. J. The Great Leap-Fraud Social Economics of Religious Terrorism Volume I Judaism and Christianity. Bloomington: iUniverse, 2011. 101-113. Book.

—. "Leap of Faith : A Cultural Heritage." Deus, A. J. The Great Leap-Fraud Social Economics of Religious Terrorism Volume I Judaism and Christianity. Bloomington: iUniverse, 2011. 9-21. Book.

—. "Leap of Faith : David Kills Goliath." Deus, A. J. The Great Leap-Fraud Social Economics of Religious Terrorism Volume I Judaism and Christianity. Bloomington: iUniverse, 2011. 74-82. Book.

—. "The Great Fraud : The Library of Alexandria." Deus, A. J. The Great Leap-Fraud Social Economics of Religious Terrorism Volume I Judaism and Christianity. Bloomington: iUniverse, 2011. 133-135. Book.

—. The Great Leap-Fraud Social Economics of Religious Terrorism. n.d. Website. 20 June 2018. <http://www.ajdeus.org/articles/130>.

—. "THE POORHOUSE : Keys to Eternal Life." Deus, A. J. The Great Leap-Fraud Social Economics of Religious Terrorism Volume I Judaism and Christianity. Bloomington: iUniverse, Inc., 2011. 247-255. Book.

—. "THE POORHOUSE : Light in a Coma." Deus, A. J. The Great Leap-Fraud Social Economics of Religious Terrorism Volume I Judaism and Christianity. Bloomington: iUniverse, Inc., 2011. 260-269. Book.

—. "THE POORHOUSE : Serving God or Serving Wife and Children." Deus, A. J. The Great Leap-Fraud Social Economics of Religious Terrorism Volume I Judaism and Christianity. Bloomington: iUniverse, Inc., 2011. 269-281. Book.

—. "THE REBELLIOUS JEWS : The Cradle of Christitianity." Deus, A. J. The Great Leap-Fraud Social Economics of Religious Terrorism Volume I Judaism and Christianity. Bloomington: iUniverse, Inc., 2011. 218-229. Book.

—. The Author. n.d. Website. 18 June 2018. <http://www.ajdeus.org/The_Author/4>.

Doherty, Earl. "Part Three: The Gospel of the Son : Chapter Eight: The Word of God in the Holy Book." Doherty, Earl. Jesus Neither God Nor Man: The Case for a Mythical Jesus. Ottawa: Age of Reason Publications, 2009. 83-90. Book.

—. "Part Two: a Life in Eclipse : Chapter Six: From Bethlehem to Jerusalem." Doherty, Earl. Jesus Neither God Nor Man : The Case for a Mythical Jesus. Ottawa: Age of Reason Publications, 2009. 57-70. Book.

—. "Preface." Doherty, Earl. Jesus Neither God Nor Man - The Case for a Mythical Jesus. Ottawa: Age of Reason Publications, 2009. vii-ix. Book.

Dupont-Sommer, A. "The Manual of Discipline And The Community Of The Covenant." Dupont-Sommer, A. The Jewish Sect of Qumran and the Essenes. New York: The Macmillan Company, 1955. 58-76. Book.

Early, Gerald. "Afrocentrism." 9 January 2015. Encyclopædia Britannica. Encyclopedia entry. 9 June 2018. <https://www.britannica.com/topic/Afrocentrism>.

Easton, Burton Scott. "Apostolic Age." Orr, James, M.A., D.D. International Standard Bible Encyclopedia. Ed. James, M.A., D.D. Orr. 1915. Entry for Apostolic Age. Website. 28 February 2018. <https://www.biblestudytools.com/dictionary/apostolic-age/>.

The Editors of Encyclopaedia Britannica. "Balfour Declaration." 27 September 2018. Encyclopædia Britannica. Encyclopedia Entry. 25 October 2018. <https://www.britannica.com/event/Balfour-Declaration >.

—. "Bar Kokhba." 27 August 2013. Encyclopædia Britannica. Website. 13 April 2018. <https://www.britannica.com/biography/Bar-Kokhba-Jewish-leader>.

—. "Biblical criticism." 10 May 2013. Encyclopædia Britannica. Encyclopedia entry. 14 June 2018. <https://www.britannica.com/topic/biblical-criticism>.

—. "Cerinthus." 20 July 1998. Encyclopædia Britannica. Website. 16 April 2018. <https://www.britannica.com/biography/Cerinthus>.

—. "Church Father." 26 December 2017. Encyclopædia Britannica. Encyclopedia entry. 14 June 2018. <https://www.britannica.com/topic/Church-Father>.

—. "Council of Nicaea." 8 February 2018. Encyclopædia Britannica. Website. 24 March 2018. <https://www.britannica.com/event/Council-of-Nicaea-Christianity-325>.

—. "Diogenes Laërtius." 16 June 2017. Encyclopædia Britannica. Website. 24 March 2018. <https://www.britannica.com/biography/Diogenes-Laertius>.

—. "Docetism." 11 April 2014. Encyclopædia Britannica. Website. 16 April 2018. <https://www.britannica.com/topic/Docetism>.

—. "Euhemerus." 21 December 2011. Encyclopædia Britannica. Website. 13 April 2018. <https://www.britannica.com/biography/Euhemerus-Greek-mythographer>.

—. "Eusebius of Caesarea." 26 October 2017. Encyclopædia Britannica. Website. 24 March 2018. <https://www.britannica.com/biography/

Eusebius-of-Caesarea>.

—. "Hasmonean Dynasty." 20 January 1998. Encyclopædia Britannica. Website. 24 March 2018. <https://www.britannica.com/topic/Hasmonean-dynasty>.

—. "Heresy." 13 April 2017. Encyclopædia Britannica. Encyclopedia Entry. 25 October 2018. <https://www.britannica.com/topic/heresy>.
—. "Hermetic writings." 3 September 2013. Encyclopædia Britannica. Article. 30 May 2018.

—. "James Henry Breasted." 16 February 2017. Encyclopædia Britannica. Encyclopedia entry. 18 June 2018. <https://www.britannica.com/biography/James-Henry-Breasted>.

—. "Marcion of Pontus." 15 November 2016. Encyclopædia Britannica. Encyclopedia entry. 17 June 2018. <https://www.britannica.com/biography/Marcion-of-Pontus>.

—. "Masoretic Text." 20 September 2013. Encyclopædia Britannica. Website article. 1 December 2017. <https://www.britannica.com/topic/Masoretic-text>.

—. "Messiah." 29 September 2008. Encyclopædia Britannica. Website. 24 March 2018. <https://www.britannica.com/topic/messiah-religion>.

—. "Neoplatonism." 15 June 2017. Encyclopædia Britannica. Encyclopedia entry. 31 May 2018. <https://www.britannica.com/topic/Neoplatonism>.

—. "Orthodox." 7 December 2017. Encyclopædia Britannica. Encyclopedia Entry. 25 October 2018. <https://www.britannica.com/topic/orthodox>.

—. "Philo Judaeus." 14 June 2017. Encyclopædia Britannica. Website. 24 March 2018. <https://www.britannica.com/biography/Philo-Ju-

daeus>.

—. "Philolaus." 27 June 2006. Encyclopædia Britannica. Website. 24 March 2018. <https://www.britannica.com/biography/Philolaus>.

—. "The Rapture." 26 October 2018. Encyclopædia Britannica. Website. 20 March 2019. <https://www.britannica.com/topic/Rapture-the>

—. "Reformation." 17 August 2018. Encyclopædia Britannica. Website. 29 August 2017. <https://www.britannica.com/event/Reformation>.

—. "Sadducee." 6 February 2014. Encyclopædia Britannica. Website. 4 May 2018. <https://www.britannica.com/topic/Sadducee>.

—. "Saint Clement I." 20 May 2013. Encyclopædia Britannica. Website. 16 April 2018. <https://www.britannica.com/biography/Saint-Clement-I>.

—. "Saint Epiphanius of Constantia." 1 December 2008. Encyclopædia Britannica. Website. 24 March 2018. <https://www.britannica.com/biography/Saint-Epiphanius-of-Constantia>.

—. "Saint Hegesippus." 23 April 2013. Encyclopædia Britannica. Website. 24 March 2018. <https://www.britannica.com/biography/Saint-Hegesippus>.

—. "Saint Justin Martyr." 1 October 2014. Encyclopædia Britannica. Website. 24 March 2018. <https://www.britannica.com/biography/Saint-Justin-Martyr>.

—. "Saint Polycarp." 20 January 2018. Encyclopædia Britannica. Encyclopeida entry. 14 June 2018. <https://www.britannica.com/biography/Saint-Polycarp>.

—. "Seleucid kingdom." 18 December 2008. Encyclopædia Britannica. Website. 24 March 2018. <https://www.britannica.com/place/Seleu-

cid-kingdom>.

—. "Septuagint." 15 June 2017. Encyclopædia Britannica. Website. 1 December 2017. <https://www.britannica.com/topic/Septuagint>.

—. "Sir Wallis Budge." 19 November 2018. inc. Encyclopædia Britannica. Encyclopedia Entry. 2 June 2019. <https://www.britannica.com/biography/Wallis-Budge>.

—. "Suetonius." 8 January 2018. Encyclopædia Britannica. Website. 24 March 2018. <https://www.britannica.com/biography/Suetonius>.

—. "Tanakh." 23 September 2013. Encyclopædia Britannica. Website. 24 March 2018. <https://www.britannica.com/topic/Tanakh>.

—. "Theophilus Of Antioch." 1 October 2013. Encyclopædia Britannica. Website. 24 March 2018. <https://www.britannica.com/biography/Theophilus-of-Antioch>.

—. "Theophrastus." 8 February 2018. Encyclopædia Britannica. Website. 24 March 2018. <https://www.britannica.com/biography/Theophrastus>.

—. "W.F. Albright." 15 September 2018. Encyclopædia Britannica. Encyclopedia Entry. 21 January 2018. <https://www.britannica.com/biography/W-F-Albright>.

Ehrman, Bart D. " The Challenge: Walter Bauer." Ehrman, Bart D. The Orthodox Corruption of Scripture: The Effect of Early Christological Controversies on the Text of the New Testament. New York: Oxford University Press, 1993. 7-9. Book.

—. "Chapter 1 The Text of Scripture in an Age of Dissent: Early Christian Struggles for Orthodoxy." Ehrman, Bart D. The Orthodox Corruption of Scripture. New York: Oxford University Press, 1993. 3-46. Book.

—. "Chapter 2 Forgeries in the Name of Peter." Ehrman, Bart D.

Forged Writing in the Name of God Why the Bible's Authors Are Not Who We Think They Are. New York: HarperCollins Publishers, 2011. 43-77. Book.

—. "Chapter 2: The Copyists of the Early Christian Writings." Ehrman, Bart D. Misquoting Jesus : The Story Behind Who Changed the Bible and Why. New York: HarperCollins Publishers, 2005. 45-69. Book.

—. "Chapter 3. Forgeries in the Name of Paul." Ehrman, Bart D. Forged Writing in the Name of God Why the Bible's Authors Are Not Who We Think They Are. New York: HarperCollins Publishers, 2011. 79-114. Book.

—. "Chapter 4: The Quest for Origins." Ehrman, Bart D. Misquoting Jesus The Story Behind Who Changed the Bible and Why. New York: HarperCollins Publishers, 2005. 101-126. Book.

—. "Chapter 6 Forgeries in Conflicts with False Teachers." Ehrman, Bart D. Forged Writing in the Name of God Why the Bible's Authors Are Not Who We Think They Are. New York: HarperCollins Publishers, 2011. 179-218. Book.

—. "Notes: Chapter 2: Note 9." Ehrman, Bart D. Misquoting Jesus: The Story Behind Who Changed the Bible and Why. First. New York: HarperSanFrancisco, 2005. 219-227. Book.

Elliott, Rich. Old Testament Textual Criticism. 1 January 1997. Website. 2 December 2017. <http://www.skypoint.com/members/ waltzmn/OTCrit.html>.

Emilie T. Sander, J. Coert Rylaarsdam and Others (See All Contributors). "Biblical literature." 2 October 2018. Encyclopædia Britannica. Encyclopedia Entry. 9 November 2018.

Encyclopedia Britannica. "Gustav Seyffarth." BRITANNICA, EN-CYCLOPEDIA. Supplement to Encyclopaedia Britannica (Ninth

Edition) A Dictionary of Arts, Sciences, and General Literature. New York, Philadelphia, London: Hubbard Brothers, 1889. 480-481. Encyclopedia entry.

The Encyclopædia Britannica Company. "Hermes." Company, The Encyclopædia Britannica. The The Encyclopædia Britannica : A Dictionary of Arts, Sciences, Literature and General Information Eleventh Edition. New York: The Encyclopædia Britannica Company, 1910. 369-370. Book.

—. "Hermes Trismegistus." Company, The Encyclopædia Britannica. The Encyclopædia Britannica : A Dictionary of Arts, Sciences, Literature and General Information Eleventh Edition. New York: The Encyclopædia Britannica Company, 1911. 370-371. Encyclopædia. EnglishGrammar.org. Kinds of co-ordinating conjunctions. n.d. Website. 29 October 2018. <https://www.englishgrammar.org/kinds-coordinating-conjunctions/>.

Epiphanius of Salamis. "30. Against Ebionites.1 Number ten, but thirty of the series." Williams, Frank. The Panarion of Epiphanius of Salamis Book I (Sects 1-46). Leiden Boston: Brill, 2009. 131-165. Book.

—. "Anacephalaeosis : Against Marcionites." Williams, Frank. The Panarion of Epiphanius of Salamis A Treatise Against Eighty Sects in Three Books Book I (Sects 1-46). Leiden Boston: Brill Academic Publishers, 2009. 294-364. Book.

Eusebius. Nicene and Post-Nicene Fathers, Second Series. Ed. Philip Schaff and Henry Wace. Trans. Arthur Cushman McGiffert. Vol. 1. Buffalo: Christian Literature Publishing Co., 1890. Book. 20 June 2018. <http://www.newadvent.org/fathers/250102.htm>.

Eusebius of Caesarea. "Ecclesiastical History or Church History, Book III, Chapter 32." Wallace, Philip Schaff and Henry. Nicene and Post-Nicene Fathers Volume I. Peabody: Hendrickson Publishers Marketing, LLC, 1890. 73-403. Book.

Finkelstein, Israel. "Digging for the Truth: Archaeology and the Bible." Schmidt, Brian B. The Quest for the Historical Israel Debating Archaeology and the History of Early Israel. Leiden, Boston: Brill, 2007. 12-14. Book.

—. "Digging For The Truth: Archaeology And The Bible." Israel Finkelstein, Amahai Mazar. The Quest for the Historical Israel Debating Archaeology and the History of Early Israel. Ed. Brian B. Schmidt. Leiden, Boston: Brill, 2007. 9-20. Book.

—. "Digging for the Truth: Archaeology and the Bible : The Rise and Fall of the Conservative Camp." Schmidt, Brian B. The Quest for the Historical Israel Debating Archaeology and the HIstory of Early Israel. Atlanta: the Society for Biblical Literature, 2007. 10-12. Book.

—. "Digging for the Truth: Archaeology and the Bible : The View from the Center." Schmidt, Brian B. The Quest for the Historical Israel Debating Archaeology and the History of Early Israel. Leiden, Boston: Brill, 2007. 14-20. Book.

—. Israel Finkelstein. n.d. Website. 5 April 2018. <https://israelfinkelstein.wordpress.com/>.

Foliard, Daniel. "Part I. From Sebastopol to Suez (1854– 1869) : 2. Labeling the East · 52." Foliard, Daniel. Dislocating the Orient : British Maps and the Making of the Middle east, 1854– 1921. Chicago: The University of Chicago Press, 2017. 52-66. Book.

Frederick Copleston, S.J. "XLIV. Jewish-Hellenic Philosophy." Frederick Copleston, S.J. A History of Philosophy Volume I Greece and Rome. New York: Doubleday, 1962. 457-462. Book.

Friedman, Richard Elliot. "Introduction Who Wrote the Bible?" Friedman, Richard Elliot. Who Wrote the Bible? New York: Summit Books, 1987. 15-32. Book.

—. "Chapter 4 The World That Produced the Bible : 722-587 B.C."

Friedman, Richard Elliott. Who Wrote the Bible? New York: Harper-Collins Publishers, 1987. 89-100. Book.

Ginzberg, Louis. "ANTIOCHUS IV., EPIPHANES." n.d. The unedited full-text of the 1906 Jewish Encyclopedia. Website. 24 March 2018. <http://jewishencyclopedia.com/articles/1589-antiochus-iv-epiphanes>.

The Gnostic Society Library. Marcion: To the Galatians. n.d. Website. 20 June 2018. <http://gnosis.org/library/marcion/Galatian.htm>. Good Birth Ministries. Introducing Dr. Gentry. n.d. 14 June 2018. <http://www.goodbirthministries.com/IntroducingDrGentry.php>.

Graber, Amanda. Paul's Contribution to Christian Theology. 29 September 2017. Website. 23 February 2018. <https://classroom.synonym.com/pauls-contribution-to-christian-theology-12084826.html>.

Green, David. 101 Preterist Time-Indicators. 2002. Website. 13 November 2017. <https://www.preteristarchive.com/Hyper/2002_green_time-indicators.html>.

Gregg, Steve. "Introduction to the Book of Revelation." Gregg, Steve. Revelation Four Views. New York: Thomas Nelson, Inc., 2013. 19-76. Book.

—. "Introduction to the Book of Revelation - The Idealist Approach." Gregg, Steve. Revelation Four Views. New York: Thomas Nelson, Inc., 1997, 2013. 68 to 72. Book.

—. "Revelation Four Views." Gregg, Steve. Revelation Four Views. New York: Thomas Nelson, Inc., 2013. 62. Book.

—. "The Futurist Approach: Everything after Chapter 3 Awaits Fulfillment in the Future." Gregg, Steve. Revelation Four Views. New York: Thomas Nelson, Inc., 2013. 19-76. Book.

—. "The Millennium Chapter 20." Gregg, Steve. Revelation Four Views. New York: Thomas Nelson, Inc., 2013. 515 - 519. Book.

Hanegraaff, Wouter J. "Chapter Fifteen. The Mirror of Secular Thought : 4. The Psychologization of Esotericism." Hanegraaff, Wouter J. New Age Religion and Western Culture : Esotericism in the Mirror of Secular Thought. Leiden, New York, Koln: E. J. Brill, 1996. 411-513. Book.

—. "Introduction." Hanegraaff, Wouter J. New Age Religion and Western Culture Esotericism in the Mirror of Secular Thought. Leiden, New York, Koln: E. J. Brill, 1996. 1-20. Book.

Hanson, K. C. The Pilate Inscription. 10 August 2015. Website. 13 November 2017. <http://www.kchanson.com/ANCDOCS/latin/pilate.html>.

Harding, Mark. "Disputed and Undisputed Letters of Paul." Porter, Stanley E. The Pauline Canon. Leiden; Boston: Brill, 2004. 129-168. Book.

Hare, John Bruno. The Works of Flavius Josephus. 2010. Website. 2 November 2017. <http://sacred-texts.com/jud/josephus/>.

Harland, Philip. Religions of the Ancient Mediterranean. n.d. Blog. 25 October 2018. <http://www.philipharland.com/Blog/>.

HarperCollins Publishers, Inc. Discover Author Matthew Sturgis. n.d. Website. 13 April 2018. <https://www.harpercollins.com/author/cr-113520/matthew-sturgis/>.

Heinrich Karl Brugsch, Mary Brodrick. "Chapter I. Introductory." Heinrich Karl Brugsch, Mary Brodrick. Egypt Under the Pharaohs : A History Derived Entirely From The Monuments. London: John Murray, Albemarle Street, 1891. 1-18. Book.

Herodotus. "Book 1. Chapter 56. Section 1-2." Herodotus. Herodotus, with an English translation. Trans. A. D. Godley. Cambridge: Harvard University Press, 1920. 1-271. Book.

—. "Book 1. Chapter 68. Section 4." Herodotus. Herodotus, with an English translation. Cambridge: Harvard University Press, 1920. 1-271. Book.

—. "Book II Chapter 123." Godley, A. D. Herodotus. Cambridge: Harvard University Press, 1920. 425. Book.

—. "Book II: Chapter 81." Godley, A. D. Herodotus. Cambridge: Harvard University Press, 1920. 367. Book.

—. "General Introduction." Godley, A. D. Herodotus The Histories Volume I Books I and II. Cambridge: Harvard University Press, 1920. vii - viii. Book.

—. "Herodotus With An English Translation." Godley, A. D. Herodotus. First. Vol. 1. Cambridge: Harvard University Press, 1920. 4 vols. 273-497. Book.

—. "The Nile-Causes of the inundation." Rawlinson, George. The History of Herodotus Vol II. New York: D. Appleton & Company, 1866. 19-27. Book.

Herzog, Ze'ev. "Deconstructing the Walls of Jericho." 29 October 1999. University of Michigan. Website. 5 April 2018. <http://umich.edu//~proflame/neh.arch.htm>.

Hicks, R. D. "Book 8. Chapter 3. PYTHAGORAS (c. 582-500 B.C.)." Laertius, Diogenes. Lives of Eminent Philosophers. Cambridge: Harvard University Press, 1972 (First Published in 1925). 320-367. Book.

—. "Book 8. Chapter 1. PYTHAGORAS (c. 582-500 B.C.)." Laertius, Diogenes. Lives of Eminent Philosophers. Cambridge: Harvard University Press, 1972 (First published 1925). 320-367. Book.

Hillerbrand, Hans J. "Martin Luther." 16 March 2018. Encyclopædia Britannica. Encyclopedia entry. 14 June 2018. <https://www.britannica.com/biography/Martin-Luther>.

Hoffeld, David. "The Science of Work | Want To Know What Your Brain Does When It Hears A Question?" 21 February 2017. Fast Company. Website. 5 April 2018. <https://www.fastcompany.com/3068341/want-to-know-what-your-brain-does-when-it-hears-a-question>.

Irenaeus. Ante-Nicene Fathers. Ed. James Donaldson, and A. Cleveland Coxe Alexander Roberts. Trans. Alexander Roberts and William Rambaut. Vol. 1. Buffalo: Christian Literature Publishing Co., 1885. Book. 20 June 2018. <http://www.newadvent.org/fathers/0103.htm>. St. Irenaeus. "Irenaeus of Lyons." n.d. Book V Chapter 20. Website. 2 November 2017. <http://www.earlychristianwritings.com/text/irenaeus-book5.html>.

Iversen, Erik. "II. The Classical Tradition." Iversen, Erik. The Myth of Egypt and Its Hieroglyphs in European Tradition. Princeton: Princeton University Press, 1961. 38-56. Book.

—. "III. The Middle Ages and The Renaissance." Iversen, Erik. The Myth of Egypt and Its Hieroglyphs in European Tradition. Princeton: Princeton University Press, 1961. 57-87. Book.

James, George G. M. Stolen Legacy: Greek Philosophy is Stolen Egyptian Philosophy. New York: New York Philosophical Library, 1954. Book.

Jews for Judaism. "Maimonides – Laws Pertaining to The Messiah." n.d. Jews for Judaism. 16 June 2018. <http://jewsforjudaism.org/knowledge/articles/maimonides-laws-pertaining-messiah/>.

Jewish Telegraphic Agency. "Solomon Zeitlin Dead at 84." Daily News Bulletin 30 December 1976: 1-4. Bulletin. 16 June 2018. <https://www.jta.org/1976/12/30/archive/solomon-zeitlin-dead-at-84>.

Jewish Virtual Library. Zadok. n.d. Website. 4 May 2018. <http://www.jewishvirtuallibrary.org/zadok>.

Jewish Virtual Library A Project of AICE. The Jewish Temples: The Babylonian Exile (597 - 538 BCE). n.d. Website. 7 March 2018. <http://jewishvirtuallibrary.org/the-babylonian-exile>.

Kelly, John N.D. "Patristic literature." 12 April 2017. Encyclopædia Britannica. Website. 24 March 2018. <https://www.britannica.com/topic/patristic-literature>.

Kenney, Edward John. "Textual criticism." 26 April 2012. Encyclopaedia Britannica. Website. 14 November 2017. <https://www.britannica.com/topic/textual-criticism>.

Kirby, Peter. Irenaeus of Lyons Book III. n.d. Website. 28 February 2018. <http://www.earlychristianwritings.com/text/irenaeus-book3.html>.

—. "The Lost Sayings Gospel Q." n.d. Early Christian Writings. Encyclopedia entry. 19 April 2018. <http://www.earlychristianwritings.com/q.html>.

Kohler, Kaufmann. "ESSENES." n.d. The unedited full-text of the 1906 Jewish Encyclopedia. Website. 24 March 2018. <http://www.jewishencyclopedia.com/articles/5867-essenes>.

—. "PHARISEES (Φαρισαῖοι; Aramaic, "Perishaya"; Hebr. "Perushim")." n.d. The unedited full-text of the 1906 Jewish Encyclopedia. Website. 24 March 2018. <http://www.jewishencyclopedia.com/articles/12087-pharisees>.

—. "SADDUCEES (Hebrew, ; Greek, Σαδδου καῖοι)." n.d. The unedited full-text of the 1906 Jewish Encyclopedia. Website. 24 March 2018. <http://jewishencyclopedia.com/articles/12989-sadducees>.

Kummel, Georg Werner. "The New Testament : The History of the Investigation of Its Problems (Nashville : Abingdon Press, 1972), 41." Ehrman, Bart D. Misquoting Jesus : The Story Behind Who Changed the Bible and Why. New York: HarperCollins Publishers, 2005. 101-125. Book.

L. Luca Cavalli-Sforza, Paolo Menozzi, and Alberto Piazza. "Chapter 1. Introduction to Concepts, Data, and Methods : 1.5 Classical attempts to distinguish human "races"." L. Luca Cavalli-Sforza, Paolo Menozzi, Alberto Piazza. The History and Geography of Human Genes. Princeton: Princeton University Press, 1994. 16-18. Book.

—."Preface." L. Luca Cavalli-Sforza, Paolo Menozzi, Alberto Piazza. The History and Geography of Human Genes. Princeton: Princeton University Press, 1994. ix-xi. Book.

Laertius, Diogenes. "Book 8. Chapter 1. PYTHAGORAS (c. 582-500 B.C.)." Hicks, R.D. Lives of Eminent Philosophers. Vol. II. New York: G. P. Putnam's Sons, 1925. 2 vols. 320 - 366. Book.

Lange, Jon. "Essay 1 : Borrowing or Plagiarism?" Lange, Jon. Masseiana Volume One : A Brief Introduction to Massey's Works. Middletown: Jon Lange, 2017. 33-47. Book.

Larson, Martin A. "Chapter 1 Judaism Section F. Eschatology." Larson, Martin A. The Story of Christian Origins. Tahlequah: Village Press, 1977. 195-295. Book.

—. "Chapter II The Essenes: The External Evidence." Larson, Martin A. The Story of Christian Origins or The Sources and Establishment of Western Religion. Tahlequah: Village Press, 1977. 195-295. Book.

—. "Chapter Three: Essene Development and Evolution." Larson, Martin A. The Essene-Christian Faith A Study in the Sources of Western Religion. New York: Philosophical Library Inc., 1980. 30. Book.

—. "Chapter Four Preparation: 195-145." Larson, Martin A. The Essene-Christian Faith A Study in the Sources of Western Religion. New York: Philosophical Library, Inc., 1980. 46-75. Book.

—. "Glossary." Larson, Martin A. The Essene-Christian Faith A Study in the Sources of Western Religion. New York: Philosophical Library, Inc., 1980. xxi. Book.

Lasserre, François. "Strabo." 7 May 2014. Encyclopædia Britannica. Website. 24 March 2018. <https://www.britannica.com/biography/Strabo>.

Lazare, Daniel. "False Testament : Archaeology Refutes the Bible's Claim to History. (Criticism)." Harper's Magazine Vol. 304, No. 1822 March 2002: 39-47. Website. <http://www.yorku.ca/dcarveth/false_testament>.

Lefkowitz, Mary. "Introduction." Lefkowitz, Mary. Not Ouf of Africa : How Afrocentrism Became an Excuse to Teach Myth as History. New York: BasicBooks, a Division of HarperCollins Publishers, Inc., 1996. 1-11. Book.

—. "The Myth of the Egyptian Mystery System." Lefkowitz, Mary. Not Out of Africa : How Afrocentrism Became an Excuse to Teach Myth as History. New York: BasicBooks A Division of HarperCollins Publishers, Inc., 1996. 91-121. Book.

Lemche, Niels Peter. "Preface." Lemche, Niels Peter. The Old Testament between Theology and History. Louisville: Westminster John Knox Press, 2008. xv-xix. Book.

Linda Schele, David Freidel. "Chapter 1 : Time Travel In The Jungle." LInda Schele, David Freidel. A Forest of Kings : The Untold Story of The Ancient Maya. New York: William Morrow and Company, Inc., 1990. 37-63. Book.

Lyall, Ian. Paul of Tarsus: Apostle to the Gentiles. Ed. Ian Lyall. Mainz: Pedia Press, 2011. Book. 14 June 2018. <https://pediapress.

com/books/show/paul-of-tarsus-apostle-to-the-gentiles-ia/>.
Lyons, Dr. Craig. "Egyptian Religion and its Realtionship to Judaism and Christianity." 1 December 2010. Bet Emet Ministries. Document from Website. 23 May 2018. <https://archive.org/details/BetEmetWebsitesInPdf/page/n17>.

M.G. Easton M.A., D.D. M.G. Easton M.A., D.D., Illustrated Bible Dictionary, Third Edition. Thomas Nelson, Inc., 1897. Book.
MacArthur, John. What Does Sola Scriptura Mean? 7 August 2015. Website. 23 February 2018. <https://www.ligonier.org/blog/what-does-sola-scriptura-mean/>.

Malkin, Stuart J. "The Essenes, Qumran, and The Dead Sea Scrolls." The Rosicrucian Digest No. 2 (2007): 33-36. Document.

Mark, Joshua J. Nebuchadnezzar II. 20 July 2010. Website. 24 March 2018. <https://www.ancient.eu/Nebuchadnezzar_II/>.

Martin, Brian L. Preterist video resources. n.d. Website. 14 June 2018. <http://www.fulfilledcg.com/Site/Video/video.htm>.

Matt Stefon, Henry Chadwick, Ernst Wilhelm Benz, Bernard J. McGinn, Sidney Spencer, and Carter H. Lindberg. "Christianity." 14 July 2017. Encyclopaedia Britannica School. Document from Website. 29 August 2017. <http://harborfieldscsd.net/hhslibrary/lmc%20webpage/Teacher%20Assignments/Religions/EB%20Articles/EB%20Christian%20philosophy.pdf>.

McCarter, J. Parnell. Historicism Research Foundation. n.d. Website. 29 August 2017. <http://www.historicism.net/>.

McDonald, Alexander Hugh. "Tacitus." 18 January 2018. Encyclopædia Britannica. Website. 24 March 2018. <https://www.britannica.com/biography/Tacitus-Roman-historian>.

Merriam-Webster. "euhemerism". Prod. Merriam-Webster.com. May 2019. 30 May 2019. <https://www.merriam-webster.com/dictionary/

euhemerism>.

—. "heresiologist". Prod. Merriam-Webster.com. 2019. 30 May 2019. <https://www.merriam-webster.com/dictionary/heresiologist>.

—. "natural science". Prod. Merriam-Webster.com. May 2019. 30 May 2019. <https://www.merriam-webster.com/dictionary/natural%20 science>.

—. mitochondrial DNA. Prod. Merriam-Webter.com. May 2019. 30 May 2019. <https://www.merriam-webster.com/dictionary/mito-chondrial%20DNA>.

Nielsen, Kirsten. "Part III. Writings (Ketuvim) IV. The Book of Daniel." Graham, Steven L. McKenzie and M. Patrick. The Hebrew Bible Today an Introduction to Critical Issues. Louisville: Westminster John Knox Press, 1998. 194-195. Book.

North, Gary. David Chilton: Free Books to Download. n.d. 14 June 2018. <https://www.garynorth.com/public/6597.cfm>.

Olson, Roger E. The Mosaic of Christian Belief: Twenty Centuries of Unity & Diversity. Westmont: InterVarsity Press, 2002. Book.

Office of the Historian. "Creation of Israel, 1948." n.d. Office of the Historian. Website. 25 October 2018. <https://history.state.gov/mile-stones/1945-1952/creation-israel>.

Onuma, Yasuaki. "Hugo Grotius." 3 April 2018. Encyclopædia Britannica. Encyclopedia entry. 14 June 2018. <https://www.britannica.com/biography/Hugo-Grotius>.

Origen. "Celsus as quoted by Origen." n.d. Early Christian Writings : Jesus and the Jewish Critic. Website. 14 November 2017. <http://www.earlychristianwritings.com/text/celsus.html>.

Oxford Biblical Studies Online. Hellenists. n.d. Website. 16 June 2018. <http://www.oxfordbiblicalstudies.com/article/opr/t94/e857>.

Oxford University Press. Oxford Biblical Studies Online. n.d. Website. 19 April 2018. <http://www.oxfordbiblicalstudies.com/article/opr/ t94/e1566>.

Peck, M. Scott. "Chapter 2: Toward A Psychology of Evil: The Case of Bobby and His Parents." Peck, M. Scott. People of the Lie: The Hope for Healing Human Evil. Second Touchstone Edition 1998. New York: Simon & Schuster, 1983. 47-69. Book.

Pervo, Richard I. "Chapter 3 Acts Among the Prophets, Apostles and Evangelists." Pervo, Richard I. Dating Acts Between the Evangelists and the Apologists. Santa Rosa: Polebridge Press, 2006. 29. Book.

—. "The Date of Acts and Some of its Souces Issues and Methods." Pervo, Richard I. Dating Acts Between the evangelists and the Apologists. Santa Rosa: Polebridge Press, 2006. 1-14. Book.

Philo. "Allegorical Interpretation of Genesis Book III." F. H. Colson, G. H. Whitaker. Philo in Ten Volumes (And Two Supplementary Volumes) I. Cambridge: Harvard University Press, 1929. 300-477. Book.

—. "Allegorical Interpretation, III (Legum Allegoriae, III)." Yonge, C. D. The Works of Philo Complete and Unabridged. Peabody: Hendrickson Publishers, Inc., 1993. 50-79. Book.

—. "Every Good Man Is Free Section 12." Yonge, C. D. The Works of Philo. London: H. G. Bohn, 1993. Book.

Plato. "Phaedo or The Immortality of the Soul." Henry Cary, M.A. The Works of Plato. London: George Bell & Sons, York St., Convent Garden, and New York, 1892. 54 - 127. Book.

—. "Phaedo Section 29." Henry Cary, M.A. The Works of Plato, A New and Literal Version, Chiefly from the text of Stallbaum. Volume I. London: Henry G. Bohn, York Street, Covent Garden, 1892. 54-127. Book.

—. "Phaedo Section 88." Henry Cary, M.A. The Works of Plato A New and Literal Version Chiefly from the text of Stallbaum. London: George Bell & Sons, York St., Covent Garden, and New York, 1892. 51-127. Book.

—. "The Timaeus Section IX." Davis, Henry. The Works of Plato, A New and Literal Version, Chiefly from the text of Stallbaum Volume II. London: Henry G. Bohn, York Street, Covent Garden, 1892. 319-410. Book.

—. "The Timaeus Section X." Davis, Henry. The Works of Plato, A New and Literal Version, Chiefly from the text of Stallbaum. Volume II. London: Henry G. Bohn, York Street, Covent Garden, 1892. 319-410. Book.

—. "The Timaeus Section XIV." Davis, Henry. The Works of Plato, A New and Literal Version, Chiefly from the text of Stallbaum. Volume II. London: Henry G. Bohn, York Street, Covent Garden, 1892. 319-410. Book.

Pliny the Elder. "Book 5, Chapter 17." Pliny the Elder. Natural History in Thirty-Seven Books. A Translation on the Basis of that by Dr. Philemon Holland Ed. 1601. Ed. The Wernerian Club. Trans. Dr. Philemon Holland. 1601. Vol. 2. London: George Barclay, Castle Street, Leicester Square., 1847-48. 47-97. Book.

—. "The Essenes (people)." Pliny the Elder. Pliny's Natural History in Thirty-Seven Books. Trans. Dr. Philemon Holland Ed. 1601. Vol. II. London: George Barclay, Castle Street, Leicester Square., 1848-49. 70. Book.

Poole, Gary William. "Flavius Josephus." 17 November 2017. Encyclopædia Britannica. Website. 24 March 2018. <https://www.britannica.com/biography/Flavius-Josephus>.

Press, Oxford University. abstract, n.1. Prod. OED Online. March

2019. 30 May 2019. <https://en.oxforddictionaries.com/definition/
abstract>.

—. Antichrist, n.1. Prod. OED Online. March 2019. 30 May 2019.
<https://en.oxforddictionaries.com/definition/antichrist>.

—. apex, n.1. Prod. OED Online. May 2019. 30 May 2019. <https://
en.oxforddictionaries.com/definition/apex>.

—. apocrypha, n.1. Prod. OED Online. March 2019. 30 May 2019.
<https://en.oxforddictionaries.com/definition/apocrypha>.

—. broach, v.1. Prod. OED Online. March 2019. 30 May 2019.
<https://en.oxforddictionaries.com/definition/broach>.

—. classical, adj.1. Prod. OED Online. March 2019. 30 May 2019.
<https://en.oxforddictionaries.com/definition/classical>.

—. credence, n,1. Prod. OED Online. March 2019. 30 May 2019.
<https://en.oxforddictionaries.com/definition/credence>.

—. deutero-, cb.1. Prod. OED Online. March 2019. 30 May 2019.
<https://en.oxforddictionaries.com/definition/deutero->.

—. eclectic, adj.1,2. Prod. OED Online. March 2019. 30 May 2019.
<https://en.oxforddictionaries.com/definition/eclectic>.

—. eschatology, n.1. Prod. OED Online. March 2019. 30 May 2019.
<https://en.oxforddictionaries.com/definition/eschatology>.

—. eschaton, n.1. Prod. OED Online. March 2019. 30 May 2019.
<https://en.oxforddictionaries.com/definition/eschaton>.

—. inconceivable, adj.1. Prod. OED Online. March 2019. 30 May
2019. <https://en.oxforddictionaries.com/definition/inconceivable>.

—. interpolation, n.1. Prod. OED Online. March 2019. 30 May 2019.

<https://en.oxforddictionaries.com/definition/interpolation>.

—. jettison, v.1.1. Prod. OED Online. March 2019. 30 May 2019. <https://en.oxforddictionaries.com/definition/jettison>.

—. Masorete, n.1. Prod. OED Online. March 2019. 30 May 2019. <https://en.oxforddictionaries.com/definition/masorete>.

—. narcissism, n.1. Prod. OED Online. March 2019. 30 May 2019. <https://en.oxforddictionaries.com/definition/narcissism>.

—. neoplatonism, n.1. Prod. OED Online. March 2019. 30 May 2019. <https://en.oxforddictionaries.com/definition/neoplatonism>.

—. Oxford Biblical Studies Online. n.d. Website. 19 April 2018. <http://www.oxfordbiblicalstudies.com/article/opr/t94/e1566>.

—. relegate, v.1. Prod. OED Online. March 2019. 30 May 2019. <https://en.oxforddictionaries.com/definition/relegate>.

—. Septuagint, n.1. Prod. OED Online. March 2019. 30 May 2019. <https://en.oxforddictionaries.com/definition/septuagint>.

—. versed, adj.1. Prod. OED Online. March 2019. 30 May 2019. <https://en.oxforddictionaries.com/definition/versed>.

—. weltanschauung, n.1. Prod. OED Online. March 2019. 30 May 2019. <https://en.oxforddictionaries.com/definition/weltanschauung>.

Preston, Dr. Don K. Dr. Don K. Preston Bio. n.d. 14 June 2018. <http://www.bibleprophecy.com/about-pri/dr-don-k-preston-bio/>.

Pritchard, James. "Historical Documents Sennacherib (704-681)." Pritchard, James. Ancient Near Eastern Texts Relating to the Old Testament Third Edition with Supplement. Princeton: Princeton University Press, 1969. 287 - 288. Book.

Quigley, Carroll. "1. Scientific Method and the Social Sciences." Quigley, Carroll. The Evolution of Civilizations : An Introduction to Historical Analysis. New York: Macmillan Company, 1961. 31-48. Book.

—. "2. Man and Culture." Quigley, Carroll. The Evolution of Civilizations : An Introduction to Historical Analysis. New York: Macmillan Company, 1961. 49-66. Book.

Reagan, Dr. David R. Daniel's 70 Weeks of Years : When did it start? Has it ended, or is there a gap in it? n.d. Website. 14 June 2018. <http://christinprophecy.org/articles/daniels-70-weeks-of-years/>.

—. Dr. David R. Reagan. n.d. Website. 14 June 2018. <http://christinprophecy.org/?staff=dr-david-r-reagan>.

Rebecca L. Cann, Mark Stoneking & Allan C. Wilson. "Mitochondrial DNA and human evolution." Nature Vol. 325 1 January 1987: 31-36. Journal.

Richard Gottheil, Samuel Krauss. The unedited full-text of the 1906 Jewish Encyclopedia. 1906. Website. 24 March 2018. <http://www.jewishencyclopedia.com/articles/4167-celsus>.

Robinson, B. A. Biblical Criticism, including Form Criticism, Tradition Criticism, Higher Criticism, etc. 19 January 2008. Website. 26 February 2018. <http://www.religioustolerance.org/chr_hcri.htm>.

—. Biblical Criticism, including Form Criticism,. 19 January 2008. Website. 18 June 2018. <http://www.religioustolerance.org/chr_hcri.htm>.

—. "Christian Reconstructionism etc. Beliefs and practices." 14 August 2009. Religious Tolerance. Website. 25 October 2018. <http://www.religioustolerance.org/reconstr3.htm>.

Robinson, James M. "Introduction." Robinson, James M. The Nag Hammadi Library. New York: HarperCollins Publishers, 2010. 10.

Book.

—. "Introduction: 3. The Discovery." Robinson, James M. The Nag Hammadi Library in English. Ed. Richard Smith. Completely Revised Edition Third. Leiden: HarperSanFrancisco, A Division of Harper-CollinsPublishers, 1990. 1-26. Book.

Robinson, John A. T. "Chapter II: The Significance of 70." Robinson, John A. T. Redating the New Testament. Eugene: Wipf & Stock Pub, 1976. 19-36. Book. 8 January 2019. <http://www.biblemaths.com/redating.pdf>.

Rossing, Barbara R. The Rapture Exposed: The Message of Hope in the Book of Revelation. New York: Westview Press, A Member of the Perseus Books Group, 2004. Book.

Russell, James Stuart. "Prophetic intimations of the approaching Consummation of the Kingdom of God: v. Woes denounced on the Scribes and Pharisees." Russell, James Stuart. The Parousia: A Critical Inquiry Into the New Testament Doctrine of Our Lord's Second Coming. London: Daldy, Isbister & Co., Unwin Brothers, The Greenham Press, Chilworth and London., 1878. 48-50. Book.

Saltet, Louis. "Epiphanius of Salamis." The Catholic Encyclopedia. Vol. 13. New York: Robert Appleton Company, 1912. Website. <http://www.newadvent.org/cathen/13393b.htm>.

Sanning, Acharya. "12. The "Historical Jesus?"" Sanning, Acharya. Suns of God, Krishna, Buddha and Christ Unveiled. Kempton: Adventures Unlimited Press, 2004. 372-445. Book.

—. "Introduction." S., Acharya. Suns of God : Krishna, Buddha and Christ Unveiled. Kempton: Adventures Unlimited Press, 2004. 1-25. Book.

Scharlemann, Robert P. "Friedrich Schleiermacher." 22 September 2006. Encyclopedia entry. 14 June 2018. <https://www.britannica.com/biography/Friedrich-Schleiermacher>.

Schmidt, Brian. "A Summary Assessment For Part 1." Israel Finkelstein, Amihai Mazar. The Quest for the Historical Israel Debating Archaeology and the History of Early Israel. Leiden, Boston: Brill, 2007. 5-8. Book.

Schodde, George H. "Old Testament Textual Criticism." The Old Testament Student, Vol. 7, No. 2 (Oct., 1887), pp. 44-48 (1887): 44-48. Journal Article.

ScriptureCatholic.com. DEUTEROCANONICAL BOOKS IN THE NEW TESTAMENT. n.d. Website. 20 June 2018. <https://www.scripturecatholic.com/deuterocanonical-books-new-testament>.

—. SEPTUAGINT QUOTES IN THE NEW TESTAMENT. n.d. Website. 20 June 2018. <https://www.scripturecatholic.com/septuagint-quotes-new-testament/>.

Sertima, Ivan Van. "Introduction." Sertima, Ivan Van. They Came Before Columbus : The African Presence in Ancient America. New York: Random House Publishing Group, 1976. xiii-xv. Book.

Shea, Christopher. "A Serious Look at New Age Spirituality." The Chronicle of Higher Education (1997): A16-A18. Document. <http://web.williams.edu/AnthSoc/native/CZ_CHE.pdf>.

Shlomo Pines, David Novak and Others. "Judaism." 24 January 2018. Encyclopædia Britannica. Website. 10 April 2018. <https://www.britannica.com/topic/Judaism>.

Shmoop Editorial Team. "Ecclesiastes Perspectives From Faith Communities." 11 November 2008. Shmoop. Shmoop University, Inc. Website. 4 March 2018. <https://www.shmoop.com/ecclesiastes/perspectives.html>.

Siculus, Diodorus. "Book I. Chapter 2." Siculus, Diodorus. The Library of Diodorus Siculus. Trans. C. H. Oldfather. Cambridge: Har-

vard University Press, 1933. 1-312. Book.
Simon, Richard. "A Critical History of the Text of the New Testament (London : R. Taylor, 1689), Preface, Part I, p. 31." Ehrman, Bart D. Misquoting Jesus : The Story Behind Who Changed the Bible and Why. New York: HarperCollins, Publishers, 2005. 101-125. Book.

Stannard, Jerry. "Pliny the Elder." 15 November 2017. Encyclopædia Britannica. Website. 24 March 2018. <https://www.britannica.com/biography/Pliny-the-Elder>.

Stefon, Matt. The Rapture. 13 April 2018. Encyclopedia entry. 14 June 2018. <https://www.britannica.com/topic/Rapture-the>.

Steiner, Margreet. "David's Jerusalem: Fiction or Reality? : It's Not There: Archaeology Proves a Negative." Biblical Archaeology Review: The Only Relic from Herod's Temple July/August 1998: 26-33;62. Magazine.

—. Welcome. n.d. Website. 5 April 2018. <https://margreetsteiner.wordpress.com/>.

Stix, Gary. Traces of a Distant Past. Magazine. New York: Scientific American, Inc., 2008. Magazine.

Sweeney, Marvin A. "The Latter Prophets: Isaiah, Jeremiah, Ezekiel; III-The Book of Isaiah." Graham, Steven L. McKenzie and M. Patrick. The Hebrew Bible Today an Introduction to Critical Issues. Louisville: Westminster John Knox Press, 1998. 69-94. Book.

Taylor, Joan E. "Part I: The Essenes in Ancient Literature; Chapter 3 Josephus." Taylor, Joan E. The Essenes, the Scrolls, and the Dead Sea. Oxford: Oxford University Press, 2012. 58. Book.

Tel Aviv University. Prof. Zeev Herzog. n.d. Website. 5 April 2018. <https://english.tau.ac.il/profile/herzog>.

The Center for Hellenic Studies, Harvard University. Chapter 1.

Textual Criticism as Applied to Classical and Biblical Texts. n.d. Website. 15 November 2017. <https://chs.harvard.edu/CHS/article/display/4742.1-textual-criticism-as-applied-to-biblical-and-classical-texts>.

Thompson, Thomas L. "Chapter One : Historical-Critical Research and Extrabiblical Sources : The Rise of Biblical Archaeology." Thompson, Thomas L. Early History of the Israelite People: From the Written and Archaeological Sources. Leiden: Brill, 1992. 10-26. Book.

—. "Chapter Nine : CONCLUSIONS, AN INDEPENDENT HISTORY OF ISRAEL : "Israel" as a National Entity." Thompson, Thomas L. Early History of the Israelite People: From the Written and Archaeological Sources. Leiden: Brill, 1992. 412-415. Book.

—. "Chapter 9 Historians Create History." Thompson, Thompson L. The Mythic Past Biblical Archaeology and the Myth of Israel. London: Random House, 1999. 200-225. Book.

Tobin, Paul. The Rejection of Pascal's Wager. Kindle. Gamlingay: Authors OnLine Ltd, 16 February 2011. Ebook.

Tomassi, Rollo. "Demystifying intersexual dynamics : Instinct, Emotion and Reason." 11 April 2018. The Rational Male. Blog. 23 May 2018. <https://therationalmale.com/2018/04/11/instinct-emotion-and-reason/>.

—. "Instinct, Emotion and Reason." 11 April 2018. The Rational Male - Demystifying intersexual dynamics. Blog. 30 May 2018. <https://therationalmale.com/2018/04/23/the-instinctual-process/>.

—. "The Rational Male." One, Chapter 1 The Soul-Mate Myth: There is no. The Rational Male. Counterflow Media LLC, 2013. 3-7. Book.
—. "Unplugging: Dispelling the Magic." Tomassi, Rollo. The Rational Male. Counterflow Media LLC, 2013. 85-87. Book.

Tree of Life Ministries. Category Archives: William Bell Feed Subscription<. n.d. 14 june 2018. <http://fullpreterism.com/category/williambell/>.

Universiteit Van Amsterdam. dhr. prof. dr. W.J. (Wouter) Hanegraaff. n.d. Website. 7 June 2018. <http://www.uva.nl/profiel/h/a/w.j.hanegraaf/w.j.hanegraaf.html>.

University of Copenhagen. Faculty of Theology Niels Peter Lemche. n.d. Website. 5 April 2018. <http://www.teol.ku.dk/abe>.

—. Palestine History and Heritage Project. n.d. Website. 7 April 2018. <https://teol.ku.dk/pahh/english/contact/>.

University of the West of England. Dr Sean Creaven. n.d. Website. 7 June 2018. <https://people.uwe.ac.uk/Person/SeanCreaven>.

Unknown. "Book Ten of the Apostolicon The Epistle of the Apostle Paul to the Philippians." n.d. http://www.apostolicon.com/Philippians.html. 20 June 2018. <http://www.marcionite-scripture.info/10Philippians.pdf>.

—. Who wrote the Bible? n.d. Website. 24 February 2018. <https://www.biblica.com/resources/bible-faqs/who-wrote-the-bible/>.

Vermes, Geza. "Appendix: The Essenes and the Qumran Community." Vermes, Geza. The Complete Dead Sea Scrolls in English. New York: Penquin Group Penguin Putnam Inc., 1997. 46-48. Book.

—."Commentary on Habakkuk." Vermes, Geza. The Complete Dead Sea Scrolls in English. New York: Penquin Group Penquin Putnam Inc., 1997. 478-483. Book.

—. "Commentary on Nahum (4Q169)." Vermes, Geza. The Complete Dead Sea Scrolls in English. New York: Penquin Group Penquin Putnum Inc., 1997. 473-477. Book.

—. "Community Rule manuscripts from Cave 4." Vermes, Geza. The

Dead Sea Scrolls in English. New York: Penquin Group Penguin Putnam Inc., 1997. 118-124. Book.

—. "III. History of the Community." Vermes, Geza. The Complete Dead Sea Scrolls. New York: Penquin Group Penguin Putnam Inc., 1997. 49-66. Book.

—. "The Community." Vermes, Geza. The Complete Dead Sea Scrolls in Engligh. New York: Penguin Putnam Inc., 1997. 26-45. Book.

—. "The Community Rule." Verbes, Geza. The Complete Dead Sea Scrolls in English. New York: Penquin Group Penguin Putnam Inc., 1997. 97-117. Book.

—."The Damascus Document." Verbes, Geza. The Complete Dead Sea Scrolls in English. New York: Penquin Group Penguin Putnam Inc., 1997. 125-143. Book.

—. "The Thanksgiving Hymns." Vermes, Geza. The Complete Dead Sea Scrolls. New York: Penquin Group Penguin Putnam Inc., 1997. 243-300. Book.

—. "The War Scroll." Vermes, Geza. The Complete Dead Sea Scrolls in English. New York: Penquin Group Penguin Putnam Inc., 1997. 161-186. Book.

Virtual Museum of Protestantism. The Reformers and the Bible : sola scriptura. n.d. Website. 23 February 2018. <https://www.museeprotestant.org/en/notice/the-reformation-and-the-bible-sola-scriptura/>. Walbank, Frank W. "Plutarch." 9 February 2018. Encyclopædia Britannica. Website. 24 March 2018. <https://www.britannica.com/biography/Plutarch>.

Wellhausen, Julius. "Introduction." Wellhausen, Julius. Prolegomena to the History of Israel: With A Reprint Of The Article Israel From The " EncyclopediaA Britannica.". Trans. Allan Menzies J. Sutherland Black. Edinburgh: ADAM & CHARLES BLACK., 1885. 1-13. Book.

Westfall, Richard S. "Sir Isaac Newton." 24 March 2018. Encyclopædia Britannica. Encyclopedia entry. 14 June 2018. <https://www.britannica.com/biography/Isaac-Newton>.

Wikipedia. Age of Enligtenment. n.d. Website. 1 June 2018. <https://en.wikipedia.org/wiki/Age_of_Enlightenment>.

—. Criticism of Christianity. n.d. Website. 26 February 2018. <https://en.wikipedia.org/wiki/Criticism_of_Christianity>.

—. Eduard Zeller. n.d. Website. 21 March 2018. <https://en.wikipedia.org/wiki/Eduard_Zeller>.

—. "Euhemerus." 13 February 2018. Wikipedia The Free Encyclopedia. Website. 13 April 2018. <https://en.wikipedia.org/wiki/Euhemerus>.

—. Francisco Ribera. 1 October 2016. Website. 14 June 2018. <https://en.wikipedia.org/wiki/Francisco_Ribera>.

—. John Robinson (bishop of Woolwich). 6 October 2017. Website. 18 October 2017. <https://en.wikipedia.org/wiki/John_Robinson_(bishop_of_Woolwich)>.

—. Luigi Luca Cavalli-Sforza. 16 May 2018. Website. 9 June 2018. <https://en.wikipedia.org/wiki/Luigi_Luca_Cavalli-Sforza>.

—. Luis del Alcázar. 25 April 2017. Website. 18 October 2017. <https://en.wikipedia.org/wiki/Luis_del_Alc%C3%A1zar>.

—. "New Age." 6 December 2017. Wikipedia. Website. 3 June 2018. <https://en.wikipedia.org/wiki/New_Age>.

—. Philip Mauro. 13 June 2018. 14 June 2018. <https://en.wikipedia.org/wiki/Philip_Mauro>.

—. Philip R. Davies. 22 March 2018. Website. 5 April 2018. <https://en.wikipedia.org/wiki/Philip_R._Davies>.

—. R. C. Sproul. 27 May 2018. 14 June 2018. <https://en.wikipedia.org/wiki/R._C._Sproul>.

Wilken, Robert L. "Tertullian." 15 November 2017. Encyclopædia Britannica. Encyclopedia entry. 24 March 2018. <https://www.britannica.com/biography/Tertullian>.

Williams, Walter. "Appendix : Why The Medu-Netcher-Hieroglyphics Have Never Been Deciphered." Williams, Walter. The Historical Origin of Christianity. Chicago: Maathaian Press, Inc., 1992. 146-150. Book.

—. "Chapter 1 - The Coming of the Europeans in Africa." Williams, Walter. The Historical Origin of Islam. Chicago: Maathian Press, Inc., 2001. 1-14. Book.

Wilson, John A. "Biographical Memoir of James Henry Breasted." National Academy of Sciences of the United States of America Biographical Memoirs Volume XVIII-Fifth Memoir (1936): 94-121. Document.

Wingren, Gustaf. "Saint Irenaeus." 27 May 2013. Encyclopædia Britannica. Website. 24 March 2018. <https://www.britannica.com/biography/Saint-Irenaeus>.

Yale Divinity School. John J. Collins. n.d. 18 June 2018. <https://divinity.yale.edu/faculty-and-research/yds-faculty/john-j-collins>.

Zeller, Dr. Eduard. "II. Jewish Greek Philosophy Section 93. The Period Before Philo." Zeller, Dr. Eduard. Outlines of the history of Greek philosophy. London: Longmans, Green, and Co., 1886. 316-320. Book.

—. "B. The Pythagoreans Pythagoras and his school." Zeller, Eduard.

Outlines of the history of Greek philosophy. London: Longmans, Green, and Co., 1886. 45-49. Book.